SPECIAL MESSAGE TO READERS

THE ULVERSCROFT FOUNDATION
(registered UK charity number 264873)
was established in 1972 to provide funds for research, diagnosis and treatment of eye diseases. Examples of major projects funded by the Ulverscroft Foundation are:-

- The Children's Eye Unit at Moorfields Eye Hospital, London
- The Ulverscroft Children's Eye Unit at Great Ormond Street Hospital for Sick Children
- Funding research into eye diseases and treatment at the Department of Ophthalmology, University of Leicester
- The Ulverscroft Vision Research Group, Institute of Child Health
- Twin operating theatres at the Western Ophthalmic Hospital, London
- The Chair of Ophthalmology at the Royal Australian College of Ophthalmologists

You can help further the work of the Foundation by making a donation or leaving a legacy. Every contribution is gratefully received. If you would like to help support the Foundation or require further information, please contact:

THE ULVERSCROFT FOUNDATION
The Green, Bradgate Road, Anstey
Leicester LE7 7FU, England
Tel: (0116) 236 4325

website: www.foundation

THE CHELTENHEM SQUARE MURDER

Regency Square in Cheltenham is home to some diverse inhabitants. One summer's evening, the square's rivalries and allegiances are disrupted by a sudden and unusual death — an arrow to the head, shot through an open window at no. 6. Unfortunately for the murderer, crime writer Aldous Barnet, staying with his sister at no. 8, had just sent an invitation to his friend Superintendent Meredith to visit him. Three days after his arrival, Meredith finds himself investigating the shocking murder two doors down and finds that six of the square's inhabitants are keen members of the Wellington Archery Club . . .

Books by John Bude
Published by Ulverscroft:

THE CORNISH COAST MURDER
DEATH ON THE RIVIERA
DEATH MAKES A PROPHET

JOHN BUDE
With an Introduction by
MARTIN EDWARDS

THE CHELTENHAM SQUARE MURDER

Complete and Unabridged

PUBLISHER SELECTION
Leicester

First published in Great Britain in 1937 by
Skeffington & Son Ltd
London

First Ulverscroft Edition
published 2019
by arrangement with
The British Library
c/o Edwards Fuglewicz Literary Agency
London

*A catalogue record for this book is available
from the British Library.*

ISBN 978–1–4448–3867–1

Published by
F. A. Thorpe (Publishing)
Anstey, Leicestershire

Set by Words & Graphics Ltd.
Anstey, Leicestershire
Printed and bound in Great Britain by
T. J. International Ltd., Padstow, Cornwall

This book is printed on acid-free paper

My thanks are due to Mr. Tom Barneby
for his help in the archery details
in this book
— J. B.

Contents

Introduction

The Cheltenham Square Murder, first published in 1937, was John Bude's fourth detective novel. Like its predecessors — set in Cornwall, the Lake District, and the Sussex Downs — it gains considerable appeal from an attractive setting, nicely evoked. This time, Bude chose the background of a spa town rather than a countryside location. Death comes to a fictitious version of one of Cheltenham's squares, and the publishers' blurb for the first edition makes clear that a touch of authenticity was regarded as a selling point: 'The author, who has actually lived in a Cheltenham square, once again utilizes topographical features to enhance the mystery.'

Bude supplies a carefully drawn plan of Regency Square, which helps the reader to follow the complications of an intricate plot.

The setting also enabled Bude to provide his detectives, and the reader, with a closed circle of suspects of a kind that was typical of whodunits written during the 'Golden Age of Murder' between the two world wars. Regency Square comprises only ten houses, and their occupants are a pleasingly varied bunch of people who are rapidly introduced in the opening pages.

As so often in books of this kind (and in real life, come to that), beneath the surface cordiality of the Square's residents all manner of tensions affect their relations, exacerbated — as Bude emphasizes in the first chapter — by 'the very fact that they live in an enclosed intimacy not to be found in an ordinary road'. When one of the residents is killed, the modus operandi is unusual: he has been shot with an arrow. One might imagine that this would narrow the field of suspects, but not so: 'all the owners of the houses in the right wing of the square were members of the Archery Club'. (This is not, incidentally, the only Golden Age detective novel to feature archery, it also crops up, for instance, in *We Shot an Arrow*, by George Goodchild and Carl Bechhofer Roberts, published two years after this book.)

Luckily for the local police, they are able to call on the expertise of Superintendent Meredith from the Sussex County Constabulary. He has been invited to spend part of his holiday in the Square with Aldous Barnet, a crime writer who is planning a book about the police and wants to benefit from the detective's expertise; the two men had become acquainted during the case chronicled in *The Sussex Downs Murder*. The amiable Inspector Long is familiar with Meredith's reputation, and not too proud to seek his help ('You cleared up the Cumberland ramp and the Rother murder . . . Two heads are better than one.'). But Meredith's superiors need to show considerable forbearance in allowing their man to stay in Cheltenham, as the investigation proves to be complex and protracted.

Bude's method is to introduce the main

suspects before the crime occurs, establishing a series of motives for murder — but for more than one potential victim. The focus then switches to the police inquiry, carefully chronicled in the manner of Freeman Wills Crofts (whose crime fiction was surely an influence on Bude), but leavened with touches of humour. Suspicion shifts from one person to another, as it becomes apparent that a startling number of inhabitants of Regency Square have something to hide.

The assured way in which the author handles his complex storyline reflects the continuing refinement of his skill as a writer. John Bude was the pen-name that Ernest Carpenter Elmore (1901–1957) adopted for his crime fiction. In 1919, after leaving Mill Hill School where he was a boarder, he attended a secretarial college — in Cheltenham — where he learned to type. He then spent several years as games master at St Christopher School in Letchworth, where archery was among the activities pursued by pupils. His enthusiasm for games is illustrated here by the fact that golf, which he enjoyed playing in his young days, also plays a part in the storyline. In addition, he led the school's dramatic activities, and presumably witnessed a local teenager called Laurence Olivier playing Lennox in *Macbeth* at the school in 1925.

This keen interest in the theatre led Bude to join the Lena Ashwell Players, as stage manager. The Players took their productions around the country, long before educational drama and public subsidy for the arts became common. He also took various acting roles in plays produced at the Everyman Theatre in Hampstead, where he lived for a time. Much of his early writing was undertaken in dressing rooms, whenever he had a moment to spare.

Bude concentrated on writing after returning to Maidstone, the town of his birth. There he produced plays for the local dramatic society, and met his future wife, Betty. They married in 1933, by which time he had published three fantasy novels under his own name, and moved to Beckley in Sussex. Here he continued to produce plays on behalf of various charities as a means of taking a break from writing. He enjoyed enough success with his crime fiction to pursue a career as a full-time author for the rest of his life.

John Bude was a craftsman whose hard work and attention to detail helped him to develop steadily as a writer. While he never became a high-profile figure during his lifetime, he was the dedicatee of *The Case of the Running Mouse* (1944), written by his friend Christopher Bush, creator of Ludovic Travers, the detective in a long-running series. The dedication to Bude said: 'May his stature, and his circulation, increase.'

Neither man, however, can have anticipated that John Bude's early mysteries would achieve an exceptionally high level of popularity nearly sixty years after his death. Yet, thanks to the appearance of his first three titles in the British Library's series of Crime Classics, that is exactly what has happened. In December 2015 his photo appeared in a lengthy article in *The Times* detailing the success of the reprints, and listing the trio of books by Bude among the top six best-sellers in the series. The article was accompanied by quotations from his daughter, Jennifer Slee, and I am most grateful for information she has supplied about her father, which has helped me to compile this introduction.

Martin Edwards
www.martinedwardsbooks.com

CHAPTER I

The Square Circle

Perhaps one of the most attractive features about that famous and lovely town, Cheltenham Spa, is its squares. Planned at a period more spacious than ours of to-day, they bear with them an atmosphere of leisure, culture, and almost rural tranquillity. They all bear a family likeness, and Regency Square, though perhaps smaller and more exclusive than others in the vicinity, typifies perfectly its Georgian origins. It consists of only ten houses erected in the form of a flattened U with a quiet, residential road ambling across its open side. These ten well-proportioned domiciles face on to the central, communal square of grass, which is shaded here and there by rare trees and graceful, flowering shrubs.

The architecture is varied, though pleasing, from the long, low façade of the White House, to the tall, flat-roofed simplicity of Number One on the opposite side of the square. None of these buildings, however, has more than three storeys, whilst most are ornamented with wrought-iron verandahs or carved stone balconies. As one faces into the square from the road one sees the left-hand arm of the U as a continuous frontage with a flat, crenellated roof and a series of four sets of stone steps leading down from four, solid-looking front-doors. To the right lies the White House in its own well-kept grounds and one other less distinguished, detached house which completes the right arm of the U.

At the base of the U are five undetached houses, the chief feature of which are the french windows on the second floor which give out on to stone balconies, supported by the pillars of porticos which hood their respective front-doors. An uninterrupted pavement runs round the three sides of the square, shaded with silver birch trees, which, combined with a number of discreet lamps, divide the pavement from the road. The general effect is of a quiet, residential backwater in which old people can grow becomingly older, undisturbed by the rush and clatter of a generation which has left them nothing but the memories of a past epoch.

Unfortunately, as in so many cases, the outward suggestions of the square are by no means compatible with the inward life lived by the people inhabiting it. Granted not one of those ten houses boasts a child. Granted that the average age of its residents is round about forty. Granted that traffic is scarce, barrel-organs unknown and wireless-sets so subdued that they are debarred from penetrating the walls of adjacent houses. But what of the yapping of Miss Boon's dogs? Of the Rev. Matthews' booming greetings which echo across the square? Of the eternal ringing of Dr. Pratt's telephone-bell? Of the doubtful hymn-singing of the Misses Watt, and Captain Cotton's high-powered motor-bike? And though, for the most part, the community live in amity, the very fact that they live in an enclosed intimacy not to be found in an ordinary road is sufficient to exaggerate such small annoyances and dissensions which from time to time arise.

There was, for instance, the controversy over the Tree. It was a minor war, which had been raging since the early winter, and now, in the middle of April, had come to a head. The Tree, a very old, almost immemorial elm, overhung the far, left-hand corner of the square, and in Mr. West's opinion it was a Menace. The feelings of the other members of the square circle were divided. The masculine, short-skirted Miss Boon upheld that as it had stood for a hundred years there was no reason why it shouldn't stand for another two hundred, an argument endorsed by Mr. Fitzgerald the bank-manager, and his pretty, though rather empty-headed young wife. The Rev. Matthews and his sister who could see the elm from their drawing-room were perfectly certain that its roots were sound, and that it would be a crime to cut it down. Dr. Pratt, on the other hand, sided with Mr. West because there was nothing he liked better than an argument with Miss Boon, whilst the caution and natural timidity of the Misses Nancy and Emmeline Watt placed them, as a matter of course, in the Menace camp. For the rest Captain Cotton didn't care a damn, Mr. Edward Buller was more interested in the stock-market and his own ailments, Miss Barnet was away, and Sir Wilfred and Lady Eleanor Whitcomb, of the White House, retained their usual aloof and non-committal attitude to the brawls of the *hoi-poloi.*

'Look here, West,' said Dr. Pratt one early spring morning, 'it's no use letting this absurd argument drift on like this. You ought to act. See the Borough Surveyor – I think it's in his demesne – get him on your side and have the tree cut down.'

'But what about Matthews? He's dead against–'

'Oh, damn Matthews. He doesn't want it cut down for aesthetic and sentimental reasons. But public safety is of far more importance than sentiment.'

'You know, Pratt,' said West apologetically, 'I hate upsetting people. It seems a pity that this matter couldn't be settled amicably.'

The doctor snorted.

'Well, if you won't see the authorities, I'll do it myself. It's your place to – you started the shamozzle. Point is, unless that elm comes down somebody's going to be killed in the long run. It's our duty to act.'

'Oh, very well,' said West wearily. 'I'll mention the matter in the right direction and see what can be done about it. I'm sick of the whole business.'

'Good!' concluded Pratt emphatically. 'You're doing the sensible thing.'

'Am I?' wondered West. 'It's all very well for you. You're making me shoulder the responsibility and if there's a row I shall be the one to suffer.'

He didn't want any more worries. He had quite enough to deal with as it was – financial worries, domestic worries, worries about the future. Ever since he had come such a cropper over those cement shares, selling when he ought to have held for a substantial rise, nothing had gone right with his finances. Buller had been handsomely apologetic over the misinformation which he had given him over those shares. Of course the man, although a stockbroker, could not always be expected to gauge the market to a T. The stock-market was a tricky business at the best of times and, of late, political unrest had undermined what little stability existed in the money world. But it had placed him in an awkward fix. If things didn't suddenly take a turn for the better and his investments show an increased profit – well, good-bye to his retirement. He'd have to look around for a job and go into harness again.

Isobel wouldn't like it. She was difficult enough now but if money got tight heaven alone knew what might happen. The old threat of a separation might be translated from a threat into an act. Things between them had become so strained since Christmas that it needed only a spark to send their domestic life sky-high. If only he could adopt a nice callous attitude toward his wife, the sort of attitude she seemed to hold for him, then the dread of this threatened split would no longer worry him. As it was he often lay awake at night trying to straighten things out. Trouble was that the others in the square knew all about it now. He had been quick to realize this fact from their politely veiled innuendos and unspoken sympathy. And it was all Isobel's fault. She was brazen, thoughtless in the calm manner in which she accepted Captain Cotton's odious advances. Hadn't he seen them sharing a tea-table on the Promenade? And the fellow was an outsider, a wastrel, an adventurer. Nobody seemed to know where his money came from or how a mere car-salesman could run a house in the square with a manservant to look after him. It seemed incredible that an intelligent, educated woman like Isobel should have come under the spell of such a vulgar upstart. The retention of that prefix 'Captain' should have been sufficient to warn her, for Pratt had told him in confidence that Cotton had never held a regular commission. Exactly what one would expect of the bounder.

Turning these unpleasant thoughts over in his mind as he made his way to the municipal offices, West almost collided with Miss Boon returning from her shopping, surrounded, as usual, by an ill-assorted pack of dogs.

'Ah, hullo, Arthur. Taking a constitutional?'

West guiltily prevaricated.

'Yes, just popping down to the bank.'

'Just been there myself,' said Miss Boon in her resounding bass. 'Fitz looks off his oats, doesn't he?'

'Fitzgerald? I haven't really noticed. Is he ill?'

'Ill! He looks as if he's seen a ghost. Or falsified his accounts. He ought to see Pratt.'

'Well he always seems happy enough – I mean in his home. If ever a couple were eminently suited to each other–'

Miss Boon shuddered.

'Horrible. The way they hang round each other's necks. I grant you they've only been married for a short time and that she's only just out of her teens, but Fitz is old enough to know better. Can't fathom what he sees in that fancy little bit.'

'She's very pretty,' contested West, edging along the pavement a little.

'Bah! Chocolate-box, Arthur. You've got low tastes.'

'And a lot to do,' added West meaningly. 'I really must–'

Miss Boon side-stepped and planted herself and her dogs implacably in his path.

'Wait a bit. I want a word with you. About that Tree.'

West felt a cold shiver run up his spine. This was the one subject he wished to avoid.

'Well?'

'Matthews and I won't have it cut down. You're old-womanish in your attitude.'

'It's unsafe. Patently so. Pratt agrees.'

'Pratt's a fool. I like him but he's a fool. If either of you dare–'

'Good-bye,' said West picking his way among the snuffling pack at his feet. 'I've got a lot to do before lunch.'

Miss Boon swung round, whistled stridently to a Cocker on the far side of the street and made off in the direction of the square.

Poor Arthur, he was always a bit edgy these days. Making a regular nuisance of himself about that Tree. So childishly insistent that he was right. Of course Isobel's behaviour was enough to drive any man to drink. Thank God *she* hadn't any domestic worries. Dogs were the only sensible housemates. They didn't argue or make trouble like human beings. She felt happy and full of vim striding along with her canine bodyguard.

But as she turned into Regency Square and made ready to mount the steps of Number One her eye was arrested by something unpleasant at the end of the square. Her expression altered. Her massive jaw advanced. Her eyes narrowed and she radiated something that was half-brother to hatred. The object of her disapproval was the retired stockbroker, Edward Buller, who had just come out on to his stone balcony and dropped into his *chaise-longue*. Being, as he himself firmly believed, an invalid, he often took up this post of vantage on sunny mornings in order to relieve the monotony of inaction by watching the activities of other people. Luckily for him Miss Boon's expression was too distant for him to recognize as also was her muttered imprecation:

'That vile inhuman brute!'

And anybody overhearing that remark would have judged that Miss Boon meant exactly what she said.

Buller himself felt in an expansive mood since he was alone and not burdened with the necessity of acting up to his role of a dying man. The finance page of his morning paper had greeted him with the bald information that overnight he had successfully made a couple of thousand pounds. One of his finest coups since the opening of the new year. Although he had retired from active stockbroking five years previously, a genuinely wealthy man, he liked to feel that he was keeping his hand in and that this hand had not lost its notorious Midas-touch. It was a familiar saying in the city: 'Buller always hits the bulls. Everything he touches turns to money.' Quite true it did. A nice little nest-egg of fifty thousand pounds tucked away in gilt-edged, these casual little snippets dropping into his hand, the house his own and no actual dependants. Of course there was that two hundred pound annuity which he had settled on his nephew Anthony, but that was a mere fleabite. Sensible boy. Had a way with him. Had the right attitude toward money. Believed that it was better to make money than to spend it. Well his nephew wouldn't regret these sentiments because he had made him his sole heir. A bit of fun to watch the boy's face when he told him last Christmas. Better to let the boy know now after what Pratt had reluctantly told him about his constitution. Go easy. Plenty of sunlight and fresh-air. Keep the windows open. A tendency, perhaps to TB. Nothing serious but serious enough in his, Buller's, opinion to talk about to his few sympathetic friends. Pity this rag-and-bobtail lot in the square didn't seem to get on with him – not that he admired them but it would have been pleasant to swap ailments whenever he felt like a chat. The old dears next door were all right though a bit pious with their church-going and hymn-singing. A little of 'em went a long way.

'Have you watered the ferns?' asked Miss Emmeline of her sister Nancy. 'The warmer weather seems to be affecting them adversely, Nance.'

Miss Nancy looked up over her embroidery frame with an air of patient martyrdom.

'Do I ever forget. Really, Emmeline, you *are* a little trying at times. We have our separate duties and I'm sure I never attempt to *evade* the responsibilities I've accepted.'

'I'm very sorry, Nance. I'd no desire to upset

you. I see Mr. Buller is taking the sun this morning.'

At this piece of news her sister laid down her embroidery and joined Emmeline at the window, where she was peeping obliquely along the façade of the house from behind a chink in the lace curtain at the projecting balcony of the adjacent building. For a moment the two sisters stared with commiseration and interest at the portly figure reclining in the chair, then Miss Nancy observed:

'I think he has got over his turn. It was terrible while it lasted, but I'm sure the spring is doing him a world of good. You were so brave that dreadful night, Emmeline.'

A tiny smirk of satisfaction rather belied Miss Emmeline's modest denial.

'I only did what I could. But Doctor Pratt was wonderful. Wonderful. I could only sit by the bedside and *pray* that the crisis would pass.'

There was a pause as Miss Nancy cautiously withdrew from the window and resettled herself in her sewing-chair. At length she looked up and asked with immense gravity.

'I wonder, Emmeline, do you think we were *right* in telling Mr. Matthews the awful words you overheard? I can't help feeling that it was a little unkind to Mr. Buller. Of course I know Mr. Matthews would never breathe a word to anybody but if Mr. West *were* to hear–'

'It was our duty,' broke in Miss Emmeline sternly, turning away from the window and picking up a feather-duster. 'I know those words were only spoken in delirium. One likes to believe there was no truth in them, but I felt I wanted advice. I naturally turned to Mr. Matthews in my distress. You must understand, Nance, that from that day I have never borne the slightest ill-will to Mr. Buller.

'But why should he *think* that he had swindled – yes, Emmeline, it's the only word to use – that he had *swindled* Mr. West of all that money?'

'I think,' concluded Miss Emmeline, flicking her feather-duster over a china-laden what-not, 'that it was a figment of his feverish imagination.'

Her sister, aware that the subject had now been closed, knew better than to try and reopen it. Instead she branched out into an entirely new conversational direction with the observation that Miss Barnet's brother, Aldous, would probably be taking his sister's house now that she had gone abroad again. They knew that their left-hand neighbour liked to 'keep the place aired.' The Misses Watt, moreover, were intensely interested in Aldous because he represented, however obliquely, a world of which they knew nothing – the world of crime. For Aldous Barnet, who lived under the South Downs in the little village of Washington, was a writer of detective stories. In the course of his occasional visits he often dropped in and chatted to them about forgeries and thefts and murders. Of course these godless things would never come their way but it was interesting to hear about the wickedness of other people from a man who was practically an authority on the subject.

Dr. Pratt, too, whose house stood at right angles to Miss Barnet's in the corner of the square, was also a willing audience to her brother's anecdotes.

He made it a custom to have Aldous in to dinner whenever he came to Cheltenham and, after their port, they settled down to an evening's survey of crime and its many ramifications. Pratt had not perhaps the naive attitude of the Misses Watt toward theft and murder, but was more interested in the psychology of criminal types. His chief, perhaps his only, hobby was a detached study of the actions and reactions of his fellow-men, a study which, after years of silent practice he had reduced to a fine art. Pratt always felt that he could anticipate to a detail what a certain man would do in certain circumstances. Or for that matter, though with less confidence, a certain woman. This hobby invested him with an air of intellectual detachment which seemed to arouse more faith in his patients than a jovial bedside-manner.

The aloofness of Sir Wilfred and Lady Eleanor, whose large, expensive, dazzling White House abutted the doctor's, was in an entirely different category. It was less intellectual and more snobbish, for Sir Wilfred's immediate forebears had by no means thought it odd to take off their coats before sitting down to their unimaginative, midday dinners. It was quite impossible to disassociate Sir Wilfred and his wife from their titles. They allowed and took no liberties, but dwelt somewhat apart from the other denizens in Regency Square, a little condescending, a little patronizing and generally disliked. Although several people in the square had approached Sir Wilfred with the suggestion that he should become a member of the Wellington Archery Club he had always refused with the simple though irritating phrase that 'bows and arrows were out-of-date.' To this sententious and absurd remark he owed quite half of his unpopularity, for Regency Square boasted a small, select band of keen archers, who were as fanatic in their own line as golfers. It was a well-known fact that many of the more vulgar residents in the vicinity referred to Regency Square as 'Archery Nook.' For all that the municipal and even county teams often called upon Dr. Pratt, Miss Boon, West, Fitzgerald and the Rev. Matthews to 'draw a bow' on their behalf.

Thus the inhabitants of Regency Square – diverse, yet as a community, typical; outwardly harmonious, yet privately at loggerheads; temperamentally and intellectually dissimilar, yet all of them chiselling away at the same hard block of granite which, for want of a better word, we call life.

CHAPTER II

Upset at Number Two

Hilary Fitzgerald glanced over the top of the ground-glass which filled in the lower sash of the bank windows. The Promenade was busy and crowded with afternoon shoppers, who ambled and chatted on the broad pavements beneath the thickening shadows of the chestnut trees. Expensive, glittering limousines were drawn up at the kerb watched over by zealous chauffeurs, who now and then opened doors and touched their hats to their fur-coated mistresses. Well-dressed middle-aged women pranced on high-heels, with a toy dog or a silent, moustached male in tow. Mahogany-faced gentlemen dawdled in the sunshine with small parcels dangling from their gloved fingers. Fitzgerald smiled a little wanly and accepted this mundane, animated scene with a nod of approval. Everything out there was going on just the same. Thank God for that! It was only in his head things were at sixes and sevens and his thoughts revolving round and round the same dark problems.

Suddenly his smile vanished and his slim, tall body stiffened. His eye had caught a glimpse of two people among that string of promenaders – two people whom he recognized instantly and with a hot surge of anger. The woman, pale, dark, distinguished with a set expression of disdain upon her almost Grecian profile, was Mrs. West. The floridly handsome man, with the bristly moustache, overwaisted suit and swaggering walk, was Captain Cotton.

'Disgusting!' he thought. 'To stroll about together in this shameless fashion. It's beyond me to say what she sees in that unmitigated swine!'

How he loathed those coarse, ruddy features, the insolent good-humour, the overweening self-confidence. The picture of that man was seldom absent from his inward vision. As he bent over his figures in the bank, as he sipped a whisky in his club, as he walked, talked, ate and dreamed – always that grinning, handsome face seemed to be leering at him. It was over a year now since Captain Cotton had come into the square and turned the bliss of his newly-married existence into a life of suspense and terrible anticipation. He could never shake the fellow off. Often when he walked home, tired, dispirited from the bank, there was a loud-voiced greeting at his elbow and the slap of that detested hand upon his shoulder. In the square they thought he was friendly with the 'Captain'. But that was through no fault of his own. The fellow was a leech, a poisonous leech, that was slowly sucking the health out of his body and the balance from his mind. How long could he stand up to this fellow's insidious attentions? How long would it be before he cracked up and threw in the sponge? And if it came to that? – he shuddered and drew away from the window. Whatever happened, for Joyce's sake, he must hang on to the last shreds of his will-power and refuse to accept defeat.

Joyce came down the steps to meet him as he drew level with Number Four. He kissed her in a perfunctory manner, slipped a hand through her arm and went into the house. She looked at him with her large, round eyes and asked anxiously:

'He hasn't–?'

He shook his head.

'Otherwise occupied, thank heaven!'

'Isobel?'

'Yes. Together on the Promenade. Quite openly now. There's going to be an almighty explosion soon.'

'Well, if *he's* blown up that won't worry us. I wonder Arthur has stood it so long.'

'We have,' he answered wryly. 'Though God knows,' he added with sudden repressed fury, 'I'd like to ... to–'

She laid a hand to his sleeve.

'Hilary!'

'Oh, all right. Don't you worry, I'll keep control of myself. But I warn you, Joyce, if this sort of thing, this nightmare situation goes on much longer, I shall go off my head.'

Captain Cotton stood just round the corner from Regency Square and squeezed Isobel's gloved hand.

'And look here, old girl, don't you worry about him,' he was saying in his thick, caressing voice. 'I've got your little Arthur taped to a T. He may yap and snarl a bit but he daren't bite. Nuisance that you have to take the brunt of his bad temper, but just you keep your nose up and he'll soon grow tired of yapping. After all there's nothing wrong in our little bit of fun, is there?'

'You know there isn't,' replied Isobel, adoringly. 'He can't expect me to sit at home all day twiddling my thumbs. And that's what it amounts to. I've loved to-day, Mark. You seem to make everything worth while. If only all these nosey-parkers–'

'Forget 'em. They're not worth a row of beans. Same time, same place to-morrow, my sweet?'

'Of course, Mark.'

He glanced furtively up and down the road and kissed her. She smiled reprovingly at him, squeezed his hand again, murmured: *'Au revoir,'* and turned the corner primly into Regency Square.

Three days later a group of workmen trundled a hand-cart into the square, laden with axes and hatchets and ropes. After a certain amount of preparation they began in an unhurried way to cut down the elm tree.

The Rev. Matthews, arrested by the sound of chopping, looked up sharply from his breakfast egg.

'Preposterous, Annie. He's stolen a march on us. I think it is singularly unsportsmanlike that we shouldn't have been consulted before the authorities decided to have the Tree down.'

His sister, a faded, anæmic creature in nondescript clothes, agreed in a toneless voice. She always agreed with Cyril. She had been agreeing with him for over forty years.

'Personally I think West should be asked to resign from the Archery Club as a protest,' went on her brother pompously. 'That may be uncharitable of me but I feel very strongly over this matter. You realize that anybody looking out of the windows of Number Five or Six will be able to see directly into our front-rooms. A disturbing thought, Annie.'

Again his sister agreed, though this time with less enthusiasm. After all so very little happened in the square that it would be quite exciting to follow the comings and goings of that queer Captain Cotton and to see Mr. Buller sitting out on his balcony.

The Rev. Matthews continued to scoop at his egg in silence. He was wondering if he hadn't been too soft-hearted in keeping to himself the remarks which Miss Emmeline had gleaned from

Buller's delirium. He had not wanted to cause trouble between West and Buller. But now–? Well, West had not been particularly considerate over this business of the Tree. It might be a good idea to give some concrete manifestation of his disapproval and, after a strong protest, tell West what Buller had said. It would show the fellow that it was a mistake to look upon parsons as meek, long-suffering, without the courage to retaliate when they had been snubbed. Yes – Buller's confession would give West something to think about. In the long run he might even apologize for his unchristian high-handedness. When he had mentioned the matter, in the strictest confidence of course, to Miss Boon, she had asserted that a thing of that sort should be brought out into the open. Out of fairness to Arthur, she said. He hadn't seen it like that at the time, only the upset it would cause, but it was encouraging to feel that he could disturb this fellow's complacency with Miss Boon's approval. It was like eating your cake and having it at the same time.

But it was some few days before the opportunity occurred for him to speak and by that time new and startling events had taken place at Number Two. The final, devastating quarrel between Arthur and his wife was impressed gently upon the square. Nobody knew anything for certain, they could only use their eyes and ears, put two and two together and make four. Miss Boon dropped the first hint with the information that when 'taking her *ménage* for an airing' the previous evening, she had heard the sounds of a violent altercation proceeding from the open window of Arthur's bedroom. Unfortunately the curtains were drawn to so that she was unable to say exactly what had been happening. This was on 30th April, just a week after the elm had been felled and carted away. About noon on 1st May Miss Annie Matthews, weeding the diamond-shaped bed in her minute front garden, saw a taxi draw up at Number Two. After a short time Mrs. West, followed by the taximan carrying a cabin-trunk, got into the taxi and was driven off. There was no sign of Mr. West. On 2nd May Dr. Pratt called on West with the offer of a 'lift' to the butts if he were intending to shoot that evening. He had found his friend slumping in an armchair with a glass of whisky at his elbow, disinclined to talk and refusing to turn out. Pratt had left him with the uneasy feeling that something had gone vitally wrong in the West household. He had seen no sign of Mrs. West. On the 3rd the cat was completely let out of the bag by Mrs. Haggard, the housekeeper at Number Two who, meeting the Fitzgeralds' maid in the High Street, informed her with a sort of breathless, well-I-never flow of words that Mrs. West had left her husband. No – she didn't rightly know where she had gone, but probably to her mother in Stroud. Of course, it was all this Captain Cotton. She'd seen this coming for months past she had, and her only surprise was that it hadn't come sooner. Lordy yes – poor Mr. West had took it bad. He was proper fond of her, and dirty dogs like that Captain Snake-in-the-grass ought to be hung, drawn and quartered.

By nightfall of that memorable day the whole of Regency Square knew of the crisis. It penetrated even the aristocratic walls of the White House, and was discreetly discussed at dinner before the servants and later more forcibly in the bedroom. All eyes were turned upon Number Five. Had Captain Cotton also disappeared? But much to the general, though unacknowledged, disappointment his high-powered motor-bike roared its customary, after-breakfast challenge through the confines of the square. Buller, who sometimes took a glass of sherry in the same pub, declared that the fellow seemed more jaunty and self-satisfied than ever. Everybody felt sorry for Arthur West, even those who had been opposed to him in the Tree controversy. Even Matthews felt dubious about handing on the information which he had received from Emmeline Watt, when he paid him a duty-call on the evening of the 5th.

He found the place in great disorder. Packing-cases were strewn about, the rooms were stripped of ornaments and pictures, the floors were littered with newspapers.

'I'm going away,' said West shortly in answer to the Vicar's look of inquiry. 'You know why, of course?'

The Rev. Matthews hummed and hawed.

'Ah, yes, to be sure. I had heard something. Nothing definite of course. A little domestic upset I take it?'

West glared at him.

'A little upset! My wife's left me, Matthews. For good. I'm leaving the square. For one thing I can't bear to live with the associations in this house and for another – you may as well know the truth – I'm so hard up that I've got to sell out.'

The Vicar was genuinely surprised. He knew that West was not a wealthy man, but he had never suspected that he was not in comfortable circumstances.

'My dear fellow, I'm very sorry to hear this. If only I could do something. But, unfortunately, Annie and I live, as you probably know, on a mere pittance–'

'Kind of you,' said West shortly, 'but it's too late now. This crash might have been avoided if I hadn't come such a cropper over those cement shares of mine. Things were not easy before, but when we began to get short of money–'

'Quite.' Should he tell West *now* about Buller's delirium? This was the opportunity. Only fair to Arthur, said Miss Boon. 'Why did you sell out so hastily?'

'Buller.'

'I see. Er ... you don't think that your loss might have been his ... er ... gain?'

'How do you mean?'

'Well, Mr. Buller knows all about the stock-market. He has inside information. Couldn't he, perhaps, have manipulated, I think that's the word, manipulated the market so that your shares depreciated.'

'Well?'

'Then when they had dropped to a very low figure, advised you to sell out and bought them in himself, knowing quite well that they were in for a sensational rise. They've almost trebled their price I believe.'

'What makes you think all this?' asked West suspiciously.

'It was something which came to my knowledge some little time back. I don't know if I ought to–'

'Well?' demanded West inexorably.

With carefully chosen words the Rev. Matthews told, in the strictest confidence of course, everything that he had heard from Miss Watt.

The following afternoon a pantechnicon transferred part of Arthur West's furniture to a couple of unpretentious, unfurnished rooms in George Street, the remainder being dumped in an auction-room ready to be sold. West himself closed and fastened the windows, bolted and locked the doors of Number Two, which in the parlance of the square was soon referred to, with commendable tact, as the Empty House. From that moment his life moved outside the circle of his old acquaintances. He even resigned from the Archery Club.

A week or so later, 1st June to be exact, Aldous Barnet's sleek, blue Alvis drew up outside his sister's house under the watchful gaze of the Misses Watt. His arrival had caused them quite a flutter of excitement. It seemed to widen for them the small world within which they dwelt, and they planned to send him an invitation to tea as soon as convention allowed. It would be pleasant to hear again about the dreadful doings of that elegant Dr. Crippen or that strange Mr. Charlie Peace who lived two lives in one.

But the Misses Watt would have been even more excited and fluttering if they had looked over Barnet's shoulder that evening as he sat at his sister's desk writing a letter.

Dear Meredith [he wrote],

Apropos of that conversation we had at the County Court a few weeks back – my offer still holds good. It would give me a lot of pleasure if you could spend part of your annual holiday with me here. I know you are keen on that book I'm planning out about the work of the County Police, but I really can't get going without your help and advice. So if you're still of the same mind as you were when we last met, what about the 10th? I think you said your holiday started from that date. Mind you, this is a proper collaboration and your name will have to go on the title page. (Officialdom permitting!) If you don't know Cheltenham you'll find it interesting.

Yours sincerely,

Aldous Barnet.

On the envelope he wrote:

Superintendent Meredith,
Sussex County Constabulary,
Lewes, Sussex.

CHAPTER III

Death at Number Six

It was on Monday, 13th June, three days after Superintendent Meredith's arrival in Cheltenham, that Captain Cotton decided to call on Edward Buller. Buller was one of the few people in the square with whom he seemed to have something in common. Perhaps it was that they were both inherent gamblers, that they both enjoyed a little flutter. He had an idea, therefore, that Buller wouldn't refuse to extend to him a little professional help and advise him about the investment of some idle capital. After a solitary dinner, served by his manservant Albert, Cotton lit a cigar and sauntering out in the square looked up at the window of Buller's study, which was on the second floor. In accordance with his usual practice Buller had left the window wide open and was, at that moment, standing at it smoking his after-dinner pipe.

'Can I have a word with you?' called up Cotton. 'Won't take up much of your valuable time.'

'Certainly. You can find your own way. The door's not locked.'

'Thanks.'

A few minutes later the two men were standing over a tray of drinks in the roomy, well-lighted room where Buller spent most of his time and transacted his few bits of very profitable business.

'Say when,' said Buller, the siphon poised over the rim of the glass.

'Whoa!' cried Cotton. 'That's just how the doctor ordered it. You probably wondered, old man, what I've come to see you about.'

'A bit of business, I hope,' smiled Buller, as he poured out his own drink. 'Take a chair and let's talk in comfort.'

Cotton crossed over to the hearth and dropped into a large, dumpy leather chair, which stood with its back to the open french window. Beyond this window was the little stone balcony where Buller generally 'took the sun' and read the *Financial Times*. Beyond the balcony lay the darkening square with orange patches of light glimmering out, here and there, in the various windows which enclosed it on three sides. As soon as his visitor was seated Buller let himself down, with a ponderous sigh, into a second armchair on the opposite side of the hearth.

'Well?' he grunted. 'What is it?'

'You hit the bull's-eye first time,' answered Cotton with a grin. 'Business. I want to find a really profitable investment.'

'Come into money, eh?'

'Struck oil, old man. Three thousand pound legacy from my dear Aunt Alice. Came as a bit of a shock as the old girl never really seemed to like the look of me. Don't blame her, of course. I never imagined myself an Apollo, you know.' And he fingered the smooth bald patch on the top of his cranium. 'But joking apart, Buller, when it came to leaving her money she found I was her sole existing relative, so she swallowed her haughtiness, bless her, and made me her sole heir. Point is – where can I best invest this little nest-egg?'

'Why come to me?' asked Buller abruptly. 'I've retired from the game.'

'Quite. Quite,' said Cotton soothingly. 'But you've still got your finger on the pulse of the Stock Exchange and I'm quite ready to recompense you your diagnosis of the patient. Shall we say five per cent?'

'I like the sound of ten per cent better,' said Buller with a broad smile. 'Ten per cent on the annual profits accruing, perhaps?'

'Or seven and a half,' corrected Cotton with a lift of his eyebrows.

'Or seven and a half,' echoed Buller, sipping his whisky with the air of a connoisseur.

'With a chance, a good chance of further business to follow, old man.'

'Have another drink?' asked Buller, rising suddenly and holding out his hand for Cotton's glass.

'Thanks,' said Cotton as Buller turned his back and walked toward the massive side-board on the far side of the room.

There Buller unstoppered the decanter, lifted the glass to the level of his eye, made ready to tilt the decanter and, in that position, remained frozen. There had come to his ears a strange, insidious sound – a faint zip, a loud click, and a long drawn-out sigh from Cotton. He swung round, puzzled, opened his mouth to speak and swayed there with his lips held slackly apart, staring. The glass dropped from his hand and was shattered on the parquet. He put down the decanter, shakily, took a couple of steps forward and again stopped dead.

'My God!' he muttered. Then louder: 'Cotton! Cotton!' Then suddenly coming to life again he stumbled towards the window and went out on to the balcony. His eyes swept hastily, excitedly over the gloom of the square, here and there broken by yellow daubs of light from the lamp-posts. He could see nothing, nobody. Everything in the square appeared to be perfectly normal, the lights still winked in the windows and from the adjacent house he heard the thin voices of the Misses Watt uplifted in some religious dirge. With the clumsy gait of an agitated and elderly man he crossed back to Cotton and thrust a trembling hand under his shirt, feeling for his heart.

The next minute he was stumbling down the stairs, along the pavement towards the unlighted house of Doctor Pratt. Just as he reached the wrought-iron gate, a car turned in at the end of the square and drove straight in his direction. As he was about to unlatch the gate a voice hailed him from the saloon which had now drawn up at the kerb.

'Hullo – who's that? Somebody want me?'

'Is that you, Pratt? Oh, thank God! It's Buller.'

'Buller?' The doctor peered forward closely into the half-gloom.

'Yes. You must come at once. Something terrible has happened.'

Pratt stepped out of the car, carrying a light overcoat and his inevitable bag of instruments.

'Well?'

'Cotton.'

'Ill?'

'No – dead. At least I think so.'

'Dead!' exclaimed Pratt in an incredulous voice. 'How? Where? Are you sure?'

Buller gripped him fiercely by the arm and began to drag him towards Number Six.

'He's upstairs in my study. There may be a chance – but–'

Pratt, the more agile of the two, raced ahead of him up the stairs and burst into the study. Without a word he strode across to the still and silent figure sitting upright in the armchair and slid a finger to the pulse. As Buller came panting into the room, he looked up.

'Tell me, quickly, Pratt – any hope?' asked Buller huskily.

Pratt shook his head.

'None. He's dead.' Then on a more strident note. 'Good God, Buller, how did this happen? What does it mean?'

'I don't know. I can't say. I was just pouring the poor fellow out a drink when I heard a noise and ... there he was – like that!'

'You saw nothing?' Pratt jerked his head toward the open window. 'Out there.'

'Nothing. Nothing at all. We must ring the police, of course.'

'Of course,' said Pratt, suddenly collapsing on the arm of the dead man's chair. 'At once.'

Buller glanced across at him anxiously.

'You look ill, Pratt. Have a drink? Upset you, eh?'

'A trifle,' said Pratt. 'It seems impossible that the poor devil could be sitting there one minute chatting and the next...' He took the proffered drink and gulped it down in one draught. 'Thanks. Now what about ringing the police? We daren't touch anything until they come.'

Just as Buller was about to take up the phone, he looked up and said: 'By the way, Barnet's got that fellow Meredith staying with him. He's a Superintendent in the County Police. Wouldn't it be as well to see if he's in and let him know what has happened? He could take a look round before the local police arrive. If there's anything to be done you may be sure he'll do it, and a minute makes all the difference in cases of this sort, Pratt.'

'All right,' agreed Pratt. 'You ring the borough police while I slip along to Number Eight and see if the fellow's there.'

Pratt's imperious ring brought Barnet himself to the door and in a few brief words the doctor explained what had transpired.

'Yes – he's here,' said Barnet. 'I'll get him to come along at once. It's irregular, of course, but if it's a major case ... well–'

A few moments later Meredith had been introduced to Buller and the four men were standing in a close group about the body of Captain Cotton. The stockbroker had got through to the local police and an Inspector was on his way. Meredith's presence in the room, however, had already introduced a calming, more official note into the tragic atmosphere. He moved quietly and deftly about the study, examining with a practised eye the general lay-out of the *mise-en-scene.* Of course, he had no official status. When the borough crowd arrived he would naturally have to take a back seat, unless they wanted his advice which, with the cynicism of an old hand, he considered doubtful. A pity, too, since this case looked promising from a purely professional point of view. It was not often that a police official was confronted, these days, by the dead body of a man with an arrow embedded in the back of his head. A clean shot, by the look of it. The poor devil must have died instantaneously.

He turned to Pratt.

'You're a doctor, sir?' Pratt nodded. 'Think the arrow has penetrated the brain?'

'Certain of it. Note the point where the arrow has entered – just half-way between the crown of the head and the nape of the neck. Deadly vulnerable, Superintendent. He must have gone out ... click! ... like that.'

'You think the body hasn't moved from the position in which it was sitting when the arrow struck?'

'Not a fraction, in my opinion.'

'Yes,' mused Meredith. 'I'm inclined to agree there. You'll notice that only the head projects above the back of the armchair and that the arrow has entered a bare inch above the top of the chair. That in itself proves there can't have been much movement.'

'A possible stiffening,' put in Pratt. 'A sudden rigidity, perhaps – but no perceptible change in the attitude, I imagine.'

Meredith made a mental note of the fact that the doctor agreed with him over this matter because, as he saw, it was bound to have an important bearing on the case.

He turned to Edward Buller.

'What time did this happen?'

'The clock had just struck the half-hour.'

'Do you usually leave your windows wide open at night, sir?'

'Invariably in the warm weather,' replied Buller with a glance in Pratt's direction, 'I'm not very strong constitutionally and my doctor here insists on plenty of fresh air.'

'Quite. I understand. And when you saw Captain Cotton had been shot I presume you looked out into the square in the hope of discovering where the arrow had come from?'

'Almost at once. But I saw nothing out of the ordinary. Certainly no sign of anybody walking about below the window. But you can see for yourself that the lamps only light the place up here and there. Anybody could have hidden in the shrubs, for instance, without my being able to spot them.'

'Hidden?' demanded Meredith. 'Aren't you rather assuming, sir, that the person who fired that arrow had criminal intentions? Why shouldn't it have been an accident?'

'Of course,' muttered Buller. 'That point hadn't struck me.'

'Personally,' went on Meredith, 'I think accident is the probable explanation. I've an idea that several of you gentlemen here in the square are keen archers.'

'That's quite right, Superintendent,' broke in Pratt. 'Five of us are members of the Wellington Archery Club.'

Meredith pulled out the note-book which he invariably carried on his person.

'Can I have the names and addresses?'

'Well at Number One there's Miss Boon.'

Meredith smiled. 'So ladies aren't debarred from your club, sir?'

'Miss Boon! My dear chap, you don't know her. It would be impossible to debar her from anything. Quite apart from that she happens to draw a very pretty bow. Better than Matthews at Number Three as a matter of fact.'

Meredith looked up inquiringly.

'He's a vicar, isn't he? I seem to remember Mr. Barnet here mentioning the fact.'

'That's right – the Reverend Cyril Matthews. Then at Number Four there's Fitzgerald, the manager of Poulson's Bank on the Promenade, and myself at Number Nine.'

Meredith ran his eye down the list with a puzzled expression.

'I thought you said there were five of you?'

Pratt gave a slight, apologetic laugh.

'Quite right. I was forgetting. Our fifth member and one of our best shots has left the square. You may have heard–?'

Barnet put in: 'You remember Meredith – I was telling you about that fellow West who lived at Number Two.'

'Oh, West. That's the chap whose wife has just left him. Another man in the case, wasn't there?'

Barnet inclined his head toward the immobile figure propped up in the armchair.

'This man,' he said quietly.

Meredith whistled.

'So that's it – eh? Umph. I hadn't quite realized that–' He broke off suddenly, went to the balcony and leaned out.

'This looks like the police-car. You'd better stay, gentlemen, until the Inspector has decided on his line of action. He'll probably want to ask you a few routine questions.'

Hardly had Meredith stepped back into the room, when the door opened and Inspector Long, followed by a uniformed policeman, entered. He was a rotund, grizzled man, with very bright blue eyes twinkling beneath a pair of almost theatrical eyebrows. Buller, for one, thought he looked far too merry to be a police official.

'Well – what's all this?' he asked with a beaming smile. 'Would you gentlemen have the goodness to sort yourselves out.'

Barnet stepped into the breach and quickly introduced Buller and Dr. Pratt. The Inspector ran a wary eye over Meredith's wiry, upright figure.

'And this?'

'Superintendent Meredith of the Sussex County Police,' said Meredith with a faint smile. 'I happened to be staying with Mr. Barnet two doors away and, hearing of the trouble, I stepped in to take a look round. No objection I hope, Inspector?'

Long's grin expanded to alarming proportions.

'I've heard of you, sir. You cleared up that Cumberland ramp and the Rother murder. Pleased to meet you.' He pushed out a chubby hand and added: 'Two heads are better than one anyway. Shanks here hasn't got a head – at least not as you'd notice.' He beamed again. 'Now, Mr. Buller, if you'd kindly accommodate these other gentlemen in another room for the time being, perhaps we can have a nose round. If the police surgeon calls, show him up, will you? He should be here any minute now.'

As soon as the others had withdrawn, Long let out a wheezy sigh of relief, poured himself out a stiff whisky, telling Shanks that it was dead against the regulations and dropped into the armchair facing the dead man.

'Well – what is it, Mr. Meredith? Accident?'

'Maybe. It's certainly not suicide.'

'Oh, that's good! That's good!' chuckled the Inspector. 'No, I've certainly never heard yet of a chap who committed suicide with a bow and arrow. He'd have to be a bit of a contortionist, eh?'

'So you noticed the arrow?'

'What, me?' Again that shaking, husky chuckle. 'There's precious little I don't notice, sir. I don't *seem* to, perhaps, but that's just my way. I notice, for instance, from the position of the arrow that the body hasn't moved more than a fraction of an inch since the arrow went home. Useful, eh, Mr. Meredith?'

'I thought so,' agreed Meredith. 'It suggests to you?'

'That the arrow was shot from the right side of the square – the right that is as you look out of this particular window.'

'Anything more?' asked Meredith.

Long shook his head slowly and said that he couldn't rightly see what the Superintendent was driving at.

'This,' explained Meredith. 'Not only has the arrow entered the skull at a considerable angle horizontally, but there's a slight vertical deviation as well. If you'll come closer, Long, you'll notice that the arrow has struck very slightly *downward*. You see the point? It couldn't have been loosed from the level of the square itself, because if one was shooting at a target in a second-floor window the arrow would enter at an *upward* angle.'

'Yes, I grasp that all right. That's a sound bit o' reasoning, sir – except for one objection.'

'And that?'

'What if the arrow was fired – I don't know properly if a chap can *fire* an arrow when you come to think of it – but suppose the arrow was shot from some point on the far side of the square, say from the other side of the main road – what about the trajectory? Seems to me, sir, from my 'umble knowledge o' things that the arrow would enter the target on the *downward* curve then. It would sort o' rise from the bow and then curve down. Maybe that would explain the point you brought forward.'

'You're forgetting something, Inspector. You yourself pointed out that the arrow was shot from the right of the square. Well, now, suppose you roughly project a line from the arrow out into the square – what then? That line is brought up short by the houses of the right wing, as it were. Here – take a squint for yourself and prove it.'

Bringing his round, childlike face within a few inches of that of the dead man, the Inspector closed one eye, as if winking, and took as true a line as he could along the shaft of the embedded arrow. It was impossible to gauge this with any accuracy because of the projection of Cotton's head, but a glance was sufficient to show that

Meredith was right.

'Darn it, sir, but you're absolutely right,' exclaimed Long in the tones of one who had expected him to be wrong. 'But I still don't–'

Meredith grinned.

'I thought you noticed everything. It's obvious, Inspector. The inference is obvious.'

'Inference?'

'Yes. The farthest of those houses – Number One – is not more than forty yards away from this window, and I have an idea that at forty yards the trajectory of an arrow would be almost flat. That's a technical point we must find out. But if that is the case then the arrow couldn't have been loosed from ground level. Without being certain on this opinion I should say it had been shot from a point level with this window – in other words from some second-storey window in the right wing of the square.'

'Now that's clever, now,' wheezed Long with an unconcealed look of admiration. 'That's really clever. You see, Shanks – from some other window? You follow the Superintendent's argument?'

'Perfectly, sir,' said Shanks in cultured tones. 'And I think it's a perfectly logical assumption.'

''E's been to the University,' explained Long, not without a touch of pride at being able to edit such an erudite inferior. ''E's good at talking but inclined to trip up on the practical side. Be a good thing for him if the Chief lets you work in with me over this case, sir. An eddication.'

'Case? What – a simple accident?'

This time the Inspector actually did wink.

'Accident? Don't you kid me, sir. 'Oo the devil

practises on his bow and arrow from his bedroom window on a dark night. Nobody but a looney.'

'Well, that,' said Meredith, 'you've got to find out. I suggest you send Shanks to make inquiries at all the houses on the right wing.' Meredith glanced at his list. 'There's a Miss Boon at Number One. She's a member of the Archery Club. Number Two's empty, of course. Then there's the Rev. Matthews at Number Three and Mr. Fitzgerald at Four. I don't see how Fitzgerald can be responsible anyway for what's happened, as his house faces out into the square in line with this. But he ought to be questioned.'

'Suppose we get 'em to meet here, Mr. Meredith? No – I don't mean in this room, of course. Lot o' people are a bit queasy where a corpse is concerned. Say downstairs with the other little lot. O.K., eh?'

Meredith agreed and as Shanks left on his errand, the police surgeon, Dr. Newark, crossed him on the stairs. He had been met and directed at the door by Mr. Buller. Alone with the police officials he got down to work quietly and methodically and his verdict differed but little from the opinion of his confrère, Dr. Pratt. Death was instantaneous. There had probably been little or no movement on the part of the deceased since the arrow struck. The arrow was probably barbed, a fact which he could easily verify by–

'Here, half a minute, sir,' cried Meredith. 'If it's all the same to you I'd rather that arrow were not removed just yet. You agree, Inspector?'

The Inspector did and Dr. Newark desisted from his intention with a shrug.

'The reason I suggest it's barbed, is that in the case of an ordinary target arrow it might easily have been deflected by the bone. The chances are that it would have glanced aside or even failed to penetrate the skull. I don't know much about archery but I do happen to know that in ordinary target shooting the arrow's not barbed. Stands to reason when they want to pull the arrow out and use it again.'

'That's rather significant,' said Meredith. 'When we do withdraw the arrow and *if* we find it barbed then it weakens the case against the theory of accident.'

'That all?' asked Newark. 'Thanks. Let me know the time and so on of the inquest, Long. Not Wednesday if you can avoid it. My hospital day. Hope you clear the matter up quickly. Rather a nasty business in a square like this. Know the chap by sight but never spoken to him. Not quite in my line, perhaps. Well, good night.'

'Good night, sir,' chorused Meredith and Long in unison.

CHAPTER IV

Meredith Gets to Work

As soon as Dr. Newark had left, Inspector Long got through on the phone to headquarters and gave a concise, though colloquial summary of what had taken place. In a short time the Chief himself, who happened to be working late in his office, came to the phone. The unusual and, so far, inexplicable aspects of the case had obviously intrigued him and he informed the Inspector that he was getting into his car, at once, and driving round to Regency Square.

'You'll like the Ole Man,' said Long in husky confidence. 'Quiet sort o' stick but got a first-class headpiece on him. First-class. No side either. Treats you as if you was a human being – not a machine.'

Ten minutes later Meredith had endorsed this opinion for himself. Alert, efficient, quiet both in manner and speech, he found the head of the borough police not only ready to condone his presence on the scene but to thank him for his co-operation.

'I understood you to say that you're on holiday here?' Meredith nodded. 'Suppose by any remote chance the Coroner's verdict is not accidental death – what about it, Meredith? Would you care to work in with Long? Without precedent, I dare say, but I think in my own division,' and an amused twinkle came into his eye, 'I think I should be allowed to *create* precedents. What do you say, Superintendent?'

'I'm on, sir, if I can be of any practical help.'

'Well, Long?'

'Two heads are better than one, sir, and his better than most,' was the Inspector's immediate reply.

'Very well,' said Mr. Hanson. 'Provided you make it all right with Lewes, Meredith, we'll consider the matter settled. Let's see, Major Forrest is your Chief, isn't he? Mention my name – we were at school together. Curious what wonders that will work even twenty or thirty years later. Now then – let's get down to business. What steps have you taken so far?'

Whilst Long was priming the Chief with all the facts which had so far come to light, Meredith stood by the open window staring out into the square. Curious business this, he thought. If accident – how the devil had anybody come to be fooling about with a bow and arrow in the dark? And from a second-storey window, too. If murder, planned and deliberate murder, what a curious choice of weapon the murderer had made! Not an easy shot, he imagined, to penetrate the skull of a man at a distance of not less than forty yards. Granted the window was big and wide open, the room brilliantly lit, but only the head of the dead man projected above the top of the leather armchair. According to Pratt all the owners of the houses in the right wing of the square were members of the Archery Club. No – wait a bit – that was not quite accurate. West was no longer in residence at Number Two. The probability was, then, that West could be ruled out. Then either this Miss Boon or the Rev. Matthews must have discharged the arrow by accident or design. Well, the moment Shanks–

He turned into the room and addressed Hanson.

'Constable just turning up with those witnesses we wanted, sir. Will you see them straight away?'

'No, I'll leave that to you and Long. If you'll take my advice, get Mr. Buller to lend you a third room and then have them in one by one. Report to me early in the morning, Inspector, and mind you get all the possible information out of these people to-night.'

When the Chief had left, the Inspector saw Buller and arranged that the witnesses should be sent in one by one to the dining-room. On the polite principle of ladies first, Miss Boon was their primary concern. She entered the dining-room defiant, angry, in a manner as belligerent as it was direct.

Glancing from one to the other of the officials, she rapped out: 'What's all this tomfool nonsense? I hear Cotton's been shot. But why drag me in? I know absolutely nothing about it.'

'Don't you worry, ma'am,' said Long, with a private wink at Meredith, 'that's about the one thing we're certain about. You know nothing, personally, see? But you may have noticed some odd little detail which, at the time, you naturally didn't associate with this ... er ... unfortunate accident.'

'Shouldn't think that man *could* die accidentally,' snorted Miss Boon. 'He was doomed from birth to die a violent and premeditated death. A congenital murderee, if you ask me!'

'Oh, go easy now, ma'am. Go easy,' soothed the Inspector with a doleful, rather censorious look. '*De mortuis nil nisi bonum,* you know. Learnt that off my dad, and in case you aren't familiar with Latin, it means, in a broad sense, "give the dead a square deal."' Adding with official cunning: 'No need to ask you if you happened to fire – er ... that is, release, an arrow across the square to-night?' Miss Boon glared at him wolfishly. She looked ready to eat him, peaked cap and all.

Long went on hastily: 'No – I thought not. Point is – did you see anybody else playing around with a bow and arrow?'

'I can't stomach your loose phraseology – and in any case I must disappoint you – I didn't.'

Meredith broke in quietly.

'Where were you, Miss Boon–?' He made a quick, mental calculation, allowing some ten minutes or so between Cotton's death and Pratt's call at Barnet's house. 'Say, between nine-twenty and nine-forty?'

'Airing my *ménage.*'

'I beg your pardon?'

'Dogs,' said Miss Boon briefly.

'In the square?'

'Most certainly not. I'm not such a fool as to *ask* for neighbourly complaints. They come without asking. I went for my usual stump – along Priory Avenue, down Queen Anne's Crescent into Victoria Road, up Albion–'

'Which would take you?'

'On my own,' said Miss Boon haughtily, 'twenty minutes. With dogs – at least an hour.' Adding curtly: 'They have reasons.'

'Quite,' smiled Meredith. 'So you couldn't possibly have been in the square when the accident happened?'

'So it appears,' barked Miss Boon making for the door. 'I presume that is all?'

'Thank you,' said Meredith.

'O.K.,' beamed the Inspector with a vague wave of his fat hand, 'Would you ask the Vicar to come in, ma'am?'

The Rev. Matthews' attitude toward the tragedy

was in direct opposition to that of Miss Boon. He entered the dining-room with a shocked, solemn and helpful air as he might have entered the parlour of a bereaved parishioner. But for all his desire to help, his information was of a negative kind. He had been sitting at that particular time in his drawing-room with his sister Annie. He had been perusing (his own word) the pages of *The Church Times* whilst his sister had been absorbed in working out a particularly ticklish hand of patience. He had not stirred from Number Three since tea-time, and as for being such an imbecile as to practise archery at that time of the evening – well, well, well. He gave the police to understand that no Christian word was forcible enough to express the absurdity of such an idea.

'The room faces the square, I take it?' asked Meredith. Matthews nodded. 'And the curtains were drawn to?' Again he inclined his head. 'And you didn't by any chance look out into the square between nine-twenty and nine-forty – I mean by drawing aside the curtain to see what sort of a night it was or anything like that, sir?'

'Most emphatically not. The events about that time are fixed in my mind because, according to her usual custom, Prudence, our maid, brought in our nightly Ovaltine at exactly half-past nine.'

'Well – that leaves Fitzgerald,' said Long with a wry face as soon as the Vicar had withdrawn. 'And his house faces in the wrong, blooming direction.'

'Hullo,' thought Meredith when the bank manager came in, 'this chap looks ill. Booked for a nervous breakdown if he isn't careful. Over-work, I suppose.'

To the Inspector's questions, however, Fitzgerald gave perfectly unemotional, sensible answers. His reaction to the news of Cotton's death was mid-way between Miss Boon's egotistic indifference and the Vicar's professional helpfulness. He said neither too much, nor too little. He and his wife had been listening in to a Symphony concert, since eight o'clock, in his study, which was at the back of the house. He had most certainly not been so foolish as to loose an arrow at random across the square.

When these three diverse witnesses had been dealt with the Inspector took written depositions from both Buller, concerning the actual incident of Cotton's death, and Pratt, in conjunction with his professional opinions after viewing the body. Meredith further questioned Pratt about West, eliciting from him when he had left his house, where he was staying now and so on. He then went on to make a few technical inquiries.

'In your opinion, Dr. Pratt – what would be the line taken by an arrow loosed at forty yards at an object on the level?'

'Practically straight. Not quite, I imagine. The arrow would probably describe a very flattened parabola.'

'So that at forty yards you wouldn't sight your arrow dead on the target?'

'No. I don't think so. You'd have to allow for a very slight gravitational drop.'

'Would it be difficult, in this case, to sight your arrow in the dark?'

'Extremely so. You see, one has to set the tip of the arrow dead on one's sighting-point. And in the dark it would be impossible to see the barb.'

'Barb?' asked Meredith quickly. 'When you say barb, do you mean that the arrow is actually barbed?'

'Good heavens – no,' smiled Pratt. 'When we're at the butts we'd never dream of using a lethal affair of that sort. Target arrows are simply fitted with a tapering metal point. In fact, although I've been keen on archery for a number of years, I've never even *seen* a barbed arrow. Except in museums. Much less have I shot with one.'

Meredith switched over to another line of inquiry.

'What sort of a shot would a man have to be to hit a nine-inch circle at forty yards, Dr. Pratt?'

'Definitely a good shot. A very sound shot indeed to do it five times out of six.'

'Could you do it?'

'Yes. But I should need an allowance of six shots to obtain, at a maximum, a couple of golds.'

'Golds?'

'Sorry,' apologized Pratt. 'That's our particular jargon for the common-or-garden bull's-eye.'

'I see. Was this Mr. West a good shot?'

'Very sound I should say. Patchy perhaps – but when he had an "on" day there was nobody in the square to touch him.'

'Thank you,' concluded Meredith, pushing away his notebook. 'I don't think we need keep you any longer, sir.' Adding as Inspector Long lumbered into the room: 'That is, unless the Inspector wants to ask you anything.'

'Nothing, thanks. Your statement covers the ground for my official report. Good night, sir.'

As soon as the doctor had left the dining-room, Meredith asked:

'Where did you slip off to, Long? Having a quick one?'

'Not me. I was ringing through to our official photographer. Thought we ought to have a few pictorial records of that bit of still life upstairs.'

'Good idea,' agreed Meredith. 'In the meantime, what about asking Buller for a screen and a sheet of drawing-paper?'

'What the 'ell for? Pardon my ignorance but I don't somehow seem to make things tally up,' said Long, pushing back his peaked cap and mopping his forehead,

'We'll collect what we want first,' answered Meredith, 'then if you'll come upstairs I'll show you.'

Five minutes later the necessary paraphernalia had been collected and the three officials got down to work behind the closed doors of the stock-broker's study.

'Now then, Shanks, I want you to drawing-pin this sheet of paper about half-way up one of the outside folds of this screen.'

Whilst the constable was engaged in this task Buller's elderly housekeeper announced the arrival of the photographer.

'Ah, hullo, Stinns – got your picture-box? We want half a dozen exposures of this little lot. May I introduce you? – Superintendent Meredith. The criminal's nightmare!'

Stinns laughed, shook hands warmly and said that he was 'pleased to meet' him. Long, in the meantime, had drawn the thick curtains across the open french windows.

The body was then photographed from several angles under the expert direction of the Inspector, who acted as assistant by working the flashlight apparatus. Stinns promised to let Long have the prints early the next morning and, after a drink (to which Buller had unnecessarily drawn the Inspector's attention), the photographer found his way downstairs and drove off.

'Now then, Shanks,' said Meredith when the door had been shut. 'Ready? Good. Let's have the screen over here. Careful! For heavens' sake don't knock against the arrow.'

Very gingerly Meredith manœuvred the screen into the required position, so arranging it that the sheet of drawing-paper was pushed flat against the shaft of the arrow without in any way disturbing it. Then, even more cautiously, he took out a pencil and drew a thick line across the paper exactly parallel with the shaft. As an extra precaution, in case anything should be moved subsequently, he removed a mat and marked in with chalk the position of both the screen and the legs of the leather armchair on the parquet. Then, satisfied, he stepped back to view his handiwork.

'What the deuce–?' began Long with an expression of puzzled amusement. 'Parlour games?'

Meredith laughed.

'Just a simple idea of mine, Long – but I think it may prove helpful. I'll explain. What we really want to know at the moment is the point from which the arrow was shot, don't we?' Long grunted. 'Very well. We can't take a proper sight down the embedded arrow because Cotton's head is in the way. But now we've marked in the exact position of the arrow on that sheet of paper we've got both the horizontal and vertical angle taped. All we've got to do now is to get hold of an expert bowman, pull the chair away, and get him to sight up an arrow parallel to that pencil line. He ought to be able to tell us, within a yard or so, the precise point from which the arrow was loosed.'

Long nodded approvingly. 'And it reads as pretty as a bedtime story. Smart, sir. That's a really smart idea. Take a note of it, Shanks.' Then with a sudden change of expression. 'Now what about withdrawing the arrow?'

'Steady!' cried Meredith. 'Don't touch it yet.'

Long winked. 'Finger-prints, eh? Is that what's worrying you, sir? I *thought* so. Well, you needn't. When I was up here just now ringing Stinns I tested the shaft myself.'

'With what result?'

'There wasn't any result.'

'What the devil do you mean – there must have been. A chap couldn't pull an arrow without handling it, could he?'

'Just as I thought. Nice smooth, polished surface, too – the sort of surface made for finger-prints. Point is – there ain't any. Not a whorl. Not a fragment of a print. Strikes me the chap who fired – darn it, there I go again – the chap who *loosed* this particular arrow must have been a bit of a dandy. He wore gloves. Curious, eh, sir?'

Meredith nodded.

'It's more than curious, Long. It's suggestive, even illuminating. It strikes me that the Coroner may not bring in a verdict of accident, after all.'

CHAPTER V

Burglary at Number Five

A few minutes later, when the gruesome task of withdrawing the arrow had been accomplished, Meredith felt more than ever dubious about a verdict of 'accidental death.' Hadn't both the police surgeon and Dr. Pratt, himself an expert in such matters, declared that a barbed arrow was never used for target purposes? Then, why, he asked himself as he gently twisted the blood-stained shaft in his gloved hands (a pair borrowed from the constable) – why was this particular arrow barbed? On the face of it, there seemed only one feasible explanation. It was barbed because whoever had shot the arrow had shot to kill! So many factors were already assembled to lend colour to this assumption. Firstly – none of the recognized members of the Archery Club had handled a bow that evening. Secondly – who, in any case, would be such a fool as to loose even a target-arrow in the direction of a lighted window? Thirdly – if anybody in the square had loosed the arrow accidentally they would almost certainly have followed its flight and seen the result of their foolhardiness. Yet nobody had come forward. Fourthly – it appeared that the arrow had been discharged from a second-storey window from one of the three houses in the right wing of the square. Yet the owners of two of the houses, Miss Boon and Matthews, had denied all knowledge of the affair. So if the arrow had been loosed from either Number One or Number Three, it had been loosed without the owners realizing it. This left Number Two – the Empty House.

'Strikes me, Long,' observed Meredith as he carefully wrapped up the arrow in a sheet of tissue paper, 'that the source of this packet of trouble must be the middle house. I think it would be as well for us to slip across now and have a look round. I don't expect to find any red-hot clue – if the arrow was shot from there, the fellow that shot it has had plenty of opportunity to make himself scarce.'

The Inspector was of the same mind.

'And to-morrow,' Long added, 'we ought to get in touch with this chap West. We already know he's a member of the Archery Club. Maybe he didn't like this chap Cotton.'

'He didn't,' said Meredith quietly. 'Although I've only been staying here three days, that bit of gossip has come my way already, Long. As far as I can make out, Cotton had turned his domestic life into a bit of merry hell. Alienation of Mrs. West's affections and so on. West would certainly seem to have darn good motive for the–'

Meredith left his sentence hanging in mid-air and smiled meaningly at Long.

'Oh, go on!' urged the Inspector vigorously. 'You needn't be frightened of shocking the lad. He's heard the word before and he'll hear it again and again. Eh, Shanks? Know what a murder is, m'lad, doncher? If not, this little tableau will put you wise. Don't you fret, sir, the Coroner's not going to get 'itched up on this job. Facts are too plain for argument. Cotton was murdered all right – yes, an' what's more – with malice, aforethought. We'll need a word with this Mr. West.'

There was a rap on the door. Shanks opened. Mr. Buller, still pale and agitated, stood inquiringly in the passage.

'Yes, sir–' asked Meredith.

'Er ... about the body, Superintendent. I don't know if it's against the law for it to be moved. But my housekeeper,' he smiled wanly, 'or for that matter, I myself, feel that – well, it's awkward ... you understand?'

'Perfectly. Don't worry, Mr. Buller. There's no official reason why Mr. Cotton's body shouldn't be moved to his own house. Let me see, it's the house–?'

'Next door – on the right,' said Buller. 'If you'd like a sheet, I'll–'

'Thanks.'

When the stockbroker had returned with the sheet, Long and Shanks shrouded the body, fetched a stretcher from the police-car and, followed by Meredith, carried the body down the stairs and out into the square. Just before Meredith negotiated the front steps he turned back and inquired of Buller:

'Will there be anybody in next door? I had an idea that Captain Cotton lived alone.'

'He does – except for his man, Albert.'

'Thanks. We'll be round again in the morning, Mr. Buller. I hope you don't object but I've taken the precaution of locking your study door and taking the key. Part of our routine, I'm afraid.'

As the little *cortège* climbed the steps which led up to the portico of Number Five, the house appeared to be deserted. Meredith, however, imagining that the manservant probably occupied a room at the back, rang the bell and told the others to wait. After a period of silence he rang again. Still no reply. Trying the handle of the front-door and finding it unlocked, he preceded the stretcher-bearers into the pitch-black hall, groping along the wall for an electric switch. Suddenly, with a muttered command for the others to do the same, he stopped dead and listened. At first he was uncertain, then in the dead silence which had fallen, he felt sure that he could hear the stealthy creak of footsteps coming down the invisible stairs. He called out sharply:

'Anybody there? Who's there?' No reply. 'Quick!' he hissed back over his shoulders. 'Dump that stretcher, Long, and flash your torch. There's somebody at the end of the passage or I'm a Dutchman. I wish the devil I could find this switch!'

But even in the short time which elapsed before Long and the constable could set down their burden, there came the quick and noisy clatter of running footsteps proceeding, as Meredith guessed, down the basement stairs, a muffled oath, more footsteps and the loud slam of a door. Coincident with this slam, too late to be effective, the rays of the Inspector's torch penetrated the gloom of the hall-way. Quick as a flash Meredith jammed down the light-switch, found another at the head of the basement stairs, plunged down, crossed through a kind of kitchen-parlour to where a door, fitted with panes of coloured glass, gave out on to an unkempt garden. Long, at his elbow, sent the rays of his lamp into every corner of the walled rectangle but, as Meredith anticipated, there was nobody in sight. At the end of the garden an open gate pointed the way which the mysterious intruder had gone, but although Shanks raced down the path and looked up and down the little lane which backed the line of houses he saw no signs of the fugitive.

'Now, 'oo the devil was *that,* I'd like to know?' asked Long in a petulant voice, as the trio went back into the house and climbed the stairs to the hall. 'Up to mischief of some sort – that's certain anyway. Couldn't have been his man, could it? – he doesn't seem to have showed up yet.'

'If so – why should he make a bunk for it like that?' demanded Meredith. 'If it was Albert then I don't see how his curious behaviour can be put down to the affair next door. He doesn't know about it. Unless, of course, somebody's tipped him the wink.'

'That's possible,' agreed Long. 'Now what about dumping the remains? I always think the bedroom's best – more homely.'

After they had tried one or two doors on the second floor, Meredith discovered which was Cotton's room and the body was lifted from the stretcher and placed on the bed. Shanks then returned the stretcher to the car whilst the others explored the remaining rooms in the upper part of the house. Opening a door which faced them at the end of the wide landing, the Inspector let out a prolonged whistle.

'Well, well, well – if this isn't a significant fact, sir, I'll resign from the Force. See that safe? See those scattered papers? Like a stage set for the second act of an Edgar Wallace, eh? Reckon this was Mr. Cotton's 'oly of 'olies – where he wrote his cheques and love-letters. Wonder if our customer has got away with anything?'

Quickly Meredith crossed to the safe, swung back the door, which was half-open, and peered in. A few scattered notes, mostly five pound Bank of England notes, lay on the floor of the safe.

'Money here right enough but whether he– Hullo – listen – who's this? Somebody coming up the stairs?'

'Shanks,' said Long.

'I know, but who's he talking to?'

Much to Meredith's astonishment the constable's companion proved to be a thin, weedy, bright-eyed little man dressed in an ill-fitting black coat and striped trousers – without a doubt the missing manservant, Albert.

'My Gawd, sir,' he exclaimed, breathlessly, the moment he entered the room, 'what's this I 'ear about the master? Dead? It ain't true! 'Swelp me – it can't be true. I was a-talkin' to 'im not a couple of hours since – just afore 'ee went in to see Mr. Buller.'

'You Albert?' snapped Long, adopting his most official tone as was his wont with persons of a lower social standing than his own. 'Captain Cotton's teetotum, eh?'

'Dunno about that,' replied Albert nonplussed, 'but I'm 'is man, if that's wot you're drivin' at.

Albert Crimp's my moniker. Been with the Captain ever since he was demobbed in '19.'

'Why weren't you in when we rang just now?' went on Long suspiciously.

'Posting a letter – box in Wellington Road at the other end o' the square.'

'Is that so?' observed Long with a wink at Meredith. 'Posting a letter. Well, well. Might I ask who the letter was addressed to?'

'You may. Chap by the name o' Freddy Flint – bookmaker if you wanter know.' Adding meaningly: *'Registered.'*

'Address?'

'14 King Street, Gloucester.' Then, as the Inspector was making a note: 'Crikey! – wot's all this? The safe's bin broken into – Captain 'ad three thasand pounds o' notes locked up in that there peter. You don't meanter tell me it's gorn?'

'Three thousand pounds,' cut in Meredith. 'Are you sure of this?'

''Course I'm sure. 'Ee come into a bit o' money from his aunt. I warned 'im it weren't safe to 'av the dough paid over in notes, but 'e always was pig-'eaded.'

'Ever heard your master speak of any other relations?'

'Never. Don't think 'e 'ad any.'

'Had he any employment?'

'Yes, sir – Johnson's Car Mart in Station Road. 'Ee was 'ead salesman for the firm.'

Meredith and Long made a few notes and elicited the following information from the agitated manservant. *(a)* That his master was not particularly popular in the square. *(b)* That he was really on speaking terms with only Mr. Buller and Mr. Fitzgerald, his immediate neighbours. *(c)* That he never entertained. *(d)* That there had been a lot of unkind talk about his master and Mrs. West.

'Now look here, Albert,' said Meredith, when the cross-examination had concluded, 'I'm going to lock this room and take the key. The body of your master has been laid out on the bed in his own room, where it will remain, of course, until after the inquest. In the meantime it would be better for you to hold your tongue about this burglary. You'll probably have to give evidence of identification at the inquest if we can't get in touch with any of Captain Cotton's relations.'

The moment they were out in the square Long turned on Meredith and observed sagaciously: 'Funny thing that Albert should have been so out of breath when he came in. Must have run back 'ell for leather from that post-box, eh, sir?'

'Quite. I thought the same thing myself. Another thing, Long – did you notice that he called the safe a peter on one occasion.'

'Criminal's slang, eh?'

'Exactly – might be worth while seeing if our friend Albert Crimp has a police record. He'd probably be too fly to leave his finger-prints on the inside of the safe – on the other hand he might not.' Adding as they drew abreast of the Empty House. 'Now for this little lot. If you'll take a look round the back I'll deal with the front of the house. I'll get Shanks to lend me a hand with his torch when he's driven the car round from Buller's place.'

As soon as the car had drawn up opposite Number Two, the three men got down to work, methodically examining every door and window on the ground floor. But at the end of five minutes they had discovered nothing in the nature of a clue. All the doors were locked and all the windows shut and fastened. Meredith then turned his attention, by means of a short ladder found in an outhouse, to the windows of the second-storey, but again without result. Although he paid particular attention to the three windows overlooking the square and *ipso facto* Buller's balcony-room, none of them gave the slightest sign of having been tampered with. These, too, were shut and fastened with metal catches on the inside. From the top of the ladder he looked across at the unlighted façade of the stockbroker's house and, although the study was unlit, it was obvious at a glance that the armchair in which Cotton had been sitting would be plainly visible from any of the three windows.

At the conclusion of this part of their investigation, after a further review of the case, both Long and Meredith felt that nothing was to be gained by prolonging their activities. They agreed to meet at Buller's at ten o'clock the following morning, after Meredith had rung through to Lewes to sound Major Forrest on the proposed scheme that he should help with the case. Long and Shanks then got into the police-car and drove off, whilst Meredith returned in a meditative mood to Number Eight, where his host was waiting up for him with a very welcome nightcap.

CHAPTER VI

Interviews

Although Captain Cotton had never been a popular or even accepted member of the Regency Square circle, his strange and tragic death sent a ripple of horror and uneasiness through that architectural U: that such things could happen *here!* that their exclusive privacy should be broken into by vulgar sightseers and avid reporters: that pictorial records of their well-loved domestic retreats should be scattered through the pages of the daily newspapers! It seemed incredible. Unjustifiable. Even damnable.

'Look here, my dear,' said Sir Wilfred over his breakfast liver-and-bacon two days after the tragedy, 'this place is becoming unbearable. God grant that I'm a democratic man – but there are limits. There are really. Some people seem to think that an affair of this sort is an excuse for familiarity. Why, only yesterday, White, my tobacconist–'

'I know,' sighed his wife. 'It's really too bad of people to be so inconsiderate. Why that dreadful man had to be killed here, in the square–' She sighed again. 'But, of course – he was that type. A hateful thing to say, but true. A sensational, *loud* type of man without any respect for the finer feelings of his neighbours. That ghastly motor-bike – ugh!'

'I think,' said Sir Wilfred after a short silence, 'that we'd better go.'

'Go?'

'Yes, my dear, to the South of France. To-day. Before we know where we are we shall be badgered – yes, even here in the White House – by these damned impertinent newspaper men. To say nothing,' he added, 'of the police.'

And apropos of this conversation on 16th June, that very day, the striped sunblinds of the White House were drawn back into their sockets and the heavy wooden shutters closed and bolted across the windows. The staff were given a holiday.

Perhaps of all the people in the square the Misses Emmeline and Nancy Watt suffered the most. By nature quiet and retiring, they suddenly found themselves exposed to all the world in the glaring limelight of notoriety. Their morning jaunt to the Pump Room, prompted less by the need to take the waters than the desire to indulge in a little pleasant gossip and listen to the music, was utterly spoilt for them. The merest nodding acquaintances came up to them, dumped themselves down on adjacent chairs, and demanded to know the latest sensational tit-bits. It seemed that their mild and rather pathetic interest in crime was to be satisfied by an ever-present and disturbing realization that they had awakened one fine morning to find themselves slap-bang in the middle of one.

Events moved too fast for them. From the rumour that Captain Cotton had been accidentally shot, the Coroner's inquest went on to prove that this couldn't possibly be the case and that the Captain had been 'murdered by person or persons unknown.' Rumour again stepped in. The Rev. Matthews was suspected of having connived with the murderer. Sir Wilfred and Lady Eleanor had fled from justice. Fitzgerald was the murderer. Dr. Pratt was the murderer. Poor Mr. West had been *arrested* for the murder stepping on to the boat at Dover. Miss Boon had shot all her dogs and then attempted to take her own life. Currents and cross-currents of suggestion and counter-suggestions crept into their shrinking ears and left the Misses Watt bewildered. They felt that at any moment, due to some horrible miscarriage of justice, they themselves might be warned that anything they had to say would be taken down in writing and (possibly) used in evidence.

'Well,' said Meredith as he dropped into a chair at the Inspector's office after the inquest at Number Five. 'That's that, Long. Of course it was a foregone conclusion. Considering the evidence we put up I don't see how the verdict could have gone any other way. Dr. Newark's point about the arrow entering the fleshy part of the skull without being deflected by the bone gave us a useful leg-up. Without that they wouldn't have accepted our expert's opinion that the arrow must have been fired from one of the three windows in the empty house.'

'Clever stunt of yours with that screen, sir,' put in Long admiringly 'It pinned our theory down and turned it into a nice, little corroborative fact. By the way, Mr. Hugh Bryant, the gentleman I got in to make the test, is an international. Draws a bow for merry England. Useful chap if we want any technical stuff.'

Meredith agreed.

'Well, now we've got our verdict, Inspector – what are we going to do about it?' Adding with genuine relief: 'Thank heaven my Guv'nor at Lewes raised no objection to my working with you fellows here. Sporting of you, too, Long.'

'Don't you believe it, sir,' replied Long with a dismissing flap of his pudgy hand. 'I've never been one to have any truck with the green-eyed monster, as the poet has it. A murder's a murder and that's all there is to it. Don't matter a rap to me 'oo gets the promotion as long as the job's tidied up. Question is, sir, can we do it? What about motive? That seems the thing to tackle first.'

Meredith suggested: 'What about your green-eyed monster, Long? Jealousy's a pretty powerful stimulant. You remember I told you about Cotton and Mrs. West? West had a motive, hadn't he?'

'Yes,' said Long in musing tones. 'I've been thinking a tidy bit about our friend West since Monday. Mark you, I haven't seen him personally yet. I rather felt it would be better to get our verdict before putting him through the hoop.' He reached forward and scooped up a sheet of paper from the desk. 'But Shanks has found out a few useful things about him. Living at 25 George Street – that's a turning out of the High Street in case you don't know, sir. Two rooms which he's furnished himself. Elderly woman by the name o' Mrs. Emmet does for him. Obviously in straitened circumstances, as the adverts say, judging from his choice of lodgings. Clean, respectable, mark you, but a big comedown after Regency Square. According to this Mrs. Emmet he's looking around for a job, too – at forty – that speaks for itself. Shanks put a few casual questions about Monday night but the ole gal seems to have a memory like a sieve. Thinks he stayed in all the evening. Thought she saw a light burning in his room. That sort of stuff. About as much use to us as a damp squib. If you ask me, sir – which by the way you've omitted to do – I suggest we pop round and have a word with West at lunch-time.'

'O.K., Long – I'll leave that to you. We don't want to fluster the chap by turning up in force. Now what about the burglary? How does that fit in with West?'

'A second motive,' said Long emphatically. 'Three thousand's not to be sneezed at by a chap who's really hard up. Pity we couldn't get any prints off the safe.'

'Did you expect to?' asked Meredith with a suggestion of sarcasm. 'If West *did* do both jobs then there *wouldn't* have been any finger-prints on the safe. There were none on the arrow, were there? If he took the precaution in the first case, he'd take it in the second. Suggests even that we're thinking along the right lines.'

'Which means,' added Long, 'that it was West who bunked down the stairs when we were carrying in the remains. Then what about Albert? Remember how short of breath he was?'

'Complicating.'

'Very.'

'Well, you see West and let me know how you

get on. I want to make a few inquiries on my own account. Can you give me Bryant's address?'

When Long had done so, Meredith strolled back to Regency Square calculating to arrive there just in time for lunch. Now that it had been proved that the arrow had been shot from the Empty House things certainly didn't look too cheerful for West. He and the house-agents, in whose hands the property had been placed, were probably the only people who had keys to the place. And since none of the doors or windows had been tampered with, a key was necessary. West was a good shot – brilliant on 'on' days. He had two sound motives for the murder. A lot, of course, would depend on what sort of an alibi he would be able to put up for Monday night. So far, at any rate, he hadn't made the fatal mistake of clearing out of Cheltenham – but that might be an argument either for or against his innocence. He might have waited until that morning, Wednesday, to see which way the Coroner's cat was going to jump. Long might find those rooms in George Street vacant.

'Mr. West in?' asked Long as the sour-faced Mrs. Emmet pushed her thin nose through six inches of space between the door and its frame.

'Not at lunch-time to nobody,' she said with asperity, reducing the six inches to three.

Long, who was in plain clothes and accustomed to this sort of reception, stuck a stout boot in the ever-closing gap.

'I think he might see me. Inspector Long, Mrs. Emmet. I wanted to catch him when he was in.'

Mrs. Emmet eyed the Inspector with obvious

suspicion, then very reluctantly swung back the door.

'Oh, very well. Up the stairs and the first door on the left. I hope there's no funny business. It's bad for letting. He's always seemed a nice, respectable sort, but, of course, there's no telling.'

'Suppose I told you he hadn't paid his dog licence?'

'I shouldn't believe you,' snorted Mrs. Emmet abruptly. 'Because he hasn't got a dog.'

Long's blue eyes twinkled under their bushy brows.

'Then, perhaps, I'm mistaken. Thank you, Mrs. Emmet – I'll find my own way out. Good day.'

Climbing the stairs, pursued by a vague odour of boiled cabbage and suet pudding, the Inspector arrived at a dingy landing, furnished with a mahogany hat-rack and a small table on which stood a stuffed owl, a vase of artificial carnations and a clothes-brush. A hat and a mackintosh hung on the rack. In answer to his knock, slow footsteps crossed the room and the door was opened, this time to its fullest extent, by Mrs. Emmet's lodger.

'Mr. West?' West nodded. 'Inspector Long – may I come in sir?'

'Certainly. I've only just finished lunch so you'll have to excuse the litter.' He smiled wryly. 'Try the basket-chair, Inspector, it's a trifle less hostile than the others. Well – what's it all about? The trouble in Regency Square, I imagine?'

'And correctly, sir,' smiled Long with his customary endeavour to put his witness at ease. 'You may not know this yet – but at the Coroner's inquest this morning a verdict of Murder was brought in.'

'Murder?' repeated West quietly, yet obviously shocked by the news. 'No – I'd no idea about this. What a ghastly business. I suppose you've no idea–?'

'None at all, sir, at present. I may as well be honest with you. We're groping. Papers may talk about an imminent arrest but that's all … balderdash. The only thing we do know is that the arrow which killed Captain Cotton was shot from one of the second-floor windows of your house.'

'Impossible!' contested West.

'Why?'

'The place is all locked up. I hold one key and Gregg and Foster, the house-agents, the other.'

'They wouldn't have lent the key to a prospective purchaser, perhaps?'

West summoned up a rather hollow smile.

'No such luck. There's no demand these days for that type of house. Number Two's a white elephant, Inspector. I was talking to Gregg only this morning. He hasn't had a single inquiry. If I had the money, I'd convert the place into flats.'

'Then how do you account–' began Long laboriously.

'I don't,' cut in West. 'Unless the place has been broken into. But I imagine it's part of your duty to tell me if this were the case.'

Long agreed and went on to explain how he had investigated the house and found everything in order. Bit by bit, his casual, seemingly irrelevant questions interspersed with his own racy footnotes and amendments, he led the conversation round to West's movements on Monday night. But, at once, a change came over the man – his former uncalculated replies gave way to more studied and cautious answers. A disturbed look crept into his eye, an uneasiness which he attempted to conceal behind a mask of bewildered surprise.

At length he burst out: 'But I've already told you, Inspector – I didn't move out of this room all the evening. Have you any reason to doubt my word? Why do you think I should *want* to prevaricate?' Long remained silent, turning the palms of his hands outward and letting them fall again to his knees. His gesture seemed to say: 'You should know best about that.' At this innuendo West became really agitated. The Inspector's obvious inference roused his simmering anger to boiling-point. 'But good God, man – you don't think I had anything to do with it? What right have you to even suggest such a thing? Was I seen in the square? In the vicinity of the square? Had I any reason to kill Cotton? The idea's not only repulsive – it's a damned insult!'

'Steady, sir, steady,' wheezed Long a trifle alarmed by the other's vehemence and quickness to take offence. 'You're jumping to conclusions. As things stand I had to put these questions. I mean nothing personal by 'em. All I want is facts. That's our chief commodity, as you probably know. Now then – you say you was in this room from five o'clock onward – just to make things more comfortable all round do you think you could lay your hand on some independent witness who'd corroborate your statement? Mrs. Emmet for example?'

'Well, she brought in my supper at eight.'

'And cleared it away?'

'Yes – about a quarter to nine as far as I remember.'

'And you didn't see her again that night?'

'No – I didn't. So you'll have to draw your own conclusions and act accordingly. If my word alone isn't sufficient to convince you that–'

'It is,' said Long bluntly, pushing himself up with a grunt of effort from the wicker-chair. 'All this, sir, is just an elimination of possible suspects – nothing more. I'm sorry you've taken offence because I don't like upsetting people. You may take it from me that I meant nothing personal, Mr. West.'

'And I'll admit I was a trifle hasty, Inspector,' apologized West, adding with surprising frankness: 'I suppose the police have already learnt something about my domestic life? The relationship, for instance, between Cotton and my wife?'

'We can't help hearing things,' admitted Long with a deep sigh for the perfidy and disloyalty of all gossips. 'For one person that we can't force to talk there are twenty that we can't stop talking. I hope things may straighten out a bit for you now, sir.'

West nodded absent-mindedly and crossing to the ornate, marble mantelshelf, began to fill his pipe from a toby-jar. Feeling that the police should hear the facts from him in preference to the garbled accounts of his neighbours, he began to talk again. Swiftly, unemotionally this time, as if he were reciting a piece he had learnt by heart. Long, ever on the alert for odd scraps of unsolicited information, dropped back into the chair and listened attentively.

It was, in its essence, a very commonplace story. An extravagant, somewhat flighty woman married to an intelligent but serious-minded man. Money difficulties arising through a bad break on the Stock Exchange – the refusal of the wife to cut her cloth according to the enforced economy resulting. An adventurer arriving on the scene, the kind of glib and practised Lothario who exercises a curious fascination upon a certain type of woman. The final, inevitable quarrel and separation.

'And here I am now,' concluded West, 'at forty-three, looking round like any youngster for a job. Any job. I've had to sink my pride and kowtow to half-educated bits of boys almost half my age. And the trouble is that I've not been trained to earn a living in the ordinary sense of the word. You don't make money out of biological research; you spend it. It seems ironical that now I could do with my inheritance to keep myself alive my capital losses have been so heavy that unless something turns up–' he raised his hand in a gesture of hopelessness. '"What a lot of time I've wasted looking at life through a microscope. Your way, the direct human contact, is safer and saner in the long run. Take that from me!'

'Well, I've never had any inheritance to lose but I do seem to rub along quite comfortable on what I get. Some people might think it a queer manner of earning a living, dealing with the misdeeds of fellow-mortals. But it's interesting. Makes you think. Instructive, too, because it brings you in touch with all sorts o' things which in the ordinary run o' life you wouldn't meet. Archery, for instance – four days ago I didn't know–' he clicked his stumpy fingers – '*that* much about the game.'

It almost seemed that Meredith's observation, as he sat in Hugh Bryant's summer-house, was an echo of his subordinate's confession.

'In a matter of this sort, Mr. Bryant, we're bound to ask the opinion of experts. Crime puts you in touch with all manner of specialized pursuits – sport, business, law, medicine, to mention a few. We can't know more than a few general facts about these things. Hence this visit.'

'And the information you're after?'

'First of all,' said Meredith, as he carefully unwrapped the arrow from its sheet of tissue-paper, 'this!'

Bryant put forward a reluctant hand.

Meredith laughed. 'It's all right, sir, I'm not asking you to handle it. I want you to take a close look and see if you can tell me anything interesting about it. Where it was bought, for instance? If the barb was added after purchase? If the shaft is much the same as those you use yourself?'

After a prolonged scrutiny, during which Meredith twisted the arrow from the tip so as to display every side of it, Bryant leant back and said diffidently:

'I can't tell you much, I'm afraid, but I should say that the barbed head, without much doubt, has been specially fitted to an ordinary shaft. This is a normal twenty-eight-inch shaft, which suggests, of course, that it was used with a six foot bow. There is one rather unusual point about the shaft, however. Did you notice that dark patch level with the nock?'

'Here,' indicated Meredith with a finger-tip.

'Yes – I thought it looked like a flaw in the wood.'

'It is in a sense,' agreed Bryant. 'Only it happens to occur at the usual point where the manufacturer's name is stamped into the wood. It looks to me as if the name has been carefully sliced away and a thin veneer of plastic wood substituted in order not to upset the flight of the arrow. Different colour, you'll notice, from the ordinary red deal of the shaft itself.'

'You see how useful an expert is,' grinned Meredith with approval. 'I shouldn't have realized the significance of that flaw. So you think the shaft came from one of the recognized makers?'

'Decidedly. Ayres, Gamages, Harrods – any of the well-known sportspeople. But arrows differ so little in appearance that it would be difficult to say where the arrow was bought without the maker's imprint.'

'And the barb?'

'There you've got me. Quite possibly it's hand-wrought. I mean it would have to be specially ordered from the sports firms because they only fit theirs, naturally, with a target pile. A dangerous procedure if the arrow were to be used criminally. If made by hand then it would not have to be of exactly the same weight as the pile which was removed. In fact, a slightly heavier arrow would be all to his advantage if he knew he would not be taking a long shot. It would enable him to take an almost point-blank aim.'

'Do target arrows vary in weight as well as length?'

'Good heavens – yes. We all have our special fads – like golfers. Personally I get on best with a four-

and-ninepenny arrow – it suits my bow, I suppose.'

'Would you consider that expensive?' asked Meredith practically.

'Expensive? I don't quite–?'

'At four and nine?'

Bryant laughed: 'Here! we're talking at cross purposes. Four and ninepence is the *weight* of the arrow. You see, they're weighed up against shillings. An ordinary shilling being the unit of measurement. Some people prefer a lighter arrow – say a four-shilling. This fellow, on the other hand, seems to have used the same weight arrow as I do myself. If you want to make sure about that point, I suggest you borrow a balance and weigh the arrow against four shillings and ninepence. In silver, of course!'

After Meredith had made a few notes about those facts which might have some bearing on the case, he began to question Bryant, who was captain of the Wellington Club, about certain of its members. What sort of shots they were, the type of bow they used, the usual weight of their arrows, and so on. At the end of fifteen minutes he had drawn up the following comprehensive list.

Miss Boon – Fair shot – 26 in. arrow – 3/6 weight – 5ft. 6 in. bow.
West – Good to brilliant shot – 28 in. arrow – 4/9 weight – 6ft. bow.
Matthews – Sound shot – 28 in. arrow – 4/6 weight – 6ft. bow.
Fitzgerald – Erratic shot – 28 in. arrow – 4/9 weight – 6ft. bow.

Pratt – Good shot – 27 in. arrow – 4/- weight – 6ft. bow.

After thanking Bryant for his information and patience, Meredith returned via the High Street to the police-station. In the High Street he called in at Boots, and with the help of one of the dispensers weighed the arrow. As Bryant had anticipated, it turned the balance at exactly four shillings and ninepence. Armed with this piece of information he went in to Long's office and found the Inspector had only just returned from George Street. After a full exchange of the results of their inquiries they fell, naturally, into a discussion of what theories they were justified in assuming from the new facts.

On the face of it Long's visit to Mrs. Emmet's had proved abortive. West had an alibi up until 8.45 p.m., but after that time they only had his own word for it that he had not left his lodgings. According to Buller, in a further cross-examination, his study clock had just struck the half-hour when the tragedy had happened. This would have left West three-quarters of an hour, at least, to have walked round to Regency Square, entered his house and loosed the fatal arrow. He, alone, of all the archers in the square, seemed unable to prove a satisfactory alibi. Miss Boon was out with her dogs – a perfectly customary habit of hers at that particular hour, though so far not corroborated. Matthews was with his sister, a fact which Shanks had cunningly elicited from Prudence, the maid, without her realizing why the question had been put. Fitzgerald had been listening-in with his wife in a back room. Their housekeeper had been out to the cinema, which meant that no disinterested witness could vouchsafe for the truth of this statement. Pratt had been out on a call and had only arrived in the square after the tragedy had taken place. Up to the moment the validity of this call had not been proved.

From this question of alibi they turned to a perusal of Meredith's list. Out of the five archers in the square only two were in the habit of using a 4/9 arrow – West and Fitzgerald. Out of these two, West, according to Bryant, was indisputably the better shot. Furthermore, Barnet had gleaned quite a lot of information from the Misses Watt concerning the personal relationships existing between the various people in the square, and, in their opinion, Fitzgerald was definitely friendly towards Captain Cotton. They often walked back from the town together after business and seemed to have the run of each other's houses.

'So you can't help but think,' concluded Long, 'that if West didn't do it then fate has bloomin' well loaded the dice against the poor blighter. Every clue we've got points towards him – like so many o' those accusing fingers you see on the front page o' magazines. I wouldn't be in his shoes, sir – not with you on the case – and that's straight!'

Meredith accepted this flattery with a non-committal smile. He realized that they had a long road to travel from mere suspicion, however well-based, to the law's more exacting demand of proven guilt.

CHAPTER VII

The Empty House

A perfect June morning. A cloudless, china-blue sky, a soft breeze which carried the scent of early roses from the gardens, a gay chorus of birds in the silver birches – Regency Square seemed fifty miles from anywhere. Seated on a newly painted, slatted bench, under a May tree, Meredith and Aldous Barnet gazed into the spacious enclosure, finding it hard work to associate this rural quiet with the murder of Captain Cotton. Twice Meredith had attempted to put his mind to thinking about the case and twice some irrelevant happening had lured him up a side-track. It was an onerous job worrying about crime on so perfect a morning. It was Barnet who eventually set the ball rolling.

'If West did it,' he said abruptly, 'why didn't he clear off at once? It seems so emphatically stupid for the man to hang around and commit a burglary two hours after the murder. You didn't remove the body to Number Five until eleven-thirty, did you?'

'No – but what about Albert? West couldn't rifle the safe until he was off the premises.'

'And in the meantime – where was West?'

'Hiding in some bushes – anywhere in the shadow where he could keep an eye on Number

Five, I imagine.'

'But the risk – think of it!' insisted Barnet. 'The chap must have had an iron nerve to have hung about a hundred yards from Buller's with the police coming and going and the whole square in a state of upheaval.'

Meredith said quietly. 'You're trying to tell me that West didn't steal the three thousand. I agree – that's very possible. On the other hand he needed the money. If he didn't pinch it – who did?'

'Albert. The curtains weren't drawn to at once in Buller's study. He might easily have been out in the square, noticed what had happened, realized that if he acted quickly he could get away with the cash before the police started to poke around Number Five.'

'A good theory,' acknowledged Meredith, 'except for one very strong objection. Long drew the curtains when Stinns, the photographer, arrived. That was just before ten-thirty. Albert, therefore, must have seen what had taken place before that time. In other words, he had a whole hour in which to open the safe before we turned up with the body.'

'A difficulty with the combination of the safe, perhaps?'

Meredith disagreed.

'With a combination it's either all or nothing. You either know it or you don't. No half-measures with these modern designs.'

'So that cinematic idea,' laughed Barnet, 'of light-fingered gentlemen in cotton gloves twiddling dials with their heads on one side is all bunkum?'

'Pure bunkum. Oxy-acetylene, if you like. Otherwise you've got to *know* the combination. Our man did in this case – must have done.'

'How does that fit in with West?'

'It doesn't. That's one of the manifold snags. He wasn't even friendly with Cotton, but we know somebody who was, Fitzgerald, the bank-manager. I've been thinking a bit about him since last night. The objection you put up with regard to West can't be sniffed at. It would have been a devil of a risk to stay in the square once the murder had been committed. This fellow, Fitzgerald, on the other hand seemed on good terms with Cotton. Often in the house and so on. On top of that as a bank-manager he'd know a bit about safes. Suppose, by any chance, Cotton had opened the safe in his presence – it's quite possible that Fitzgerald might have noticed the combination. I grant you we cross-questioned him before ten-thirty, but the idea of breaking into the safe may not have occurred to him at once. Even if it had it was essential for him to return to Mrs. Fitzgerald and get her to fix him up with an alibi while he was doing the job. Again he probably knew something about Albert's habits, and knew that Albert would go along to the post at his usual time. He simply waited his opportunity, watching from an unlighted window of his own house, then slipped in next door and did the job.'

'Well, it all sounds very plausible,' admitted Barnet. 'But a trifle up in the air perhaps. You're not going to fix him up as the murderer as well, eh?'

'I don't think so – I still have my suspicions

about West. Strong suspicions. He had motive, the ability to shoot, a key to the Empty House. His alibi is uncorroborated. The points against him stick out a mile!' Meredith sighed profoundly. 'But how the devil I'm going to ram those facts home by good, honest proof ... well, well, well.'

For a time the two men puffed at their pipes, silently appreciating the delights of the summer's morning and the narcotic influence of tobacco. The Misses Watt, two dark little figures like black-beetles, crawled across the square, which was bisected with a diagonal gravel path, and bowed their recognition from a distance. Dr. Pratt's car swished off on some errand of mercy – by the excessive speed at which he drove, a life-and-death case. Miss Boon came down her front steps, baying deep commands at her pack and made off in the direction of the town. Mr. Buller appeared with a newspaper on his stone balcony.

'A pity about that tree,' said Barnet, breaking in on Meredith's ruminations. 'I miss it. It leaves a gap over in that corner.'

'Tree?'

'Yes – used to be an elm over there. A real veteran. Some of the people here got scared and had the thing cut down. I believe West was the main agitator.'

Meredith grunted and retired again behind a secure wall of silence. He wanted to apply his mind to this case, solidly, exhaustively, before taking further action. Why on earth had Barnet wanted to break in with that chatter about the tree? West was probably right anyway – elms were notoriously unsafe. Too shallow rooted. Over in that corner. An elm tree. Oh, damn the tree. If West had left George Street at – funny that a murderer should worry about the safety of a tree. Seemed illogical. Oh, damn the tree! If West had left George–

Suddenly Meredith sat upright, knocked out his pipe and demanded.

'When was this tree cut down?'

'What tree?'

'That elm you were talking about just now.'

'Oh, that. Some time in the middle of April I think. My sister wrote about it. Why?'

'Just an idea. Shall we stroll over and take a look?'

Puzzled, but intrigued, Barnet accompanied Meredith across the grass to the stump of the elm, which the authorities had decided not to uproot.

'Well, I'll be–' began Meredith. 'There may not be anything in it – this idea of mine, I mean – but do you notice anything significant about the position of this stump?'

'Not at the moment,' acknowledged Barnet, 'though I'm quite prepared to believe that you're going to tell me something that ought to be obvious to the meanest intelligence.'

Meredith laughed. 'I am, Mr. Barnet. This tree, before it was cut down, must have stood in a direct line *between the windows of West's house and Buller's study*. West was the man who agitated to have it removed. If that isn't a suspicious fact–'

Barnet contested: 'Why not a simple coincidence? The point I'm getting at is this – if West planned this murder two months ago, how did he know that Cotton would visit Buller? It was an extraordinary rather than a usual event for Cotton to visit Number Six. How the deuce could West be sure of this. And further,' added Barnet with greater emphasis, 'how did West happen to be in the Empty House at the exact hour?'

'Cotton may have seen him in the town that day and mentioned the fact,' argued Meredith. 'I grant you there are plenty of holes in my theory. At this stage there are bound to be. But since everything at the moment points to the fact that West might be the murderer, the cutting down of this elm simply helps to underline the fact.'

For all his glib arguments, however, Meredith was keenly worried by Aldous Barnet's objections. He felt the need to get away on his own and wrestle with all the various conflicting details of the case.

'Look here,' he said to Barnet, 'do you mind if I take my pipe for a stroll in Pitville Gardens. I always think better when I'm walking around.'

Crossing, therefore, into Evesham Road, Meredith ambled toward the entrance lodge, paid his twopence and entered the gardens. There were not many people about – a few nursemaids with their charges, a few elderly ladies airing their toy dogs, one or two gardeners potting out plants for the summer borders. He wandered down to the little ornamental lake, with its weeping willows and arched stone bridge, like the conventional background of a Japanese print. Children were throwing pieces of bread to a gay flotilla of ducks. In the distance, beyond a fine, rising sweep of lawn, he saw the massive portico of the old Pump Room, crowned with its three outsize statues and enormous green dome.

He thought: 'Now let's see if I can reconstruct West's movements on the night of 13th June. He left George Street sometime after a quarter to nine. We know that because Mrs. Emmet cleared his supper away about this time. He walks round to Regency Square, taking care not to be seen, enters Number Two, takes up his position at a second-storey window and waits till Cotton is seated in the armchair. He opens his own window, of course, sights up his arrow and looses it. He then either creeps out into the square and hides in the bushes, or possibly stays at the window, until he sees the coast is clear for his entry into Number Five. He dashes up the stairs, opens the safe, takes out the money – wearing gloves, of course – meets us as we're bringing in the body and makes his getaway via the basement and the back gate.' Meredith paused in his stride for a minute, resting his elbows on the parapet of the bridge and watched a couple of black swans paddling drowsily in the sparkling water. A new thread of thought began to unwind from his brain. 'The bow and arrow! Now how on earth could he have walked through the streets with a six-foot bow under his arm without attracting undesirable notice? And what did he do with the bow after he had committed the murder? He certainly wouldn't have taken it with him on that burglary expedition to Cotton's place. Hidden it in the house somewhere? That's the most plausible explanation. And the bow and arrow had been planted in the Empty House ready for use when required? That again seemed likely. And the chances were that the bow still remained hidden somewhere in the house. West would not find it easy to smuggle the thing through the town to George Street. I think a thorough search of the house is indicated. Key from the agents. The sooner the better.'

His mind made up Meredith hurried off to the offices of Gregg and Foster, whose board he had noticed in the garden of Number Two, and after revealing his official status obtained the keys. Ten minutes later he was hard at work combing through every room in the Empty House. He left nothing to chance. He examined every possible hiding-place – chimneys, cupboards, floor-boards, out-houses, cellars, everything. He even climbed up into the roof and dabbled in the water cistern. Noticing a skylight let into the ceiling of the attic landing, he erected a tower of crates, opened the skylight and climbed through on to the flat crenellated roof. With his customary care he investigated, not only the roof area above the Empty House, but that of Numbers One and Three, divided only by a low stone coping. But there was no sign of the bow. Disheartened he returned to Clarence Street to see if Long were in his office.

Long was very much there – 'up to his eyes in work,' as he expressed it, but perfectly ready to shelve everything in order to chat with Meredith.

'Since seeing you yesterday I've had a row with my missus,' he began with a doleful grimace. 'I tell you – this murder case has darn near wrecked my conoobial bliss – not that you'd notice it anyway. All on account o' that bloomin' arrow that you handed me to take care of. Exhibit Number One, as you might say.'

'I don't quite see the connection,' said Meredith, puzzled.

'Well it was like this. Yesterday evening when I went off dooty I took the arrow along home with me, see? Thought it might be safer there than 'anging around the office with all these prying youngsters on their toes to get the low-down on this case. I tell you it's been merry hell here these last few days. Nothing but damfool questions. "When are you going to make an arrest, Inspector?" "Can we see the photographs o' the dead man with the arrow in his 'ead," and so on. Sickening. At any rate, just afore joining my wife in bed I unwrapped the arrow down in our parlour and had another look-see. 'Course, I didn't find anything new, so I took it up to the bedroom and planked it down on the dressing-table. Then I undressed, turned out the light and 'opped into bed. I was just about getting down to a comfortable eight hours when my wife catches 'old of my arm and lets out a couple of squeaks. "'Erbert," she ses, "there's somebody in the room. I can see a light shining over there." Naturally I cursed like the devil thinking that it was only a bit o' woman nonsense. But jigger me! when I did sit up in bed there *was* a light in the room. Just a glimmer. Not more. I called out sharply – in my best official voice, as it were – "'Oo's there? Better not move. Get me?" Then leaning over I switched on the light.'

'Well?' asked Meredith.

'There wasn't anybody there,' said Long with

comic anticlimax. 'Not a sign of anything out of order, moreover. I turned out the light and, believe it or not, that glimmer was still visible over by the dressing-table. In a second I had 'opped out of bed to investigate, telling my missus not to worry, and that it wasn't anything in the spook line whatever she suspected. I was right about that. It wasn't. The light was coming from the arrow.'

'The arrow?' said Meredith incredulously.

'Yes – two dabs o' luminous paint at each end. Makes you think, eh? You know well enough why they were there.'

'I can make a pretty shrewd guess after my various chats with the archery experts,' agreed Meredith. 'Those spots of light were necessary, I take it, to sight the arrow in the dark.'

'Exactly. 'Course they didn't show in daylight, and we hadn't thought to look at the exhibit in the dark. Fairly scared my missus I can tell you. I'm on my best behaviour up at home to-day.' Long groped under the knee-hole of his desk and waved a large bunch of flowers under Meredith's nose. ''Ere, what do you think o' those?'

'Lovely.'

'Yes – and I hope my old woman agrees. Otherwise I'm booked for a lively week.'

'Tried to trace the purchase of the paint?' asked Meredith.

'Yes – Shanks has been at it all the morning trying all the likely places in the town. But we can't expect much, can we? The paint may have been bought anywhere – Gloucester, Stroud, Cirencester, any-damn-where for that matter. He's had no luck so far. Perhaps your news is a bit more encouraging, sir?'

'Mostly negative,' acknowledged Meredith, and proceeded to hand on what little data he had gathered. After a full discussion of all the new facts Long said:

'I did find out something this morning. Nothing much – but curious. I was round at Johnson's Car Mart where Cotton was employed. Raking around for information *re* 'is past life, habits, friends and so on. What d'you think his screw was round there?'

Meredith calculated quickly, after a mental picture of Number Five and Albert, the manservant: 'Oh, about five hundred a year, I suppose.'

'Four quid a week! Four bloomin' quid a week and no extras. Johnson's don't believe in working their chaps on the commission basis. Now I ask you – how the 'ell did our friend manage to run his house, a motor-bike and general teetotum on four quid a week?'

'Private income perhaps.'

Long nodded with approval. 'Just what I said to myself. To clear up the point I went round to Williamson, the manager of the Provincial where Cotton banked. Nice chap – friend of mine. Always obliging and *very* confidential. Cotton had a current account there with a credit balance of twenty odd pounds. That's all. Not a hint of any income save what he was drawing from the Car Mart.'

'Umph,' commented Meredith.

'And that's not all, sir,' went on Long. 'Directly after breakfast I 'opped round to see Albert and pump him about that legacy. Appears this aunt o'

Cotton's lived in Cirencester. Alice Bateman was her name – a maternal aunt, see? So I got in touch with our chaps over at Cirencester and asked if they knew anything about the ole gal. Oh, yes – they knew her right enough. Well-known character in the locality. Loopy. Not dangerous but queer in her manner. Died a month back.'

'That fits in with Cotton's statement anyway.'

'Quite. Quite. But listen to the rest of it. The ole gal, who lived alone, didn't die natural. She was found gassed. 'Course, there was an inquest, and it came out in the proceedings that she hadn't got a bean. Not a brass farthing. They reckoned that was why the poor ole dear slipped out of her mortal coil, as Shakespeare says. What about Cotton's statement now? Legacy be–'

'Exactly. So that three thousand has got to be accounted for in some other way. And I reckon that wherever that three thousand came from it wasn't from any legitimate source. Otherwise Cotton wouldn't have troubled to invent that story. Strikes me he ran the house on a similar sort of income.'

Long, who was of a like mind, went on to point out that for all his inquiries the 'Captain' didn't appear to have a solicitor or to have left a will. In his opinion, an opinion which seemed to coincide with that of most of the people who knew Cotton, 'the chap was a regular dirty dog.' Previous to his arrival in Cheltenham he had – at least according to Albert's statement – been living in a flat at 23a Broadhurst Gardens, Hampstead, a turning off the Finchley Road. Money had not been quite so plentiful at that period, complained Albert, and he often had to wait a couple of months for his wages. His master had then been mixed up with a firm of antique dealers. The moment they arrived in Cheltenham, however, his master's finances seemed to take a decided turn for the better. Albert had no idea as to the origin of this sudden affluence. All he bothered about was his wages.

'Which suggests,' said Meredith judicially, 'that, whatever his underhand game, he didn't put it in operation until he arrived here. The question is – what was his ramp? What about blackmail? From what I've gathered about his character that seems the most feasible explanation.'

'With West as the plucked pigeon?' suggested Long. 'He's lost all his money of late. Another motive for the murder, too. Although he told me he'd lost it on the Stock Exchange.'

Meredith pondered a moment. 'I think the most likely victim is Fitzgerald. Remember he was the only man who appeared to be friendly with Cotton. A queer friendship when you come to think of it. I can't somehow see Fitzgerald 'mixing' well with a bounder like Cotton. Only a theory, of course, but worth thinking about.'

There was a brief silence before Meredith broke out with: 'Good heavens! it hadn't occurred to me in that light before. I was putting forward a theory to Mr. Barnet this morning that Fitzgerald could easily have been our burglar. You don't think it possible that the money taken from the safe was his own "hush" money? The fact that it was all in notes suggests it. Fitzgerald would know, I reckon, where Cotton dumped the cash. He was probably in the room when Cotton locked away the various instalments of his silence money in the safe. Do you know, Long, I believe we're on the right track here. It's even possible that Fitzgerald committed the murder!'

'What about his alibi?'

'We've only got his wife's word for it that he was listening in to that concert. No independent witness. If Fitzgerald could have got into the Empty House, loosed the arrow and sneaked back to Number Four – he'd have only been away for about fifteen minutes at the most. I grant you he's not supposed to be a crack shot but what's to have prevented him from practising in secret? Again, living next door to Cotton, he was in a good position to see him leave for Buller's place. Cotton may have even taunted him with the news that he was going to ask Buller's advice about the investment of that three thousand.'

'But if he committed the murder why didn't he nip in and pinch the dough at once?'

'Because he was intelligent enough to guess that the police would probably want to interview him. So he naturally waited until after our cross-examination.'

'I wonder if you're right,' said Long with a husky sigh. 'First West, now Fitzgerald. Strikes me, sir, we might just as soon draw up a list of everybody living in the square, shut our peepers and 'ave a jab at it with a pin.'

Meredith laughed.

'There's something in that, Long. We're still groping, I admit.'

CHAPTER VIII

Mystery on the Roof

Tucked away behind numbers four, five and six of Regency Square, dwarfed by the spacious Georgian architecture of the surrounding houses, was a small, old fashioned cottage which, before Cheltenham's rise to popularity as a spa, had probably stood in the midst of broad, green fields. In it lived the widowed Mrs. Harrington with her small son, Percy. Four times a week Mrs. Harrington visited Number One and tidied up the litter left by Miss Boon's incorrigible pack. Unfortunately an acute attack of asthma had put Mrs. Harrington to bed for a few days, with the result that Miss Boon, out of the kindness of her heart, was now visiting the cottage in order to tidy up the litter left by her charwoman's incorrigible son Percy. To do this she walked out through her own back gate into the narrow lane (where the dustbins lived) which ran parallel with three sides of the square. This walk took her past the back-garden of Number Four, Fitzgerald's house.

On the afternoon of 1st July, drawing level with the high wall belonging to Number Four, Miss Boon was surprised to hear the sound of low-pitched voices coming from just inside the closed garden door – surprised because one of the voices belonged to Joyce Fitzgerald and the other to

Cotton's manservant, Albert. In the ordinary course of events Miss Boon was not unduly interested in other people's affairs. In their dogs and canine ailments – yes – but not in their doings or quarrels. But the secretive and hostile exchange of words proceeding behind that wall was so inexplicable that even her sluggish curiosity was aroused. With one ear to the wall she stopped and listened. As luck would have it the spaniel which she had on a lead gave her a perfectly legitimate excuse for waiting, outwardly impatient, in the lane.

Even with her hand cupped to her ear she was not able to hear the whole sequence of this mysterious conversation. It came to her as a series of disjointed phrases, both startling and intriguing.

First there was Joyce's voice, quiet yet charged with repressed anger – the impatient voice of somebody struggling with stubborn obstinacy.

'Found out even now … of course ... must hand it over ... you know where it's hidden…'

Then Albert's sibilant objection.

'Not me ... a 'undred pahnds ... worth that, eh miss? ... one 'undred pahnds down and...'

'...that it's impossible ... my husband's already paid ... that was for the Captain … expect you benefited...'

Then Albert again.

'…'elp 'is bleedin' worries … know 'e did the murder ... motive any 'ole hows.'

On hearing the dread word 'murder' Miss Boon grew tense and alert. As one who still guided the destinies of a Girl Guide Troop she knew exactly what to do. Hastily she pulled out a memorandum pad and pencil from her hand-bag and jotted down the main points of what she had just heard. The rest of the conversation she copied out word for word with the dog-lead slipped over her wrist. Luckily for her attempts to write the spaniel was still completely occupied.

'How dare you....' she wrote rapidly, '...what proof?... If you think you can...'

'Easy now, miss ... I won't ... you pays up ... keep quiet about 'im being out...'

'And the other matter? ... before the police look through...'

'...a 'undred I said ... no more nor less ... get that straight...'

'...last word?'

'It is, miss ... otherwise I might 'av a word ... that 'ud be bad, eh? ... you an' your 'usband...'

Aware of a conclusive tone in Albert's voice Miss Boon did not dare wait a moment longer. It was obvious that Albert had slipped into Number Four via the back gate of Number Five. It would be awkward if she were seen. Dragging the resistant dog along, regardless of its unmoving legs, she hastened round the corner, retracing her steps to Number One.

What did it mean? What was it that Joyce insisted should be handed over? What did Albert mean by his reference to the murder? Was he suggesting that Fitz ... poor old Fitz? Impossible! Unthinkable! But for all that Miss Boon was deeply perturbed. She felt that something underhand, something criminal even was in progress, and had been in progress for some time, between the two adjacent households. No wonder Fitz had been looking off his oats. No wonder Joyce's pretty, though rather simpering and unintelligent features, had looked a little drawn.

She thought: 'I must see Pratt about this. He's a bit of a pompous ass but he'll know what to do. Yes – I'll see him now. Harrington must wait!'

She stumped back through the square and rang the doctor's bell resoundingly.

'Urgent,' she said to the maid. 'No excuses. I must see the doctor without delay. Where is he – having tea?'

'Yes, ma'am.'

'I thought so. Send in another cup and I'll take it with him. Well, bustle along!'

The maid tactfully scurried off, whilst Miss Boon, calling loudly to her spaniel, banged down the hall and burst decisively into Pratt's drawing-room.

'No – don't get up,' she boomed. 'I want to talk. I've just heard something extraordinary. Want your advice. Now get on with your tea, my dear man, and listen.'

Save for a momentary interruption when the maid entered with the extra cup and saucer, Miss Boon spoke without a break for five minutes. Her monologue included the verbatim notes which she had made of that perplexing conversation. At the end of those five minutes Pratt got up without a word and crossed over to the phone.

'What are you up to?' demanded Miss Boon suspiciously.

'I'm ringing up next door to see if that chap Meredith is in.'

'Damned abominable laziness, Pratt. You're

sure this is a police matter?'

Pratt nodded emphatically as he dialled the number.

'I certainly am. Don't you realize that this may have some important bearing on their investigations?'

If Meredith was intrigued by Miss Boon's staccato collection of facts he allowed no vestige of it to appear on his features. With his usual methodical care he took a copious series of notes, copying out word for word the most vital section of her evidence. Once clear of the doctor's house, he slipped up to his own room and sat by the open window poring over the strange and unexpected information which had just come to hand. What precisely did it mean? Why were this ill-assorted couple in such close and secret confabulation behind the wall of Number Four?

The longer Meredith studied the notes the more he was struck by two of the principal phrases. No less than three times Albert had made mention of a ''undred pahnds.' And later he had stated this bald and simple fact: 'Know 'e did the murder.' The more he puzzled over the matter the more Meredith felt that these two phrases were interrelated. It suggested – surely he was right in supposing this? – that Albert was coolly, calculatingly blackmailing the Fitzgeralds. Blackmailing the bank-manager because he had some hold over him concerning the murder. A later phrase seemed to offer further enlightenment ... 'keep quiet about 'im being out.' Out where? In the square possibly. Out in the square, some time after eight on that fateful night, although Fitzgerald swore he had been indoors listening-in to that concert. Did it mean that Fitzgerald had called in to see Cotton, found that he was out at Buller's, seen the Captain in the open window, returned to his house, fetched the bow and arrow, sneaked along to the Empty House, somehow forced an entry and committed the crime? And had Albert, perhaps, seen him either going or returning from West's place with that tell-tale bow?

'Here, but wait a minute,' argued Meredith. 'I'm going too fast. What possible motive could Fitzgerald have for wanting Cotton out of the way? Cotton wasn't making up to *his* wife. An ideally happy couple according to the square... But, confound it, he must have had a motive if he *did* do it!'

Meredith again returned to a concentrated perusal of his notes. Was there anything in his wife's words which hinted at a possible motive? Nothing as far as he could see. No – wait a bit! Miss Boon had said something about 'my husband's paid ... for the Captain.' Yes – here it was '...my husband's already paid ... that was for the Captain ... expect you benefited...' This obviously suggested that the bank-manager had already paid out something and not, in his case, to Albert but to Cotton himself. If this were so then there were two distinct cases of blackmail to be investigated. And if it could be proved that Fitzgerald had been paying out silence money to the Captain, here was a cast-iron motive for the murder. But what hold had Cotton over his neighbour? Something detrimental which he knew about his past life? Something criminal connected with his job at the bank? Misappropriation? A woman in the case? What?

Curious how, in talking to Long the week before, he had put forward this precise theory and coupled it with the further theory that Fitzgerald had rifled the safe to get back his own 'hush' money. Did it mean that the murder, too, could now be fixed on the same man?

As usual, Meredith attacked this supposition by setting up all the 'againsts.' As far as he could see the strongest objection to the bank-manager being the criminal was the difficulty he would have in entering the Empty House. All the doors, save the front, were bolted on the inside. All the windows were locked. The front door opened with a Yale. Surely it hadn't been possible for Fitzgerald to take a wax impression and have another key made? Always a risky procedure because of the necessary confederate. Then how the devil had he got in? There was no other–

Meredith let out a muffled exclamation and clicked his fingers. Good heavens! the skylight! The flat roof. Wasn't it possible that Fitzgerald had made an overhead journey from Number Four to the Empty House? There and then he decided to stroll round and, surreptitiously, take a look. In order to help the police investigation West had sensibly surrendered his own key to Number Two and Meredith now made use of it. Setting up the crates and climbing out once more through the skylight on to the roof, he took a rapid survey of Fitzgerald's possible route. He was interested at once. The roof of Number Four, unlike that of Number Three which it abutted at right-angles, went up to an apex. In the triangular face thus formed above the flat roof of Matthews' house was a small window. Screening himself as much as possible behind the chimney-stacks, not wanting to arouse anybody's curiosity, Meredith worked his way along the roofs to this small window. He noticed instantly that it was ajar and that the cement wall directly beneath it was scored with a number of light, and obviously recent scratches. His interest deepened. Did it mean that he was on the right track? Those scratches certainly suggested that somebody had used that little window as a means of getting out on to the roof. But who exactly had–

Meredith suddenly lent down and let out a small grunt of satisfaction. Imprinted on the grimy cement, with which the flat roofs were covered, clearly discernible, were a series of footprints. Footprints with certain peculiar characteristics. Whoever had climbed out of that window had certainly worn rubber soles and heels, the pattern of which consisted of a number of hollowed circles surrounding an embossed centre about the size of a sixpence. The prints both came and went from the window and, with little difficulty, Meredith was able to follow this mysterious track. But what did it mean? Despite all his fine theories the footsteps did not terminate at the skylight of the Empty House. They proceeded a short distance across the roof of Number Three, skirting a chimney-stack, turned toward the front of the house and were brought up short by the low, crenellated coping. But why? What on earth was the point of this unknown prowler standing mid-way along the

Vicar's roof and looking down into the square? It was obvious that the man – or woman? – no, the footprints were surely those of a man? – that the man had stood at this point for some time. Quite an accumulation of match-ends and cigarette-butts littered the spot. Meredith collected one or two of the butts – Craven A cork-tipped. Well and good – all he had to do now was to find this gentleman who smoked that brand of cigarette and wore that particular sort of rubbers on his shoes.

A little later he was on the phone to Long.

'For reasons which I'll let you know later, it's absolutely necessary that you arrange to interview Fitzgerald in your office. A further cross-examination, perhaps, with regard to his movements on the night of the murder. That might prove useful anyway now. I'll come round and let you know what's happened since I last saw you. Can you arrange to have Fitzgerald round in about an hour's time?'

As the bank-manager came into the Inspector's office at Clarence Street, Meredith was shocked by his appearance. If he had thought him ill on the night of the murder, what about the poor devil now? He looked like a walking skeleton. Even his voice was utterly without animation, a dead, disinterested monotone. Long asked him to sit down and the cross-examination politely and methodically proceeded. No – he was sorry but he had only his wife's statement to corroborate his own evidence about his movements on the thirteenth. Yes – it was certainly unfortunate but one couldn't very well manufacture evidence when it didn't exist, could one? Was he very friendly with the late Captain Cotton? No hardly that. The friendship – if indeed it existed – was very one-sided. But it was quite true that he often visited Cotton and that Cotton often came in for a drink in the evenings. His wife's attitude toward the Captain? Well, frankly, she detested him. She thought he was an unpleasant and shifty type. There was a pause whilst Long ostensibly jotted down a few notes. Meredith picked up the cigarette-box from the desk and offered it to the bank-manager.

'Smoke, sir? Oh – sorry. I hadn't noticed. Long, you've run short of cigarettes.' Meredith fumbled in his own pockets. 'Confound it – I'm in the same state. Sorry about that, Mr. Fitzgerald.'

'Here – have one of mine,' said Fitzgerald, holding out his case.

'Thanks,' said Meredith.

Suddenly Long looked up and said: 'You've never by any chance let Cotton have any money, have you, sir?'

A fleeting expression of alarm crossed Fitzgerald's features.

'Of course not,' he protested. 'What on earth put that idea into your head?' He smiled wanly. 'I may be a fool but not quite such a fool as that, Inspector.'

'And you don't think your wife–?'

'Joyce? Good heavens – no!'

'Did you know Cotton before he arrived in Cheltenham, sir?'

'No – luckily.'

'And previous to your appointment here you

were at–?'

'Poulson's Swiss Cottage branch in the Finchley Road.'

Meredith pricked up his ears and exchanged a quick glance with the Inspector.

'Did you know Mrs. Fitzgerald then, sir, or hadn't you met?'

The manager hesitated a moment, clearly embarrassed by this unexpected question; then he said flatly: 'Yes – we met in Hampstead and when I had been down here for six months we were married.' Adding quite extraneously Meredith thought: 'My wife is an orphan, you know. She lived with her aunt for a time but when we met in Hampstead she was living on her own. She had a job in the West End.'

Long said amiably: 'I expect you think all these questions a bit unnecessary, eh, sir? Most witnesses do – but, believe me, it's often some entirely chance question which lets in the daylight.'

After a few more polite exchanges of this sort, Fitzgerald took his departure. Instantly Meredith crossed to the door and picked up a smooth, damp rubber mat which had been specially placed just inside the office.

'Well?' demanded Long anxiously.

Meredith spread the mat out on the desk.

'What do you think of that, Long? Conclusive, isn't it?'

'And that cigarette you so cunningly cadged?'

'Craven A, Long – cork-tipped.'

Long whistled.

'Now what's his little game, I wonder? Did 'e do the murder? If so why didn't those bloomin' footprints o' yours end at the skylight? Notice how fidgety 'e was when we started to pump him about his previous job. Hampstead, eh? Cotton lived in West Hampstead, didn't he? Must have been within a stone's throw of each other at that time. And they never met! Well, well, well – what a coincidence. Three people, all more or less living in each other's pockets in Hampstead. One of 'em moves to Cheltenham and hey presto – the other two follow in father's footsteps.'

'Yes, I've got the same feeling,' said Meredith slowly. 'I've got the glimmerings of an idea. Just a spark. You don't think that Mrs. F was living with Cotton when Fitzgerald first met her?'

'Oh, tut-tut! Is she that sort o' lady?'

'I'm not sure,' went on Meredith after a moment's thought. 'Only, you see, if Fitzgerald did do the murder he must have had a motive. Now my idea is – taking into consideration that conversation Miss Boon overheard – that Cotton was receiving money from him. He had some hold over Fitzgerald, and I'm beginning to think now that this hold had something to do with Joyce Fitzgerald.'

'You mean the Captain knew they weren't married and threatened to let the cat out of the bag unless Fitz paid up?'

'Yes – that's one possibility.'

'And he'd naturally be a bit pipped – I mean Cotton – if 'is bit o' goods had 'opped off with another man. That type always are. Think their own powers of attraction can't be resisted. I seen some o' that, I can tell you.'

'There's an alternative supposition, too,' went

on Meredith. 'What if Cotton and the girl *were* married? That's possible. I've an idea that Cotton would have found Mrs. Fitz rather in his line. Well, suppose she got fed up with her husband's immoralities and cleared off, eventually meeting Fitzgerald and falling in love with him. Isn't it possible, Long, that when Fitzgerald got the job here, he thought he'd be far enough away from Cotton to take the risk?'

'You mean, for appearances sake, they went through a marriage ceremony?' Meredith nodded. 'Bigamy on her part, eh?' Meredith nodded again.

He went on to explain further: 'Cotton finds out what has happened, sees his chance to turn a dishonest penny and takes a house next door to his legal wife. Quite a nice little situation. Pleasant for poor old Fitzgerald with his reputation to keep up for the sake of his job. The bank authorities, you bet, wouldn't stomach any sort of a scandal.'

'And when the opportunity comes Fitz puts his unwelcome neighbour out of the way?' exclaimed Long, obviously impressed by Meredith's theory. 'Then why did those footsteps only go as far as the middle of the coping on Matthews' roof?'

'Do you think he could have shot the arrow from that point?' asked Meredith.

'You should know the answer better than me,' protested Long. 'You took a look round from up there this afternoon.'

'Yes, and was fairly well satisfied that Cotton couldn't have been hit with any certainty from that point. As a matter of fact Buller was seated in the same armchair in just the same position. I could just see the crown of his head and his bald patch. But only just – if Buller moved at all half his head disappeared behind the window-frame. Besides, what about the arrow? The angles, both the vertical and horizontal would have been quite different. No, Long, if Fitz did kill Cotton then, in some way, he must have entered the Empty House.' Meredith sighed. 'I wish the devil we could find out what Albert saw on the night of the thirteenth. He's got *some* damaging evidence up his sleeve – damaging that is for Fitzgerald. Do you think we could frighten him into speaking?'

Long rubbed his chin reflectively, then leaning forward selected a couple of memo-slips from a tray on the desk.

'I took Albert into a pub the other day, partly to find out what he really knows and partly to get a line on him. Usual stunt with a specially polished glass to get his finger-prints. Not the first time Gertie has helped me in this way. Also got Stinns to plant himself behind the laurel bushes in front of West's place and get a few useful snapshots. Fitz, his wife's, Matthews, Miss Boon's and, o' course, Albert's. I had the finger-prints photographed and sent them up to the Yard, together with an enlargement of the chap's dial. Result came to hand this morning. 'E's been identified. Two convictions for theft. And that's not all – the Yard have got him docketed alongside our friend the Captain. They know they've worked together. Confidence stuff mostly. Cotton's never been convicted but the Yard have got a few details of his career filed away. He's always been too fly for them to make an arrest.'

'Well – what's your idea?'

'Oh, have him along here and put him politely but firmly through a bit o' third degree. I've an idea that Miss Boon's evidence can be used to good account. Shall we say eight o'clock here this evening if we can lay our hands on him?'

At eight o'clock precisely Shanks ushered a somewhat alarmed and wary Albert into the Inspector's office. After Meredith had handed him a cigarette, Long got down to work.

'Remember the autumn of 1929, Albert?'

'1929?'

'Yes – remember it?'

'Why should I?'

'Oh, I only thought you might do. No particular reason. Or even the summer of 1932. You didn't see much o' that summer did you, Albert? In cramped quarters, eh?'

''Ere, 'arf a mo – wot's this all abaht? You've got nothing–'

'O.K. O.K. Forget it,' said Long soothingly. 'That's past history anyway. I'm more interested actually in something that happened this afternoon. You're a careless sort o' chap, Albert. If you take my advice next time you want to pluck a pigeon do it indoors – otherwise the feathers are inclined to fly about. You never know 'oo's going to pick them up. The constable here, for example, might be walking down a lane behind Regency Square and 'ocus-pocus ... a few feathers come floating over the wall from Mr. Fitzgerald's garden. O' course you weren't ever in his garden were you, Albert?'

'Don't talk silly. You know I wasn't.' Albert

looked uneasily from Meredith to the Inspector and cast a suspicious glance at Shanks, who was standing with a poker-face in the doorway. '"Ere, wot are you trying to lay on me?'

Long picked up a slip of paper and examined it casually. Clearing his throat ostentatiously he read: '"...a 'undred pahnds ... worth that, eh miss? ... one 'undred pahnds down and..." And what, Albert? Pity some o' the feathers floated out o' the constable's reach. But we've got a tidy lot in the bag, believe me. Well,' rapped out Long on a sharper note, 'are you going to speak?'

Albert's shifty eyes slithered cunningly over the three men. Meredith noticed that the hand attending to his cigarette was trembling. He had gone a little pale, too, about the gills. He had the appearance of a weak-kneed man who suddenly finds himself trapped in a very ugly corner.

'Well – come on! Out with it!'

'I didn't say nothing like that,' protested Albert in a wavering voice. 'You got it wrong. It musta been somebody else wot was talking wiv Mrs. Fitz. I never–'

'Mrs. Fitz!' snapped Meredith, swinging round on Albert's cringing figure. 'Who said anything about Mrs. Fitzgerald? That was a bad give-away, m'lad. That's just the proof we were after. The sooner you let us have the truth the better. Get me?'

Albert flared up weakly: 'Wot if I was talking to 'er – nothing wrong in that is there?'

'Only if you were being foolish enough to try and get money from her by threats,' added Long smoothly. He rose and planted himself squarely in front of the man. 'Look here, m'lad, if you've got any sense in that head o' yours you'll tell us all you know. You've got something to tell us – we've a good idea what it is too – but we must have a signed statement. Well?'

'What d'you wanter know?' asked Albert sullenly. 'Maybe I can 'elp if I wants to.'

'First of all,' said Long briskly, 'were you with the Captain when he lived in West Hampstead?'

'Yus.'

'Ever see Fitzgerald at that time?'

'Maybe.'

'He came to the Captain's flat perhaps?'

'I'm not saying 'e didn't am I?'

'What about Mrs. Fitzgerald?'

'Wot, Joyce?' Albert grinned. 'She's a bit o' orlrite ain't she?'

'Seen her before I dare say?'

'Wot me? Watcher think? You ain't telling me that you didn't know, eh?'

'Know what?' rapped out Meredith suddenly.

'That she an' the Captain was living together in 'Ampstead.'

'Living together,' echoed Long impatiently, 'O' course we knew that.' He winked at Meredith. ''E doesn't quite realize what we do know, does he? Married weren't they?'

'Wot the 'ell d'you think all the fuss 'ud be about if they *wasn't* spliced? Ole Fitz wouldn't 'av parted so easy unless the Captain 'ad *that* 'old over him.'

Long assumed a terrific air of disinterest.

'How long had this blackmail been going on?'

''Ere easy!' cried Albert in alarm. 'That ain't a

nice word to use. Just a friendly business arrangement wot the Captain fixed up with Ole Fitz when 'e first took that 'ouse in the square. Let's see – eighteen months back we come 'ere.'

'And now,' broke in Meredith quietly, 'that your master's no longer in the business you thought you'd take over the stock and goodwill and do a little speculating on your own account. Is that the idea, Albert?'

The little man moved uneasily on his chair and looked down fixedly at his boots.

'Well a bloke must live some'ow these days,' he mumbled, adding on a brighter, more assertive note. ''Tain't as if I've made anything out of it ... yet.'

'Luckily for you, m'lad,' was Long's immediate observation. 'And I suppose this document that Mrs. Fitzgerald – or rather Mrs. Cotton was after was her marriage certificate?'

'It didn't take much outer you to think o' that,' commented Albert drily. ''Course it bloomin' well was. She 'ad an idea that the perlice or some relation might go through the Captain's papers an' find the thing, see? Then the cat 'ud be properly aht of the bag for all 'er ole pot-an'-pan's money wot 'ad been paid aht to the Captain.'

'You know where this certificate is, of course?'

'I do,' said Albert promptly.

'Where?'

''Ere,' replied Albert diving into an inside pocket and holding out a stout, sealed envelope. 'If I 'ands this over you'll make it orlrite for me, eh? Shows I wanter to go straight, don't it, if I 'and over the evidence. Mrs. Fitz'll tell you that no money's bin paid aht.'

Long looked across inquiringly at Meredith who, after a moment's hesitation, nodded.

'O.K.,' said Long. 'We'll call it a deal, Albert, provided nothing else comes to light in the future. Get that? Now then let's have a look.'

Taking the envelope he dropped back into his desk-chair, whilst Meredith crossed over and stood by his shoulder. The envelope was inscribed: Duplicate Marriage Certificate – J. R. C. – M.C. – and securely fastened at the flap with sealing-wax. Breaking this seal, Long thrust in his hand and drew out a single sheet of paper which he spread out on the desk. Meredith craned over. Albert, overcome with curiosity to see this valuable document which, so far, he had not troubled to slip from its envelope, also approached the desk and leaned over.

Simultaneously all three men let out an exclamation, scarcely able to credit the evidence of their eyes. *The sheet of paper was blank!*

CHAPTER IX

The Fitzgeralds Talk

'Blimey!' breathed Albert, passing a vague hand over his forehead, then drawing out a handkerchief to mop it. 'Diddled, eh?'

'Somebody's been,' observed Meredith with a puzzled look. 'Can't see the point of this trick, can you, Long?'

'Not yet, sir.'

'Where did the Captain keep this envelope?'

'In a little desk in 'is bedroom,' explained Albert. 'Always kept 'is desk locked an' after 'e was done in I pinched the key orf the bunch on 'is westkit, took the envelope aht and 'id it in my own room.'

'You don't think–' began Long in an inspirational voice.

'Half a minute, Long – let's finish with Albert first. He's still got something to tell us.' Meredith drew out his note-book. 'For instance – what about this? A little more of that unfortunate conversation of yours, Albert. You said something to Mrs. Fitzgerald about knowing that her husband did the murder. Your exact words were: "Know he did the murder ... motive any-old-hows."'

''Ere, 'arf a mo!' cried Albert excitedly. 'I never said that! At least not as you've took it dahn. You've only got part of wot I said. Wot I actually said was: "For all I know 'e did the murder. 'E 'ad a good motive, any ole 'ows." Meaning on account of 'is business transactions wiv the Captain, see?'

'Then you've no other reason to suspect that Mr. Fitzgerald murdered your master? You said something about seeing him out that night – what did you mean by that?'

'That's right! I did see 'im aht. And when I 'eard abaht the murder it looked fishy to me.'

'Yes – but out where? In the square?'

'Yus – in a manner of speaking. 'E was up on the roof when I saw 'im.'

'The roof!' exclaimed Long and Meredith in unison.

'Ain't I jus' said so? On the parson's roof looking over the edge 'e was. When 'e saw me come aht of Number Five 'e dodged back quick.'

'What time was this?'

'Abaht a quarter-past nine – just afore.'

'How d'you know?'

'Because I was going aht to post a letter and the post goes at nine-fifteen, see? So I knew I 'ad to look nippy.'

'But, good heavens,' broke in Meredith, 'when we saw you that night at eleven-thirty you told us you'd just come back from posting a letter. It wasn't the same letter by any chance, was it?'

'Yes,' cut in Long sharply, 'and why were you so out o' breath when you arrived?'

'Had you been back into Number Five since you went out with that letter?' demanded Meredith.

'If so, where had you been 'iding yourself all that time?' asked Long suspiciously.

'For two hours, Albert. Did it take you two hours to post that letter?'

Bombarded by these penetrating, quick-fire questions Albert grew confused and finally blurted out in a whining voice:

'Orlrite, I'll tell you. I wasn't up to nothing slippery if that's wot you're trying to lay on me. Fact is, I did post that there letter to my bookie same as I told you. After that I went up the road a bit and saw Charlie Hogg wot keeps the "Goose and Fevvers." Friend o' mine is Charlie. Well, I nipped in, see, and 'ad a couple. We got talking abaht 'orses and you know wot *that* is. When I looks at the clock I sees it's bloomin' well arpas eleven. The Captain 'ad warned me afore abaht these 'ere evenings along wiv Charlie, so I nips aht and 'ops orf back as quick as I could.'

'Well,' said Meredith, 'we can easily check up that statement by a visit to Hogg. In the meantime, Albert, we'll take your word for it. Anything else you want to ask, Inspector?'

As Long shook his head, after cautioning Albert to notify the police of any change of address, he dismissed the unhappy man and plunged at once into a discussion of that strange certificate.

'What's your idea about this trick, Long – any suggestions?'

'Well, it *did* occur to me,' said Long with the ponderous humility of a man who feels he's right and desires to give the opposite impression, 'that Cotton was frightened that the real certificate might be pinched.'

'By Fitzgerald?'

'Yes, or Albert. So he locks this envelope away in his desk and puts the actual certificate away in his safe or deposits it at his bank.'

'That's possible,' agreed Meredith. 'But surely not in his safe? We didn't find it when we went through it that night. And nobody, except Albert and the Fitzgeralds, would have troubled to have taken it along with the three thousand. If Fitz stole the money then he didn't find the certificate, otherwise his wife wouldn't have had that little talk with Albert.'

'Perhaps Albert pinched it. All this may be a blind,' suggested Long. 'He may have the actual certificate tucked away safe and sound – just biding his time to make use of it.'

'On the other hand, if Albert's alibi is a true

one,' argued Meredith, 'he wouldn't have had a chance to break into the safe. He left the house at nine-fifteen. Cotton was killed at nine-thirty. He wouldn't have rifled the safe *before* the murder, would he? Moreover, as he realizes we can question Hogg or anybody else in the pub, I think he's telling the truth.'

'Have you any alternative explanation then?' asked Long.

'The only other plausible reason for the trick, as far as I can see at the moment, is that Cotton hadn't got a marriage certificate at all.'

'But why?'

'Because he wasn't married to Joyce Fitzgerald.'

'Yes, but Albert's just told us–'

'I know all about that, Long. Albert obviously thought they *were* married. So did Joyce herself. See the point?'

'You mean Cotton had faked the marriage ceremony?'

'Well, it's an idea, isn't it? He was probably infatuated with the girl – yes, or even just physically attracted – but, you see, that type of chap usually shies away from marriage. He may have suggested that Joyce should live with him and received the cold shoulder. So to satisfy the girl's morality he goes through a false marriage ceremony and probably flourishes the faked certificate under her nose.'

'That's just the point, sir,' argued Long. 'If Cotton had faked a certificate why wasn't it in the envelope?'

'Because he wasn't such a fool as to suggest any motive for blackmail. Suppose we got suspicious and felt pretty certain that he was blackmailing Fitzgerald; suppose we got a search warrant and went through his papers? What then? If we'd found that certificate we'd have wondered about his wife, shouldn't we? Where was she? Why wasn't she living with him? Was she dead and so on. Inquiries would have been made and we'd have probably hit on the motive for his blackmail.'

'But why keep the envelope at all?'

'Well, he probably had to show Fitzgerald something when he first started his game. Since the girl *thought* without any shadow of doubt that she was married to him, Fitzgerald would take it for granted that the envelope contained the certificate. Quite obvious the girl thought it did – that's what she was trying to wheedle from Albert.'

'And the next move, sir?'

'What about cross-questioning the girl herself? She could tell us all about the ceremony. We could follow up her statements and find out if it was faked.'

Long nodded in agreement.

'Yes, and after we've seen her, what about another little chat with Fitzgerald? He didn't tell us anything about being out on that roof to-day, did he? Fishy, eh? He couldn't have been up there for any lawful purpose. Unless,' added Long with a twinkle, ''e was potting at stray cats with his air-gun!'

As it was then late they decided, therefore, to call on Joyce Fitzgerald as soon as her husband had left for the bank on the following morning.

The tall windows of the Fitzgeralds' sitting-room

were open to the morning sun when Meredith and Long were shown in by the maid shortly after ten. Almost at once Joyce Fitzgerald joined them. It was obvious to the men that this visit had both surprised and agitated her and, although she politely asked them to be seated, she was very ill-at-ease. Long had asked Meredith to do the cross-questioning, as he had an inherent dislike of interviewing women. Meredith, seeing that the girl was in a decidedly jumpy condition, decided to go cautiously at the start. He did not want to frighten her into a defensive mood. Quietly and methodically he asked her all sorts of questions regarding her husband's relationship with the dead man, switched over by degrees to Albert and mentioned, at length, the strange conversation in the garden of Number Four. Immediately the girl's attitude changed. She began to bristle with suspicion, making careful replies, obviously wondering what Meredith was leading up to.

Suddenly Meredith stood up and said with a disarming air of frankness: 'Look here, Mrs. Fitzgerald, there's no point in beating about the bush any longer. We've learnt quite a lot about Captain Cotton and his servant during these last few days. We know, for example, that you and your husband were acquainted with these two men before you came to live here in Cheltenham. We know – or at least we have very strong reasons to believe – that Cotton had been blackmailing your husband. We even suspect that the motive for this unpleasant game had something to do with you. Now, Mrs. Fitzgerald, are you prepared to be honest with me? To tell me everything about your previous relations with Captain Cotton? I assure you that in the long run complete frankness on your part will considerably help us to clear up the mystery surrounding the Captain's death. I think, too, that in return we shall be able to do something for you. Well?'

'What exactly do you want me to tell you?' asked Joyce, in a tremulous voice. 'I feel all this would have been easier and fairer to me if my husband had been present.'

'Yes – I appreciate that – but we specially wanted to see you alone before we interviewed Mr. Fitzgerald. To begin with,' added Meredith, slipping a hand into his pocket, 'have you ever seen that before?'

Taking it from the Superintendent's outstretched hand, Joyce glanced at it and looked up in astonishment.

'The certificate! Where did you find this? How did you get hold of it? I suppose now you must know... You must have learnt that...'

Meredith broke in on her confusion: 'That you were at one time Captain Cotton's wife? Is that what you were going to say?' She nodded mutely, turning over the envelope listlessly in her hand. 'Open it,' suggested Meredith.

With fumbling fingers Joyce felt in the envelope and drew out the blank sheet. Again she was overcome with amazement and perplexity.

'But what does it mean? Where is the certificate? I saw Mark seal it up in that envelope. My husband and I felt certain that–' She tailed off with a puzzled shake of her head, unable to credit the trick which had been played upon her.

Omitting no detail, Meredith carefully explained how the certificate had come into the possession of the police and put forward his overnight theory as to why this mysterious trick had been played.

'But it's impossible! Surely?' cried Joyce. 'Never really married? But what about the ceremony – how could Mark have faked that?'

'Suppose you help us to answer that question by telling us exactly what happened. You first met Cotton – when?'

'About six years ago,' began Joyce, suppressing her feelings only by an effort. 'I was in my first job then up West in a dressmakers' shop. One evening Mark sat next to me in a cinema and we got talking. I thought he seemed quite a decent sort of man and, as I was very lonely, I went out with him quite a lot. After a few weeks he put a proposal to me which upset me considerably and for a time I would have nothing to do with him. He constantly wrote and phoned to me, until in the end I gave in and we began to meet again. By this time I was really beginning to grow fond of him and when, a little later, he suggested we should get married, I seriously began to consider the advantages. You see, Mr. Meredith, my prospects were pretty grey. I wasn't earning much and it's not much fun living on your own in a bed-sitting-room. For all that I refused to decide at once. Things drifted for a month or two, but finally Mark began to press me for a definite answer. Well, to cut that part of my affairs short – we were married that spring at a Registrar's Office. Mark was very much against a church marriage and as I had no strong ideas myself I agreed with him.'

'The proposal for a civil marriage came from him first, Mrs. Fitzgerald?'

Joyce nodded and went on: 'Yes, and Mark made all the subsequent arrangements – fixed the day, the place and the time, everything. On the actual morning he called for me in Belsize Road where I had my room, tucked me into a taxi and we drove off to the Registrar's Office.'

'Alone?'

'No – Albert was with us as he was to act as one of the witnesses. Mark explained that the Registrar himself was arranging to supply the other.'

'I see. And where exactly was this office?'

'Well that's a difficult question to answer. We seemed to turn off Baker Street somewhere and wander about through a lot of side streets. I didn't know my way about Town very well and I was naturally so excited that I never troubled to ask Mark the name of the street. I don't know why but I had an idea it was somewhere near Euston Station. I may have actually seen the station – but I really can't remember much. All I know is, that when we got there we went into a very dingy room on the ground-floor of a big building, like a block of offices. There was very little furniture in the room – just a desk, one or two upright chairs and a strip of carpet. The Registrar himself was an elderly, ordinary-looking sort of man. He seemed to mumble through the ceremony as if he were bored with the whole thing. The witness must have been even more nondescript because the only thing I remember about him was that he had reddish hair.'

For a moment Meredith remained silent; then:

'Well, frankly, Mrs. Fitzgerald, what you've told me only strengthens my suspicions that the ceremony *was* faked. We can find out for certain, of course, through Somerset House. If you'll just give me the necessary details – date, year, Christian names, your maiden name and so on, I'll get in touch at once with the Metropolitan Police.'

'And all this terrible trouble we've been through – the worry, the constant fear that Mark would go to the police, the incessant need for secrecy – it's all been in a sense unnecessary?'

'Quite. You see how your frankness may help to clear the air, Mrs. Fitzgerald?'

Joyce nodded and then, after a moment's hesitation, blurted out: 'But the murder! Who could have murdered Mark? My husband and I have been asking ourselves this question ever since that ghastly evening. Have *you* any idea, Mr. Meredith?'

'None,' said Meredith emphatically. 'But it doesn't mean we're not going to find out.'

'Worried, eh?' asked Long, as the two men walked in step across the square and made for Clarence Street. 'Still a bit tickled up over the murder. And not without cause. Noticed you didn't say anything about the rest of Albert's information – I mean about her hubby being out on the tiles that night. Dare say she wondered how much of that conversation *was* overheard. Dare say she wondered if you knew about Albert's unhappy remarks. She *knew*, since you told her, that the police had information about the blackmail section of that chat. Uneasy, eh? Anxious to know if we suspect anybody? Betcher a box o' cigars to a burnt match, sir, that ole Fitz did it.'

'Suppose we have him round, Long, when we get back to the station? He's got to be pumped about his actions that night. The sooner the better to my mind.'

After Long had put through a long-distance call to the Yard with regard to the tracing of the marriage licence, he dialled Poulson's Bank and asked Fitzgerald if he could slip round to Clarence Street for a few moments. The manager promised to do so without delay and, in less than five minutes, he was seated in the Inspector's office. This time it was Long who set the ball rolling. In the background Shanks sat, unobtrusively, with his note-book and pencil at the 'ready.'

'Now, sir, I'm not going to bother you with a lot of unnecessary facts – but we've had some definite information which we're bound to investigate. It concerns you. Quite briefly, sir, we want to know what you were doing on the roof of Mr. Matthews' house somewhere about nine-fifteen on the night of 13th June.'

'13th June?'

'Captain Cotton's unlucky day, sir – the day of the murder.'

'On the roof? But what on earth gave you the idea that–'

'From information received – witness swears to 'is identification. Well, sir?'

'But it's ridiculous, Inspector! What on earth should I be on the roof for?'

'That's just what we wondered. I might add that we have obtained corroborative evidence of the facts stated by witness.'

'What d'you mean by that?' asked the manager on a note of anxiety. 'How could you have such evidence if I wasn't there?'

Long lifted his broad shoulders and, staring at the ceiling, began to rub his triplicate chins.

'I'm waiting, sir – so's the Superintendent here.'

'But good heavens – what for? What do you want me to do?'

'Tell the truth – that's all,' said Long bluntly. 'I warn you from the start, sir, that the dice are loaded, *'eavily* loaded against you. Now, if you didn't wear rubbers like that on your shoes, for instance–' Long pointed to the manager's outstretched feet and smiled when he quickly placed them flat on the floor. Suddenly Fitzgerald rose and took a turn or two up and down the room. He seemed to be struggling inwardly to come to some vital decision. How much did the police know? Was this all bluff? Should he speak? These were the queries which Meredith imagined he was posing himself. What would be the result of this obvious conflict with his conscience? The truth? Or a pack of clever lies? Anxiously, without moving, the two officials waited. Then without warning, Fitzgerald, from whose face the last vestige of colour had drained, began to speak. At first in a jerky mutter, barely audible, then as he progressed, stimulated by his own words, his voice gaining strength and clarity. Long nodded and Shanks, taking the tip, began to write swiftly.

'All right. I won't keep up the pretence any more. I know exactly what you're referring to. You've got to accept my explanation as the truth. Yes, the whole truth and nothing but the truth. I *was* on the roof that night! But I swear to you, gentlemen, that it had absolutely nothing to do with Cotton's murder. With Cotton – yes – but not his death. There's a lot to tell. You may have guessed part of what has been happening already. Blackmail! That's the whole ugly situation in a nutshell. One word. Blackmail! A hellish crime, believe me. It saps you – your strength, your self-respect, your financial resources, any attempt to enjoy a little happiness. I'll tell you how I first met Cotton and my wife. The whole business really began then…'

And little by little, some of it fresh, some of it stale, Fitzgerald announced the bald facts which had led up to Cotton's hold over him. Hampstead – Joyce's unbearable marriage – Cotton's unceasing neglect and mental cruelty – their own intimacy – the offer of the Cheltenham job – the chance to forget the past and start again, together, as man and wife – Cotton's arrival at Number Five – his threat to divulge their secret – an initial payment of 'silence' money – further demands – further payments – worry – incessant fear and the dreadful feeling of insecurity.

'At last I could stick it no longer. I'd already paid out something in the region of two thousand pounds. I saw myself being forced to sell up my house to meet Cotton's demands. I didn't know which way to turn. Could I borrow the money? Mortgage the house? What? In the end, driven nearly crazy by the situation, I did something that I've regretted ever since. I began to misappropriate money from the bank. Once I had started that game I seemed unable to turn aside. I only plunged deeper. Two months ago I found, to my horror, that I had borrowed from the bank to the tune of three thousand pounds. Three thousand! And no immediate prospect of putting the money back where it belonged. Then an idea occurred to me. From my visits to Cotton I knew where he kept his safe and I was certain that a large proportion of the cash I had paid over to him was being hoarded in that safe. In short – I decided to steal my own money back – or rather the bank's. A mad idea, perhaps, but it seemed the only solution to my problem. Cotton might suspect me but if I did the job properly I reckoned that he'd never be able to prove that I was the thief. At the same time I was struck by another possibility. What if the certificate of marriage were also kept in the safe? Couldn't I get hold of that as well? I knew exactly what sort of an envelope it was in, Cotton had often flourished the damned thing under my nose. You see he knew that he was, physically, the stronger man and he rather enjoyed riling me in this manner. Of course he might have a duplicate of the certificate. He could get another document from Somerset House – but all I thought of then was breathing-space. Time in which to sit down and think things straight again. The point was how to break into the safe? It was a combination safe and, although my profession has taught me a good deal about safes, I naturally didn't know the cipher which would open Cotton's. At length I hit on a plan. I noticed that when Cotton pulled down the blinds of his study he only pulled down the big blind in the centre. The window, as you may know, is a bay. This meant that it was possible to see into the room at night through either of the smaller windows – *provided one could look into them from the right angle.* Well, after a cautious review, I discovered that I could get an absolutely uninterrupted, front-view of the safe from the roof of Matthews' house. I began to creep up there after it was dark, via my landing-window, and keep watch. I'd already bought a specially powerful pair of binoculars, with which I hoped to read the combination of the safe when Cotton next opened it. You can imagine how often my watches proved futile. How often I waited up there for Cotton to go to his safe. Eventually, however, my luck changed and I was able to note down the first part of the cipher. If Cotton hadn't moved on that occasion I should have had the complete combination in my hand. Then, on 13th June, Cotton walked with me to the bank and announced, in a sneering sort of way, that as his capital had now reached substantial proportions he intended to invest it. He told me that he was going to see Buller after dinner that evening and ask his advice. This put me on the *qui vive.* I thought to myself that it was very possible Cotton would go through the contents of his safe that evening. My only fear was that he might do this before it was dark. My luck still held, however, and shortly after nine o'clock, when I had been up on Matthews' roof for about twenty minutes, the light went on in Cotton's study and I saw him go to the safe. This time I was able to read the rest of the cipher. But before I had time to make myself scarce, Albert came out of the front door of Number Five. I dodged back as quickly as I could behind a chimney-stack, but from what you were telling me just now I rather suspect that Albert was your witness. Well, that – in short – is the situation in which I have been existing these past two years. You can imagine that it's not been all honey. It's up to you now to take what proceedings you think fit. I shall, of course, make a clean breast of the affair to my directors.'

'Yes, but half a minute, sir,' put in Meredith, aware of the conclusive tone in the manager's voice. 'You've not told us the whole story – surely? You say you were able to complete your reading of the cipher that night. Did you by any chance put this knowledge to good account, Mr. Fitzgerald?'

'You mean did I open Cotton's safe? Well, that's rather an extraneous question, isn't it, Mr. Meredith? You know the safe was burgled. The whole square have been talking about the theft. And since I've confessed to having the combination ... well...'

Meredith nodded.

'We suspected, of course. Not at first but as our investigations went on. But I'd rather like to hear your account so that I can check up on details. Purely official routine.'

'Very well – here's exactly what happened. Understand, I had no intention of breaking into the safe on that particular night. The idea came to me only after I had received your summons to answer some questions at Buller's place. When I realized that Cotton was dead and that Albert was out of the house, I saw what a god-sent opportunity I had to put my plans into operation. I want you to understand that my wife knew absolutely nothing about these plans. When I had kept watch up on the roof I had to invent excuses for my absence and creep up to the top landing without her knowledge. It was the same that night. When I reached home after your cross-examination, I turned things over in my mind, came to a decision to act without delay and told my wife that I was going for a stroll round. I often did this before going to bed as I've not been sleeping too well. She naturally didn't suspect anything. I put on a pair of wash-leather gloves, took a good look at Cotton's house from both the front and back, saw there were no lights burning, found the front door unlocked and crept up to the study. I knew my way about the house, of course, because of my frequent visits to satisfy Cotton's demands. I got down to work with the help of a small pocket-torch, referred to the notes I had jotted down and soon had the safe open. It was at that moment that you and the other officials turned up and rang the bell. I grabbed up the packets of bank-notes as quickly as I could, switched out the torch and began to grope my way down the stairs. Unfortunately my arrival in the hall coincided, as you probably remember, with your entry. However, I managed to slip down the basement stairs, run down the garden, out through the gate and into my own garden. I actually heard your man calling out that he could see no signs of anybody in the lane. He was only a couple of yards away from the spot where I was standing, holding my breath. After the excitement had died down I crept into my own house through the kitchen, along the hall, slammed the front door and walked in to my wife. That, I think, explains everything you want to know.'

At the conclusion of this lengthy statement Fitzgerald dropped, exhausted and shaken, into a chair and mechanically took the cigarette which Meredith tactfully offered him.

'You were up on the roof until what time?' asked the Superintendent.

'About twenty-past nine, I think.'

'And you noticed nobody else prowling about up there? No sounds or anything out of the ordinary?'

'It's queer you should mention that about sounds, because I *did* hear something. A sort of hollow bump – rather like a sash-window being shut.'

'From which direction did this come?'

'From One or Two, I thought. It sounded as if it came from West's place. But, of course, it couldn't have come from there, could it?'

'Hardly,' agreed Meredith, thinking to himself: 'The skylight – somebody may have just sneaked into the Empty House and shut it.' Aloud he went on: 'Well, sir, I can't say exactly how you stand with regard to the law. I imagine it rests with your directors whether proceedings are taken or not. But I'm sure, from our point of view, that you've done the right thing in telling us the whole truth. I've an idea, too, that we can hold out a strong hope that the whole matter of your wife's marriage may be cleared up to your advantage. She'll doubtless have something to tell you about this when you get home. In the meantime, would you kindly read through and sign this statement? Thanks. I don't think we need take up more of your time after that, Mr. Fitzgerald.'

CHAPTER X

April House

'Well, that's that,' said Meredith, when Shanks had retired to escort the bank-manager to the door. 'D'you think he was telling the truth, Long?'

'Yes, sir – quite frankly I do. Quite apart from his statement, there's the hooman element to take into consideration. I've always upheld that the hooman element tells you just as much about a witness as his facts. In this particular case, for instance, it was obvious that the poor devil 'ad really been through the hoop. 'E'd been suffering. It cost him an effort to speak out as he did, but once 'e was off the mark I'll betcher a penny to the Bank of England that he was telling the truth. Too much circumstantial detail about his story, in my opinion, for it to have been a fairy-tale.'

Meredith felt inclined to agree with the Inspector and went on to point out that all the facts known to the police seemed to fit in without a flaw to Fitzgerald's statement. The tracks did not lead to the skylight of the Empty House, but to a point where, as the manager had explained, a clear view could be got through the side-window of Cotton's study. Further he had seen Albert coming out of

Number Five, a strong, corroborative fact since the police had not named their witness before the interview began. Finally he had confessed, not only to the theft from Cotton's safe, but to a falsifying of his books at the bank in order to lay hands on that badly-needed three thousand. If he had been lying then surely he wouldn't incorporate in his false statement a confession to two crimes, both detrimental to his career? In any case, argued Meredith, this part of his confession couldn't have been a lie because he had mentioned that encounter on the dark stairs and his subsequent flit through the basement and out of the garden gate. Take it all in all both Long and Meredith felt fairly satisfied now that the manager had had no hand in the murder.

'Another blind-alley,' said Long miserably. 'First West and now Fitzgerald. We seem to start off on a line of investigation with a handful of sizzling-hot clues and find the darn things going cold on us. We don't seem to be able to shake West's alibi. No further incriminating facts have come to light in the meantime. Where the devil are we now? At a full-stop, eh, sir? I don't see how we're bloomin' well going to make things *move* again after this second squib has fizzled out.'

'Disheartening, Long. I quite agree about that. But at any rate it's cleared the air a bit. If we can assume that neither West nor Fitzgerald did the job, then we can pretty safely say that it must have been one of the other archers in the square – namely Miss Boon, Matthews or Pratt. We have corroborative evidence that Matthews was in his sitting-room at the time the murder was committed. Shanks wheedled that, you remember, out of his maid, Prudence. She swore that she took in her master's Ovaltine at exactly nine-thirty. That leaves Pratt and Miss Boon. We've now got to check up their statements – see if their alibis really hold water. To save time, Inspector, I suggest that you find out all you can about Miss Boon, whilst I tackle Pratt.'

''Ere, that's a bit thick, sir! I can't stomach dealing with the female element. Particularly when it comes to an ole dragon like that Miss Boon. General Boon suits her style better, what with her parade manner an' army o' mangy mongrels.'

Meredith laughed.

'Yes and you'd better cross-question her dogs, too, while you're about it. Perhaps she's taught one of them to shoot with a bow and arrow.'

Long sighed and concluded in a funereal voice: 'If I get murdered for my pains I only 'ope that you get landed with the investigation. Oh, Lord – what a harpy! I wonder she don't wear trousis and a trilby!'

Pratt, thought Long as he walked back to the square for lunch – what about Pratt? He was away, at the time the murder was committed, visiting a patient. His car entered the square as Buller ran along to his house to tell him the fatal news. Shanks had been detailed to find out a few particulars about this call – name and address of the patient, time the doctor left after the visit and so on. Fishing out his note-book, Meredith turned to where he had copied down the bare outline of Shanks' excellent statement. Yes – here it was, tabulated thus:

Name of patient – Antony John Wade.
Address – c/o Mrs. Violet Black (widow),
April House, Leckhampton Road.
Occupation of Patient – None.

Mrs. Black, landlady, states that Pratt left house at (about) nine-fifteen. Wade unable to confirm this as asleep before doctor left. Wade been in doctor's hands for some weeks. Suffering from insomnia, general debility and nerves. On the evening of 13th June, Wade, who was suffering from some form of abdominal pain, asked Black to phone Pratt. Doctor arrived shortly before nine o'clock – gave Wade morphia injection to induce sleep.

Studying these notes intently, so intently that he only just avoided walking into a lamp-post, Meredith could not help feeling that on the face of it Pratt's evidence was genuine. He had been attending Wade for some weeks and so far there was nothing to suggest that there was any personal relationship (with the possibility of criminal collaboration) existing between the two men. On the other hand could Mrs. Black have been mistaken about the time? Fifteen minutes might have made all the difference. But until Meredith was able to study a town map at leisure he was unable to say how long it would take a car to travel from Leckhampton Road to the square. He had an idea that it was an outlying street, probably, as its name suggested, under Leckhampton Hill.

Arriving at Number Eight he found Aldous

Barnet in an armchair, reading a newspaper and sipping a pink gin.

'Join me in one before lunch, Meredith? No? Sherry then? I'm afraid I've picked up the pernicious habit of imbibing pink gins through my brother in the Navy. It's a pre-lunch ritual in the mess, y'know. Well, how's the murder? Anything fresh?'

Meredith turned down his thumbs and scowled.

'A fresh dead-end – that's all.'

'Something here in the local rag which might interest you,' smiled Barnet. 'There's been another murder in the locality.'

'What!' exclaimed Meredith, incredulously. 'A murder? When? Why didn't Long know about it? Who's the victim?'

'A sheep.'

'Sheep?'

'Yes, and the interesting part about it is that the unfortunate animal met its end in the same way as Cotton. It was found with an arrow sticking out of its head. Read the paragraph for yourself if you think I'm leg-pulling.'

Taking the paper, Meredith settled himself down in a chair and read as follows:

An extraordinary happening has occurred on the farm of Mr. Wilfred Bates of The Dower House, Winchcombe. Last Friday a labourer employed on the farm found a ewe half-lying in a stream which runs through the middle of the estate. The animal, when found, had an arrow embedded in its brain and appears to have been shot at some spot distant from the stream itself. In the opinion of Mr. Bates the animal, maddened with pain, must have jumped over a low stone wall and run for nearly half-a-mile before it died. The local police are at a loss as to how the accident could have happened. Inquiries are being made in the district.

'Well?' said Barnet. 'What do you make of that?'

'It's certainly a bit of a coincidence,' observed Meredith. 'I mean people who wander around with bows and arrows are not particularly numerous. I wonder who've got the job in hand? The Winchcombe lot, I suppose.'

'Do you think there's anything in it?'

'Might be. I can't see the slightest connection yet but that doesn't mean that there isn't one. I'd like to have a look at that arrow, for example. This article doesn't go into details – but I'm wondering if that arrow was fitted with a barb or not?'

'Umph,' grunted Barnet with an understanding nod. 'Have another drink?'

Although Meredith was decidedly puzzled by the death of Mr. Bates's ewe, he was more immediately concerned with Dr. Pratt. Shortly after lunch he called in next door, found the doctor in and ready to spare him a few minutes of his valuable time.

'Can give you just ten minutes,' said Pratt glancing at his wrist-watch. 'I've got a hospital job at 2.30. What's the trouble?'

'Briefly this, Mr. Pratt. Some time back we took down a general statement concerning your actions on the night of 13th June. You signed the statement. To be quite frank with you, we find, at this point in our investigations, that it will be necessary for us to go more thoroughly into this statement.'

'Well, of all the damned...' began Pratt hotly. 'You don't mean to say that *I'm* a suspect? That's rather a poor sort of a joke, isn't it? How could I possibly have done the beastly job when I was over at Leckhampton at the time?'

'That's just our argument,' answered Meredith amiably. 'But I want you to clinch it for us. Have you any idea of the time you left Leckhampton Road?'

'9.15, as I stated.'

'I understand Mr. Wade, your patient, was asleep when you left?'

'Exactly. I'd just pumped a little morphia into him to ease the pain and give him a sound night.'

'What was his trouble?'

'Acute indigestion due to his general nervous condition. The lad's been going the pace and now his chickens have come home to roost. Warned him to steady up, but you know what it is with these youngsters.'

'Do you know Mr. Wade socially?'

'No.'

'Which way did you drive back to the square?'

'Down the Leckhampton Road, along the Bath Road by the college, into the High Street and home via the Winchcombe Road.'

Meredith jotted down a few notes then looked up and asked: 'How's your patient now?'

'On his feet again, thanks.'

'I see.' Meredith rose. 'Well, that's all, Mr. Pratt. Sorry to have wasted your time.'

Barnet's dark-blue Alvis 'sports' was waiting by arrangement to take the Superintendent out to Leckhampton Road. Barnet was at the wheel.

'Now, sir, if you'll keep your speedometer needle somewhere round the thirty mark, I'll make a note of our time. Let's see it's now 2.25 exactly. Pratt says he took this route.'

Whilst Meredith was naming the streets which he had jotted down, the long, lean car began to nose its way out of the square. Threading his way dexterously through the High Street traffic, at this hour crowded with bicycles, Barnet drove by the college – its lovely weathered stone mellow in the afternoon sun – and cruised on down the Leckhampton Road. Suddenly Meredith called out: 'Whoa! Here we are – April House, on the right, sir. We've taken just under fifteen minutes.'

'Good God! April House,' muttered Barnet sardonically. 'Where do these people get their names from? April? It looks more like December in a black frost!'

There was certainly nothing spring-like about the square, grimy façade of Mrs. Black's establishment. A few pinched laurels and wilting geraniums straggled up behind the unpainted iron-railings, and in the lower bay stood a flourishing, ugly aspidistra. Meredith rang a rusty bell which jangled somewhere in the interior of this architectural monster, and drew the stern-faced Mrs. Black to the door.

'If it's rooms you're wanting,' she said without preliminary, 'then I'm full up. Have been these last six months. But I dare say Mrs. Williams at Number–'

'That's all right. I really want to see Mr. Wade – if he's in. I should also like to have a word with you, Mrs. Black. I'm a police officer.'

Mrs. Black stepped back a pace, shocked and startled.

'Police? Oh, don't say Mr. Wade's been up to tricks! He's a lively gentleman, I'll admit, but I'm sure his heart's in the right place.'

'Can I come in?' asked Meredith pointedly.

'This way, sir,' said Mrs. Black deferentially piloting the Superintendent into the room with the aspidistra and bay-window, a room which smelt of soot, camphor and hair-rugs. Meredith was waved into a rigid, springless armchair draped with a lace antimacassar. Mrs. Black edged herself primly on to a black horse-hair sofa, carefully avoiding the silk-covered cushions which adorned it.

'Well, sir?'

'I want you to cast your mind back, if you can, to 13th June, Mrs. Black. Perhaps I can help you to remember the date by reminding you that it was the evening Mr. Wade asked you to ring for the doctor.'

Mrs. Black brightened a little, less impressed by the law, now that it had come down to such homely details.

'That's right – the night his pains came on so bad that he could hardly bear with himself. Poor lad. "Ring Doctor Pratt at once," he called down to me, "else I shall go off my head, Mrs. Black." "You'll go off to bed," I ses, "and at once. You've no right to be on your feet," I ses. Meaning what I said too. He made some fuss about that but I did manage to get him in bed with a hot bottle before I rang the doctor from the call-box up the road.'

'Doctor Pratt had been attending him some time, hadn't he?'

'Yes, sir – on and off for some weeks.'

'Did they appear to know each other well? I mean do you think they knew each other socially – quite apart from being doctor and patient?'

'Well, they always seemed sort of free-and-easy in their talk. But young Mr. Wade's like that anyhow. Always chipping people. I've never heard him say anything about meeting the doctor outside this house.'

'What's been Mr. Wade's trouble?'

Mrs. Black glanced round instinctively and lowered her voice before making a reply.

'The doctor says as it's some form of nerves and acute indigestion, but between you and me – not that I'd breathe a word to anybody else about this – but it's my opinion that the young man is a *little too fond of the drink!* Not that he's ever given me cause to complain though he does come home a little the worse for it more often than not.'

'I see. Before this attack came on on 13th June d'you think he'd been drinking then?'

'I couldn't rightly tell about that, sir.'

Meredith switched over to another angle of approach.

'What time did the doctor arrive?'

'As far as I can recall somewhere around nine o'clock, sir.'

'And he left?'

'Just afore 9.15.'

'You seem more sure about the time he left. Any reason, Mrs. Black?'

'A very good one, sir. After the doctor had done with Mr. Wade he came down and called me into the hall. We had a few words about the poor young fellow – told me something about his food, to keep him in bed a day or two and so on. Then the doctor looked up at my grandfather clock and said: "Good gracious, Mrs. Black, that can't really be the time!" "Well, sir," I ses, "I've known that clock for the last twenty-five years and I've never known it wrong." But to satisfy him I stuck my head into the kitchen to see what the clock said out there. As both clocks were the same I knew they must be right. Yes – a minute or two before 9.15 the doctor left. I'll swear to that, sir.'

At the conclusion of this speech there was the click of the front-gate shutting and the sound of a voice pleasantly raised in song. Meredith glanced out of the window and saw a young man in a double-breasted blue suit and a soft hat coming rather unsteadily up the path. It was obvious at a glance that the young man was, if not well lit, at least glowing with a benevolent alcoholic spark.

'Mr. Wade?' inquired Meredith.

'That's him,' answered Mrs. Black tersely without having to glance out of the window. 'He always croons when he's been at it.'

Meredith got up. 'Would you catch him before he goes up to his own room and ask him to have a word with me in here? Alone, if you've no objection, Mrs. Black.'

The landlady bustled out and after a short, muffled conversation, the door was opened and young Wade drifted in with an outstretched hand and an amiable smile on his face.

'Hullo, old boy. The geezer says you want to put me through a spot of third degree. I suppose you wouldn't like to come up to my room and knock one back before we get down to it. This bally room gives me the jitters.'

'That sounds good to me,' answered Meredith with a grin. 'Suppose you lead the way.'

Once up in the bed-sitting-room, Wade produced a bottle of whisky from the wardrobe and a couple of glasses. After he had poured out two stiff drinks and swished in a little soda, he flung himself back on the bed and nodded Meredith into an armchair.

'Well, what's the charge, old boy, rape, murder, arson or obliterated number-plate? If the last then it's a clear case of mistaken identity. I haven't a car. Can't afford a car. Can't afford anything really.' Then lifting his glass. 'Except this.'

'You know Pratt, don't you?'

'Dear old Pratt – 'course I do. Damn good scout is old Pratt. Owe him God knows what for his professional services – say, I got round that corner all right. Can't be as squiffy as I thought I was. Try it out again if you don't believe me. Profeshio – profess'nal – on second thoughts, old boy, let's leave it.'

'He's been treating you, hasn't he?'

'What – old Pratt! Not him. Never met him in a pub. S'matter of fact I ran up against that young blister Cannington–'

Meredith grinned.

'No – I mean treating you professionally. You've been ill?'

'Ill! I've been feeling like death warmed up these

last few weeks. Old Pratt says my bally engine wants decarbing or something. But honestly, old boy, I've been in pain. Had to have a shot of morphia one evening. Don't ask me if I liked it! I floated, old boy. Like a balloon. Lovely.'

'Was that when Mrs. Black had to suddenly phone up?'

'That's the idea. And though you won't believe it the old geezer stung me twopence for the call as soon as I came up from the depths. I may be tight sometimes but she's tight always. Tight as a clam when it comes to the dibs.'

'When did you first meet Pratt?'

Wade looked across at the Superintendent with a vaguely suspicious look of inquiry.

'I say, old boy – if you don't mind my asking – what's all this about? Has the old witch-doctor been up to some mumbo-jumbo or what? If so – wash me off the slate. I've never seen the fellow outside this room. Given him the happy hand up the Prom once or twice. That's all. Have an idea he'd consider me low company outside working hours. S'matter of fact my old Uncle Buller put me on to him. Nice lad, my uncle. Collects ailments.'

'Buller?' broke in Meredith, surprised. 'You don't mean Edward Buller in Regency Square?'

'I do, old boy. That's Uncle Teddy. My deceased father married his deceased sister. D'you know him? Damn it! Of course you would! Wasn't thinking. It was in my Uncle Teddy's house that Cotton copped that packet. Nice chap the Captain. One of the stoutest. But couldn't he shift it. Left me standing, old boy – *just* standing, that is.' Adding with a look of amused incredulity. 'Here you're not trying to tell me that old Pratt is suspected of–?'

'I'm not telling you anything,' said Meredith. 'You're telling me – or at least I hope you will.'

'Sounds like Mae West. Anyway, what's the next question on the list? Something snappy, I'll bet. Have another drink?'

'No, thanks. To come back to 13th June.'

'13th June?'

'The night Mrs. Black phoned the doctor for you. What time did Pratt leave that night?'

'What time did–? Ah, you've hipped me this time, old boy. I can't supply. Not an idea. You see the last I remember of Pratt that evening was a blurred outline before I passed out under the morphia. He may have stayed to kiss me good-night, but I doubt it. You know what these doctor lads are – all hurry and heartiness. You'll have to ask the geezer.'

'I have.'

'I see. So all you want from me is corrorob ... crobb...'

'Corroborative evidence.'

'Thanks. Have another drink.'

Meredith grinned and shook his head.

'No time. I've got to move. No, don't trouble to come down. I can find my way out.'

'You're lucky, old boy.' Wade pushed himself up unsteadily from the bed and thrust out his unoccupied hand. 'Well, it's all been very jolly. Call round again if you feel bored. Always like to keep on the right side of the law. You're *sure* you won't have another?'

'Quite,' said Meredith, shaking the hand and

beating a quick retreat to the door. 'Thanks for the information.'

Wade picked up the whisky bottle and looked at it closely.

'Well, I've heard it called lots of names before but never that. Cheero.'

'Well?' said Barnet eagerly as Meredith stepped into the Alvis.

'Interesting but negative,' said Meredith with a nod toward April House. 'The evidence simply backs up Pratt's statement. For all that, I'd like to make a second test run and see what our average time is for the journey.'

On this occasion, owing to a traffic jam in the High Street, they did not draw up in Regency Square until seventeen minutes later. As the outward journey had taken just under fifteen minutes it meant that Pratt's arrival in the square, just as Buller was rushing along to his house on the night of the murder, fitted in perfectly with his statement.

'So Pratt,' thought Meredith, disheartened, 'can more or less be ruled out, too. Matthews having a sound alibi – it looks as if Miss Boon might have something to tell us.'

He rang through to Clarence Street and got in touch with Long.

'Have you seen the lady yet?'

'The lady!' The Inspector's voice quivered with indignation. 'It's all very well for you to laugh. You don't know what I've been through. I'm only just getting my second wind now. Phew!'

'I take it you had a rough passage, eh?'

'Rough! Stormy, sir. A typhoon. Doubting her

word. Daring to suspect *her* of having a hand in the crime. Half a mind to take the matter into the courts. Insulting and libellous conduct, et cetera, et cetera. 'Course I did what I could to pour oil on troubled waters and only succeeded in stirring up more trouble. After putting me properly through the hoop she shuts up like a clam and refuses to answer a question. That's how things are now, sir. Strikes me that if she has anything to tell us it's going to be darn difficult to get it out of her. I suppose,' added Long in wheedling tones, 'that you wouldn't like to take a 'and, sir? Frankly, she's not in my line.'

Meredith laughed.

'O.K., Long. I'll see what I can do. Any other news?'

'Yes – Yard report. Unable to trace marriage of Cotton and Mrs. F. – no licence on Somerset House files. So we were on the right track there. I'm getting Shanks to hand on the information to the Fitzs. Poor devil can do with a bit o' *good* news for a change, eh? And what about your end – any luck in that Pratt investigation? None? That's bad, sir. I mean, much as I dislike that female Mussolini, I don't think some'ow that she did it.'

Although Meredith was of a like opinion, he realized that it was an essential part of the routine to re-examine Miss Boon with regard to her actions on June 13th. Metaphorically squaring his shoulders, therefore, he strolled across to Number One and rang the bell. A terrifying canine chorus broke forth, gradually increasing in volume, as heavy footsteps stumped down the hall. The door opened and Meredith was almost swept off his feet by an avalanche of dogs, behind which, like the mountain from which the avalanche had sprung, stood Miss Boon. Her formidable jaw was advanced.

'If official – good afternoon,' she snapped before Meredith could put in a word. 'If not – come in and have tea. *Which?*'

'Unofficial,' replied Meredith hastily. 'I want some advice.'

'About?'

'Dogs,' said Meredith.

'This way,' said Miss Boon, shrilly blowing a whistle and striding into a near-by room. 'No – down, sir! Down! Mat, Toby! Mat, sir! Under your chair, Prince. Now Flossie – stop that! Sofa!'

As soon as the excited pack had been drilled into some semblance of order and deposited in their correct places about the room, Miss Boon went out and returned with a large brass tray full of tea-things.

'Milk? Sugar? Both. Good. Have a bun? Now what's the trouble?'

'It's my aunt's Airedale,' began Meredith glibly. 'It's gone off its food.'

'Tried condition powders?'

'Certainly. It was the first thing my aunt thought of.'

'Sure it's not distemper?'

'Distemper! I don't think she thought of that.'

'Idiotic, of course. If it's a young dog–'

'It is,' said Meredith quickly.

'Then it's almost certainly distemper. Some people have no right to keep dogs. Your aunt isn't senile, is she?'

'Possibly,' said Meredith politely. 'What shall I write and tell her to do?'

'Diet first – milk, bovril, eggs, minced meat. Nourishing, understand? Bathe the eyes. Frequently bathe the eyes. Best thing is a solution of boracic acid, creolin and water. Can't go far wrong then. But in your aunt's case I imagine a vet ought to be called in. For the dog, I mean.'

'Thanks. That's very helpful of you, Miss Boon. I had an idea you'd know.'

From the mythical Airedale of Meredith's aunt the canine conversation spread out to embrace other, more material dogs, including, of course, Miss Boon's own property. She discussed their ailments with a physiological frankness which might have shocked any man other than a police officer. She began to warm to Meredith. He had a second cup of tea. Another bun. It cost him an effort to eat it, but, from a sense of duty, he persisted. Gradually he steered the conversation round to Cotton and Cotton's death. Miss Boon seemed unaware of the fact that the interview was, in a sense, no longer unofficial.

'It was a pity that you should have been absent at the time the murder was committed,' said Meredith. 'I'm sure you're very observant. You might have been able to put us on to a clue.'

'My dear man – your confrère who was here this morning not only thinks I might supply you with a clue, but with a murderer as well. Frankly I believe that fat-headed idiot suspected *me*. I wonder you don't keep him on a lead and muzzle him. A menace – that man. Utterly brainless, of course.'

Meredith, with a pang of disloyalty, agreed.
'I suppose you noticed nothing, either on your walk or on your return to the square?'
'Nothing untoward if that's what you mean. Now if that inhuman monster Buller had been the victim I might have been able to put you on to something good.'
'Oh?'
'Yes. His nephew, Antony. He inherits, you know. Always a sound motive so I understand from detective stories. In this case very apt as the young fellow hasn't a bean.'
'But you didn't see him that night, did you?'
'Did I not! Careering down Victoria Road in a car. Missed my darling Flossie by inches. He was probably bottled. He usually is, you know!'
'But has he a car?' Meredith suddenly felt, not only deeply intrigued, but immensely excited by this unexpected bit of news.
'He had that night.'
'You're sure it was Buller's nephew?'
'Would I tell you if I wasn't.'
'Let's see, his surname is–?'
'Wade. Lodges out by Leckhampton Hill. Lives on an allowance provided by his uncle. But bone-lazy. A waster of the Cotton brand. In my opinion simply waiting for his uncle to kick the bucket.'
'Did you notice what sort of car it was?'
'No. I never notice cars. They all look alike to me.'
'You've no idea of the time you saw Mr. Wade?'
'Just after 9.30. You see, I do the same round every night. I always turn into the end of Victoria Road at about 9.30.'

Meredith nodded, glanced at his watch and simulated surprise.

'Ten past four!' he exclaimed. 'Much as I am enjoying our chat I really must be off. Kind of you to advise me about my aunt's dog. I'm sure she'll be grateful.'

'The dog will,' contested Miss Boon as she led Meredith to the front door and nodded him a brusque: 'Good-bye.'

Wade? Good heavens – what did it mean? Wade was asleep in bed at April House that evening. He had no car. Or had he? Was he rather less poverty-stricken than he made out? But how the devil, even if he had a car, had he managed to be within the vicinity of Regency Square when, according to the evidence, he was asleep in the Leckhampton Road? Something was vitally wrong somewhere. What? Who had been lying? Wade? Mrs. Black? Pratt? Or was Miss Boon putting up this curious story for some nefarious purpose of her own? This darn case was getting complex, to say the least of it!

CHAPTER XI

Death Flies Again

Miss Boon's evidence opened up for Meredith an entirely new line of investigation. From the various statements he had received he felt fairly safe in assuming that Wade, for all his seemingly unshakable alibi, must have played some part in the murder. Miss Boon had seen him just after 9.30 in the Victoria Road. On consulting his street map, however, Meredith found himself up against another curious fact. Victoria Road lay to the north-east of the square – Leckhampton Road to the south-east. In other words, if Wade had just committed the murder and was then on the run, he certainly wasn't making for his lodgings. Did it mean, perhaps, that he was garaging his car, in secret, at some other part of the town? He might have realized that a car was going to be essential to his scheme for putting Cotton out of the way and, in order to deceive the police, kept up the pretence of not being able to afford one. A search of the garages in the north-east district of the town might, therefore, prove profitable.

Next, motive? Why had Wade wanted Cotton out of the way? As Miss Boon had aptly said, if it were Buller who had been murdered – then the motive would have been only too obvious. Wade was to inherit from his uncle; he was not particularly affluent, to judge from the amenities of April House; possibly in debt. Yes – if that arrow had entered Buller's head – then Wade might easily have been the murderer. But so far nothing had come to light to suggest that he had anything against Cotton. If anything, they were the sort that would get on together. Wade had said as much. And even if the motive were forthcoming, the problem still remained as to how he had fooled Pratt and Mrs. Black, left his sick-bed and reached Victoria Road by 9.30.

Had Miss Boon been mistaken in her identity?

From his judgment of the woman's character, Meredith felt inclined to dismiss this possibility. Was she in some way incriminated? Had she made some arrangement with Wade to provide her with an alibi on the night of 13th June and, unaware of his sudden illness, stuck to her story with rather unfortunate consequences? But, damn it, she wasn't the sort of woman to kill a man with malice aforethought! In a temper, perhaps – but not in cold-blood. Very well – accept her evidence as the truth. How the devil had Wade managed to slip out of April House after an injection of morphia? He'd be incapable of driving a car – let alone in a suitable state to make a difficult shot with a bow and arrow. So far there had been no suggestion that he *was* an archer. No – even if there were a case to be made out against him, at present it was a very thin one.

Was Pratt implicated, after all? Had he lied about that morphia injection? If so he had covered up his tracks with devilish cunning. His alibi had now been tested and proved valid. There seemed no reason to doubt the fact that he and Wade did not know each other socially. But a morphia injection *was* a morphia injection, and, unless Pratt had been lying, Wade couldn't have been seen by Miss Boon.

'I think,' said Meredith to Barnet after dinner that evening, 'that I'll slip in and have another word with Pratt.'

But the doctor could not be shaken from his former statement. He was quite certain that morphia had been injected and that the drug had taken effect before he left his patient's bedside.

So far as he knew, Wade had no car. His uncle, so he believed, had made him an allowance of three pounds ten a week, with the idea that if his nephew wanted any luxuries then he'd have to buckle to and earn them. Of course, it was well known that the boy was to inherit, but in the meantime his uncle refused to give him a penny more than his allowance. No – so far as he knew, Wade was not an archer. He certainly wasn't a member of the Wellington Club. Not that he, Pratt, knew very much about the boy's private life. He was not attracted to that type.

After running Long to earth at his home, much to his wife's disapproval, they discussed every point of the case into the small hours. Tired out, Meredith went back to the square, more depressed than he had been at any moment since the case opened.

In the morning he decided to run out to Winchcombe and investigate the strange death of Mr. Bates's ewe. He was still hoping it might give him a pointer. Barnet, ever ready to help and to add to his knowledge of police procedure, offered to drive the Superintendent in the Alvis.

It was a dull morning. Dark clouds were massing over the ridge of the distant Malverns, and the silvery curves of the Severn were only visible when an occasional shaft of sunlight penetrated the murk and glittered on the water. From the crest of Cleeve Hill the town, embowered in its wealth of fine trees, looked sombre and unattractive. The uplands themselves, with their bare, cropped pasturage and grey-stoned walls, seemed strangely bleak for July. For all that,

Meredith could not stifle a note of appreciation when the car sidled into the long and winding street of the village. There was not a modern touch to disturb the ancient charm of the place with its cluster of crusty, lichenous roofs, its gargoyled church and its more than satisfying example of the art of Inigo Jones. He had often heard of these Cotswold villages and in Winchcombe he was not disappointed.

He found the local police station, explained who he was to the sergeant and the reason for his visit. The sergeant was impressed.

'Yes, sir – we've got the arrow all right. Can't for the life of me see how it happened. We suspect that it was one o' the village lads up to mischief.' He rummaged in a cupboard and handed Meredith the weapon in question. 'That's it, sir. A bit amatoorish by the look of it. Looks as if the 'ead was hand-made, eh?'

Hand-made, thought Meredith experiencing a sudden thrill. By God! – he was right in coming out to investigate! The arrow *was* barbed. It might have been the same arrow that had been drawn from the dead man's head. Identical. Same length. Same sort of barb. Yes – and level with the nock was the same veneering of plastic wood where the maker's imprint had been carefully pared away with a knife. Whoever had killed that sheep had killed Cotton. But why the sheep? Was it the work of a maniac?

'The spot where this animal was supposed to have been shot,' asked Meredith, 'was it off the beaten track?'

The sergeant nodded: 'As lonely a spot as any

in the district. Lies over beyond Cleeve Hill in a deep valley.'

'And no stranger was noticed about that day?'

'None as far as we can gather, sir. We questioned the gentlemen up on the golf-course in case the chap had come over Cleeve Hill way. Nobody here in the village saw anybody suspicious like. He must have made off over the wolds towards Naunton or Stow. After all, if 'e was carrying a bow–'

'When he saw what had happened,' cut in Meredith, 'he may have *cached* it somewhere. D'you mind if I hang on to this arrow? Refer to borough headquarters if you make an arrest and the case comes into court. It may be rather useful to us. Thanks.'

From Winchcombe Meredith got Barnet to drive direct to April House. Wade was luckily out so the Superintendent was able to interview Mrs. Black without putting the boy on his guard. Once more he found himself sitting in that prim, camphorated parlour – more dingy than ever on account of the brewing rain-storm.

'It's about that night of 13th June again,' he explained to the landlady. 'Did you see or speak with Mr. Wade after the doctor had left that evening?'

'I never *saw* him,' said Mrs. Black, 'though when I went up to bed myself at ten o'clock I called out through the door to ask if he was comfortable and if there was anything he'd be wanting. As I didn't get any answer I guessed he was still asleep.'

'To be expected after a dose of morphia. What time did he wake in the morning?'

'Not until well past eleven, as far as I can remember.'

'And you heard no unusual sounds during the night?'

'No, sir.'

'How do you lock your front door?'

'With a Yale lock, sir.'

'Mr. Wade has his own key?'

'Yes, sir.'

'It never occurred to you that Mr. Wade might have been out that night after the doctor left?'

'Oh dear no – after what the doctor had told me about his being fast asleep I don't see how he could have gone out without me knowing. Besides he'd had that sleeping draught, hadn't he?'

'Quite.' Meredith rose and moved meaningly toward the door, followed by the landlady. 'I'd rather you made no mention of this interview to Mr. Wade. Understand, Mrs. Black?'

The woman gave her solemn promise and Meredith went out to the waiting Alvis. As it was then lunch-time they returned to the square, where the Superintendent took a hasty meal and hurried off to Clarence Street to see Long.

'Well, sir – any forrader?' asked the Inspector.

'Nothing new except this.' And he unwrapped the arrow and placed it on the desk. 'Borrowed it from Winchcombe. It's identical with the one which killed Cotton.'

Long grunted. 'Can't understand this twist at all. Unless the chap's got a screw loose there seems no point in murdering a bloomin' sheep. Went a long way to do it, too. Funny. 'Ow about this lively lad, Wade? Something fishy there as I said the other night.'

'Yes – but what motive?'

'I've been thinking about 'm in conjunction with the crime. No – don't look surprised, sir. I do a spot o' thinking in my leisure hours. You don't think it was a case of mistaken identity?'

'What, on Miss Boon's part?'

'No – on Wade's. You don't think that when he shot that arrow 'e thought he was drawing the bead on 'is uncle? See what I mean – just a head sticking up above the back of that armchair. And 'oo's chair was it? Not Cotton's. His uncle's. 'Oo did he expect to be sitting in that chair? Not Cotton, did 'e? Nine times out of ten his uncle *would* have been sitting in that particular chair. When I've been into the square since I've seen him sitting in it myself.'

Meredith jumped up as, stimulated by the Inspector's suggestion, another fact flashed into his mind.

'Good heavens, Long! – I believe there's something in that idea. D'you remember when I was investigating those footprints up on Matthews' roof I took a look at Buller's window? He was sitting in the same chair, and I noticed that his bald patch showed above the back of it. Cotton had a bald patch!'

'Yes,' went on Long, flattered by the reception his theory had received. 'And when Cotton got it in the neck, Buller was over in the corner of the room pouring out the drinks. Remember 'is evidence? So Wade wouldn't have seen the second person in the room unless 'e'd been watching from the Empty House for some time. Naturally he wouldn't risk that. I reckon 'is idea would be to nip in, take aim, watch for the result and then 'op it quick.'

'But that damned morphia!' exclaimed Meredith irritably. 'How the devil are we going to get over that? If it had been an ordinary sleeping-draught it could have been counteracted with an emetic. I've known that trick to be played before. But an injection, you can't get that out of your system.'

'Then Pratt *must* be in it,' contested Long. 'After all we've only got 'is word that the boy was asleep when he left the room. Mrs. Black didn't see 'im again that night.'

'I know all that, Long – but even then how did he get out of the house? Pratt didn't leave until 9.15. If Wade was to get over to Regency Square in time to commit the murder at 9.30 then he must have left *before* Pratt.'

'Is there a back stairs to the 'ouse?'

Meredith shook his head.

'I should have noticed if there had been when I went up to Wade's room. Why d'you ask?'

'Well – from what you've told me – Pratt came down from the lad's room and 'ung about in the front-hall for a time talking to Mrs. Black. Suppose, for the sake of argument, Pratt *was* a party to the crime – couldn't this chat 'ave been pre-arranged so as to give Wade the chance to nip out the back way?'

Meredith nodded slowly.

'That's more than possible, Long. He may have shinned down a water-pipe into the garden and had his car waiting in a road behind the house. There may be footprints, indications of some sort

– what d'you say to taking a Leckhampton bus and settling our minds on this point? A vital clue if we hit on anything.'

'I'm all for that, sir.'

Mrs. Black was plainly agitated on receiving a second police visit so shortly after the first.

'Oh dear, sir – it's all so upsetting. Gives me the creeps to feel that something might have gone wrong in *my* house. If only I knew what the trouble was! It can't be nothing to do with Mr. Wade. He wouldn't hurt a fly.'

Setting her fears at rest with some non-committal answer, Meredith, ascertaining that Wade was still out, asked to be shown up into his room. Once there he dismissed the landlady and beckoned Long to the window.

'Well if we are going to find anything we're only just in time. You realize, of course, that it hasn't rained since the 13th? But in a minute or two it's going to rain cats-and-dogs.' Between them they slid up the sash and craned out. 'Good Lord!' was Meredith's immediate exclamation, 'crime made easy, eh, Long?'

'A shed! Darn it, even I could make a getaway over that roof. Shall we climb out and run the tape over it?'

Meredith threw a leg over the sill and dropped lightly on to the rubberoid roof of the lean-to, followed more cautiously by the Inspector. Going down on their hands and knees they examined the grimy surface. Several long, clearly-defined scratches suggested that something or somebody had recently been up on the roof. But it was impossible to say if the scratches had been made by boots. It was not until they peered over the guttering of the shed and examined the loamy soil of the border directly below, that Meredith let out a cry of satisfaction.

'Footprints, Long! Here – directly behind that laurel bush. Deep impressions, too – just as we might expect.'

'By jingo! – that's where 'e jumped down right enough,' observed Long, with a low whistle, 'and there's the gate at the end of the garden through which 'e got into the road at the back.'

They dropped down, one by one, to the ground and investigated the narrow, deserted road on the far side of the garden-gate. It offered a perfect parking-place for somebody who was anxious not to draw attention to their car. Back in the house Meredith put a final question to Mrs. Black.

'That gate at the end of the garden – do you lock it at night?'

'No, sir – never.'

'Thanks, I suppose you've no idea where we're likely to find Mr. Wade at this hour?'

'Well, it's possible he may be in Parker's billiards-saloon in Grange Street. He's very partial to a game of billiards is Mr. Wade.'

'Right – we'll have a look for him there. And remember, Mrs. Black, not a word about these visits.'

'Know where this place it?' asked Meredith of Long when they were clear of April House.

'Somewhere round the back o' Montpellier Gardens. It's your idea that we should tackle the lad straightaway, is it?'

Meredith nodded and pointed out that, with the

circumstantial evidence now incriminating Wade, the sooner he was questioned the better. But their luck was out. The proprietor of the billiards-saloon said that he had been there for an hour after lunch, but had left some twenty minutes earlier. He had an idea that he had gone to the cinema show at the Gaumont Palace in Winchcombe Street.

'Damn!' said Meredith as they left the building and turned towards the gardens. 'We can't comb through a cinema audience. We'd better send a man out to keep watch at April House, with a request for Wade to show up at the station as soon as he returns home.'

'O.K. I'll prime Shanks up with 'is description. As it's just come on to rain he'll enjoy a couple of hours cooling 'is heels in the Leckhampton Road. Pity we haven't got a photo of the lad.'

'We have,' grinned Meredith, pulling a post-card out of his pocket. 'I borrowed this off Mrs. Black's kitchen mantelpiece when she wasn't looking. But we need this ourselves. In any case Shanks has only got to make an inquiry the moment he sees a young man enter the house.'

'Yes – but what do we want the photo for?'

'You and I are going to fill in our time walking round to the garages to see if we can trace that car.'

'Walking!' gasped Long. 'What in this rain?'

'Better than cooling your heels in the Leckhampton Road,' retorted Meredith with a malicious smile.

But although for two solid hours they cross-questioned the proprietors of some dozen garages in the vicinity of the Leckhampton Road, they learnt nothing about the car. Long, in the meantime, had phoned up Clarence Street and sent Shanks out to April House. At half-past five the two men decided to abandon their quest until the next day and separated to get some tea. After they had eaten Long was to go back to the station to wait for Wade's appearance, when he was to phone Meredith in Regency Square.

It was a terrible evening – gusty and rainy, unusually chilly for the time of the year. After tea Barnet and Meredith settled down to a long discussion of the book in which they were collaborating. Cotton's murder had prevented them from really getting down to it, and although Meredith had arrived over three weeks before, only the barest outline of its scope and contents had been decided on. As luck would have it, however, Major Forrest, the Chief Constable at Lewes, had raised no objection to Meredith prolonging his stay until the police either made an arrest or decided to abandon the case. But all the time he was talking to the crime-writer Meredith was listening for Long's call. He felt more and more certain that Wade knew something about the murder. There were one or two leading questions which that young fellow was going to find mighty difficult to answer. At half-past eight, however, he was still listening. Outside it was still pouring with rain and an early dusk was settling over the square. And then, just when Meredith had given up hope of seeing Wade that night, the phone-bell rang.

Excusing himself to Barnet, Meredith picked up the receiver.

'Hullo? That you, Long? He's there? Good. I'll

come right round. Keep him chatting about the weather until I arrive.'

Hurrying into his mackintosh, the Superintendent opened the front door, put down his head and went down the path. Just outside the gate, however, he collided with a hatless, coatless female, who was running along the wet pavement. The woman looked up and Meredith recognized Mrs. Gannet, Buller's housekeeper.

'Hullo. Hullo. What's the hurry?'

The housekeeper, recognizing him in turn, clutched wildly at his sleeve.

'Oh, my Gawd, sir! You must come quick! Something terrible has happened. The master's been– Oh, my Gawd, 'e looked awful. I can't bring myself to say it.'

'Here – pull yourself together,' snapped Meredith. 'Hysterics won't help. Where were you off to?'

'To fetch the doctor, sir.'

'Mr. Buller ill? Come on – what is it? Had a fit or something?'

'I wish to Gawd it *were* only that. *'E's dead.*'

'Dead!' exclaimed Meredith, thunderstruck. 'Here, you run back indoors. I'll fetch Pratt. Quick now!'

Rushing up to the door of Number Nine, Meredith pressed the bell, tapping his toes with impatience as he waited for an answer.

'The doctor in?' he asked the maid the moment the door opened. 'He must come at once. Urgent.'

Hearing his raised voice, Pratt, himself in a dinner-jacket, came out into the hall.

'Hullo – what's up?'

'Buller. Serious as far as I can gather.'

'Buller? But I've only just left him.'

'Got it from Mrs. Gannet. She was coming here.'

Pratt snatched his hat from a peg and took up his professional bag.

Once out of the maid's hearing, Pratt demanded:

'What is it?'

'Dead – I think.'

Pratt let out a whistle.

Together they raced up the stairs to Buller's study, in the window of which they had noticed a light burning. Mrs. Gannet was waiting for them outside the door. Pratt flashed her a look of inquiry. She nodded.

'In there, sir.'

They went in.

Buller was sitting in the leather armchair nearest the wide-open window. One hand gripped the lapel of his velvet smoking-jacket. The other was closed over an unlighted cigar. His mouth was slightly agape. In three strides Meredith was across the room with the doctor close at his heels. Simultaneously their eyes met.

'Good God!' breathed Pratt in a shaken voice. 'It's impossible!'

But the slender, vicious-looking arrow which projected from the back of the stockbroker's head offered a flat contradiction to the doctor's involuntary statement.

CHAPTER XII

Suspect at Number One

Instinctively Meredith glanced at his watch. Eight-forty-three. He turned on the doctor.

'When you say you've just left Buller – what do you mean?'

'Just that,' answered Pratt. 'Five minutes ago I was in this room and now–'

'All right,' snapped Meredith. 'Stay here and keep an eye on things. I'll be back in a moment.'

Ignoring Mrs. Gannet who was still hanging about on the landing, Meredith dashed down the stairs and out into the square. Running as hard as he could, regardless of the wet, he slipped through the front gate of the Empty House and took the steps two at a time. He tried the door. Locked. Hastily he glanced over the façade of the building still dimly lit by the fading daylight. All the windows were shut. Without wasting a second he proceeded to the back of the house. The back door, too, was locked. He glanced up again. Not a window was open. Curious. Had the murderer been too quick for him? Or did it mean that, this time, the arrow had been loosed from some other vantage point?

At the sound of footsteps he peered into the darkening murk and recognized Matthews.

'Look here, sir – there's been more trouble over

at Buller's place. Can't stop to explain now. I want you to fetch Fitzgerald along and keep watch on this house. As quickly as you can, sir,' he added, noticing the Vicar's apparent inability to grasp the need for urgency.

'Oh, dear – yes – of course,' burbled the Vicar from under his dripping umbrella. 'Of course.'

He disappeared with a dignified trot and returned in a few seconds with the bank-manager.

'One at the front and one at the back if you will,' said Meredith briskly. 'And if anybody comes out, nab him.' Then, noticing the Vicar's look of alarm: 'Or failing that get a line on his identity. Back later.'

It did not take the Superintendent a minute to reach the phone in Barnet's study. Whilst he was getting through to the police-station, he said over his shoulder: 'Buller's copped a packet. Nip in next door and see if you can be of any use to Pratt, will you, sir?' Then into the phone: 'Hullo! Hullo! That you, Long? Meredith speaking. No – can't be bothered with him now. Hold him there for the time being. Buller's just been shot. Cotton business all over again. Got that? O.K. Now listen – I want a man rushed to George Street. Friend West. Understand? See if he's out. If so, stop him before entering the house and lug him round to the station. Then, of course, I want you here with the police surgeon. Also Shanks. No time for more now. But for heavens' sake get a move on!'

Back in Buller's study he found Pratt making a cursory examination of the body. Barnet was watching him with an air of professional interest.

'Well, doctor – what do you make of it?'

'Cause of death, eh? Well – that's obvious isn't it? The only difference between this case and the other is the man sitting in the chair. By God – it's incredible! Like something out of Edgar Wallace. Shakes you up a bit – this sort of thing when it occurs frequently.'

'What about that arrow, Meredith?' asked Barnet in the true Watsonian manner. 'From what direction–?'

'Yes – that's just what I'm trying to gauge,' cut in Meredith. 'Off-hand I should say it was loosed from exactly the same spot. Curious.' He turned on Pratt. 'You say you were in this room five minutes before Buller was shot?'

'Yes. He'd asked me in to dinner, but as I had some work to do on a paper I'm writing I couldn't stay late, I'd only just taken off my outdoor things when you rang.'

'Then Mrs. Gannet must have come up to the study the moment after you left?'

'That's more than probable. You see Buller asked me to send her up with a glass of water on my way out.'

'Water?' said Meredith in a tone of incredulity.

Pratt smiled faintly: 'To take a pill with – those pills you see there. Anti-acid pills, as a matter of fact. Buller was inclined to be dyspeptic.' He pointed to the little smoking-table beside the armchair. 'It looks as if Mrs. Gannet did as I asked – there's the glass of water.'

'–and there's a car,' broke in Barnet as he strode across to the open window. 'Police, I think.'

The next minute Long and Shanks entered, the

former in plain clothes. The eyes of the two officials met. Meredith gave a slight shrug.

'Police surgeon's on the way,' announced the Inspector as he walked across to view the body. 'Anything, so far, to give us a pointer, sir?'

Again Meredith shrugged. He turned to Barnet and the doctor.

'I wonder if you'd mind–?'

'Not a bit,' said Barnet instantly. 'Come in and have a drink, Pratt? I'm sure we can do with it. We'll be there if you want us.'

As soon as the door had closed Long said vehemently: 'Well, of all the bloomin' surprises. You could have knocked me down with a feather. Buller, eh? Strikes me my little theory of mistaken identity is going to be proved up to the 'ilt. Cotton was a misfire, as you might say. This is the real thing. Any idea, sir?'

'Flummoxed,' replied Meredith tersely. 'What's your opinion about the arrow?'

'Come from the same spot, hasn't it?'

'What do you say, Shanks?'

'Undoubtedly, sir. I'll bet my bottom dollar it was shot from the Empty House.'

'Maybe – but about three minutes after the murder was committed all the doors were locked and all the windows shut. The chap made a quick getaway all right. By the way Shanks – get on to Gregg, the estate-agent, at his private address and tell him I want the key to Number Two sent round here at the double.'

'Very good, sir.'

Whilst Shanks was putting through the call, a second car drew up in the square below and a moment later Newark, the police surgeon, pushed his head round the door.

'Hullo? Same setting, eh? Bit of a coincidence, Meredith. I hope you're not going to make a habit of this! Just having a nice hand of bridge.' He crossed over to the body. 'Umph – might have made a carbon-copy of my findings in the Cotton case and saved time. Hit in precisely the same spot. About the same amount of penetration. The old chap couldn't have known much about it. Shall we get this arrow out – nasty sight.'

'Hey, steady sir–!' began Long in great agitation. He swung round on the Superintendent. 'What about making use of your apparatus again before we remove the arrow?'

'The screen and the sheet of paper? All right. Can you lay your hands on the necessary things, constable?'

'Housekeeper got them from this desk, sir,' said Shanks, crossing over and pulling out a drawer. 'Here's the foolscap and the drawing-pins. The chalk's in that pen-tray. Shall I fix things as before?'

Whilst the constable was pinning the sheet of paper to the screen, Meredith marked in the exact position of the armchair. The screen was cautiously pushed into place, the line of the arrow scored across the paper and the position of the screen, in turn, chalked on the parquet. The armchair with its tragic occupant was then drawn out toward the centre of the room. Newark, who had been watching these operations with quizzical amusement, again approached the dead man.

'Well, what about the arrow now – shall I–?'

'Whoa! Whoa!' broke in Long again. 'Not so fast, sir. We've got to–'

Newark smiled. 'Oh, I know, Inspector – those precious fingerprints.' He pulled a pair of thin, rubber gloves out of his case.

'Any objection if I use these and only handle the extreme tip? None? Good. Well – here goes!'

His gruesome task completed, Newark handed the arrow to Meredith who stood by ready to receive it in an open sheet of newspaper. The officials stood round in a close group examining it.

'Just like the other, isn't it?' said Long with the air of a connoisseur. 'Same sort of thingummy on the end. Maker's name carefully erased. And ... 'ere, Shanks, turn out that light, will you?' added Long, struck by a sudden thought. Then, when the room had been plunged into darkness: ''Ullo, different in one respect, any'ow. None of that spooky paint daubed on the shaft this time. Wasn't intended for night-work, eh, sir?'

'So it seems,' said Meredith. 'But if the light wasn't on in this room when the doctor left then it must have been a darned tricky shot. It was getting darkish when I came out into the square and the rain wouldn't have helped the visibility. What about testing for prints, Long?'

Whilst Long was drawing on gloves preparatory to making the test with his magnifying-glass and powder preparation, Newark had returned to a further examination of the body.

Looking up, he said: 'Seems to be rather more stiffening of the limbs than in Cotton's case. I'm rather wondering now if he went out as quickly as I first thought. Thickness of the skull may have something to do with it. Position of the vulnerable point may be slightly different. Notice that he's had time to lift his left hand and clutch the lapel of his coat. Involuntary reaction, no doubt, but it argues a fraction of a second between the moment of penetration and actual death.' Newark grinned pleasantly. 'But you needn't worry, Meredith – I shan't make a "nice" point of that at the inquest. The cause of death is obvious. That's all our friend the Coroner will want to know. Well – if you can do without me – I'd like to get back and finish that hand of bridge. I was all booked for a Little Slam when your damned call arrived. Good night.'

When the surgeon had left Shanks returned from the phone.

'Key will be here in a few minutes, sir.'

'Good. Any luck, Long?'

'So far,' said Long, looking up from his delicate operations, 'the surface seems about as smooth as a baby's bottom. Did you expect anything else? It's a routine job, of course, but nowadays nine times out o' ten it's a bloomin' waste of energy!'

'What about a photographer?'

'Well, I haven't called him,' acknowledged Long, 'but if–'

'No. Not necessary. The two cases being so similar, we've got half our data ready made.' Meredith turned to Shanks. 'You might see if the two gentlemen watching the Empty House have had any luck. Tell them I'll be across in a minute with the key. Then go on to Number One and take a statement from Miss Boon. Usual thing – where has she been during the last half-hour? Has she noticed anybody in the square? We may have to visit her later.'

When Shanks had left, the Inspector looked up from his fingerprint test and turned down a thumb.

'Nothing doing. Our friend's been just as careful as he was in the Cotton case.' Adding with deep admiration, 'You know 'e uses his brain. Got it all taped out to a T. The coolest customer, I reckon, I've ever been up against. What now, sir?'

'Let's get the body out of the room. I want to have a word with Mrs. Gannet and this sort of thing always proves a distraction when you're cross-questioning a woman of her type. See if she's outside, borrow a sheet and find out which is his bedroom.'

In a few minutes Long returned with the sheet and the two men carried the body across the passage and laid it out on the bed. Snatching up a towel Meredith went back into the study and carefully cleaned all the bloodstains off the armchair. Then, throwing the towel into the wastepaper basket, he asked the housekeeper to come in. She was obviously on the verge of fainting and it was not until the Inspector had made her sip a little brandy and propped her up with cushions on the settee, that a little colour came back into her cheeks.

'Feeling better, Mrs. Gannet?' asked Meredith paternally patting her on the shoulder. 'A terrible shock for you – we realize that – but you've got to help us by answering a few questions. I understand the doctor had been dining with your master this evening?'

'That's right, sir,' replied Mrs. Gannet in a husky

whisper. 'He came across about seven o'clock. Dinner was at half-past as usual. After dinner he and the master came up here for a smoke, but from something he said at table the doctor couldn't stay late.'

'What was that?'

'Something about working on a paper – whatever that might mean.'

'What time did they leave the table to come up here?'

'About five-and-twenty past eight. The kitchen clock struck the half-hour just as I started to clear away.'

'And the doctor left the house?'

'About ten minutes later.'

'You saw him before he went?'

'Yes, sir. He called down for me to take up a glass of water to the master.'

'Was this usual?'

'Oh, yes, sir. Three times a day, after meals, the master always took his stomach pills. Suffered unnatural in that way, poor man. No matter what I'd cook, his meals never seemed to agree with him.'

'But surely, Mrs. Gannet, if it was usual for your master to take these pills, you would have placed the glass of water ready in the study?'

'That's just the funny part about it. I thought I had taken a glass up. Surprised me no end when the doctor called down. I'm not usually forgetful.'

'And you went up with the water the moment after the doctor had left?'

'Immediate, sir.'

'Was the light on in the study when you entered?'

'No, sir, it wasn't. There was still a bit of daylight left, of course, and thinking the master didn't want it switched on I walked across and put the water on his smoking-table.'

'And then you noticed?'

Mrs. Gannet shuddered and buried her face in her hands as if to shut away the scene that she was, once more, visualizing.

'Then I noticed that awful thing sticking out of his head. I called out sharp, but he didn't answer. I was terrified. I remembered what had happened to the Captain.'

'Did you touch the body?'

'Oh, no, sir – I daren't. I couldn't have brought myself to do it. But I knew he was dead right enough.'

'And then, of course, you rushed off for the doctor?'

'That's right, sir.'

'This window was open when you came in?'

'That window's always open,' said Mrs. Gannet with emphasis. 'Wet or fine. It's only kept shut in the very cold weather. One of the master's fads it was – supposed to be good for his health.'

'Tell me, Mrs. Gannet, did your master ever smoke before he took his medicine?'

'No, I don't think so, sir. Most times he'd come up here, swallow his pill directly after his meal and then light his cigar.'

'You noticed he had an unlighted cigar in his hand this evening?'

'No, sir – I didn't notice that.'

'All right, Mrs. Gannet – that's all for the present, thanks. If you take my advice you'll go and lie down for a bit. Is there anywhere you could stay for the night?'

'I've a married sister in Mont Road. She'd have me all right.'

'Very well. You'll have to stay for a bit in case we want anything. Later the constable can take you and your luggage round to Mont Road.'

'Thank you, sir. If you don't mind then, I think I'll go and pack a few things. It will take my mind off the master, if you see how I mean?'

As soon as Mrs. Gannet had gone out Meredith pushed away his note-book and turned to Long: 'I think it would be a good idea to get your friend Bryant, the archery expert, round here. Tell him to bring his bow and arrow. We've got to make dead sure that the arrow was loosed from the Empty House. Now that we've got the direction taped I've an idea that there's a deviation in the horizontal angle – compared with the shot that killed Cotton, I mean.'

'O.K. He's in the book. I'll ring at once.'

'Then come and join me over at the Empty House. I expect that's Gregg's messenger at the door now.'

Hurrying across the square through the teeming rain Meredith found his two helpers still anxiously on guard but drenched to the skin. In his excitement the Vicar had closed his umbrella and forgotten to open it again. They had nothing to report. There had been no sign of life in the house. They had heard no suspicious noises. Thanking them for their co-operation and warning them that they would be called upon to make a statement later, Meredith dismissed them. Just as he was turning the key in the Yale lock, Shanks joined him on the steps.

'Was she in?'

'I'll say she was! I've managed to extract a statement, sir, but only with the greatest difficulty. Nothing much to report, I'm afraid. Has seen or heard nothing out of the ordinary. She's been in all the evening doing a crossword.'

'All right, Shanks – we'll leave Miss Boon for the time being. I want to have a look round in here. Got a torch?'

Shanks switched on a pocket-lamp and the two of them made a meticulous examination of the whole house. The wind was striking gustily against the window-panes and making them rattle in their sashes. It was practically impossible to see out into the square through the streaming wet glass. Meredith naturally paid most attention to the front-room on the second storey, on the look out for footprints which should have been discernible on account of the rain. But he found nothing suspicious. A further inexplicable point suddenly occurred to him. If the arrow had been loosed from the house, then one of the windows must have been opened. The wind was driving the rain directly against the front of the house. Then why, in heaven's name, wasn't there a wet patch on the floor? Every floor in every room was as dry as a bone. Meredith tried the effect of an open window and in an instant the boards were soaked. No footprints. No window opened. Then surely the arrow had not been discharged from the Empty House?

Back in Buller's study he found that Bryant had turned up with his bow, obviously thrilled to be called in on such a sensational occasion. As Meredith entered the room he was down on one knee sighting up an arrow parallel with the pencil line which had been drawn on the foolscap.

'Well, Mr. Bryant – what's the verdict? Sorry to drag you out on a night like this but we need your expert judgment.'

Without turning his head, his eye still fixed on his aiming-point, Bryant said decisively: 'One thing's certain. Buller wasn't shot from the Empty House.'

'You're sure?' snapped Meredith.

'Dead sure as far as this particular test is concerned. If I loosed this arrow it would disappear, as far as I can see, through a second-storey window of Number One.'

'Miss Boon's,' exclaimed Meredith, surprised.

'What, 'er!' added Long. 'She couldn't have done it, surely? What motive had she got?'

'Well, unless Buller moved in his chair after he was shot the arrow was certainly loosed from her house,' contested Bryant, rising. 'I naturally haven't the faintest idea why she wanted to kill him.'

'Perhaps Buller did move,' suggested Long. 'Remember what Newark said about the stiffening of 'is limbs? He seemed to think that death might not have been instantaneous, didn't he?'

'On the other hand,' put in Meredith, 'from my investigation in the Empty House I should say that the arrow couldn't possibly have come from there. Strikes me Miss Boon will have to answer a few questions. It's certainly curious.'

As soon as Bryant had left, Meredith and Long set out to take statements from Fitzgerald and Matthews. The former's alibi differed little from the one he had put up on 13th June. He and his wife had been in all the evening, he reading a book, she sewing. As their maid did not live in he was, he confessed, in no position to put forward an independent witness. Matthews had been along to the Public Library in search of a reference book. He admitted that the library closed at eight and that he had not arrived at the square until after twenty to nine but, as he hastened to point out, there was a simple explanation for this. He had whiled away a good twenty minutes in the Newspaper Room, which did not close until nine o'clock. No – he had not encountered anybody suspicious on turning into the end of the square.

'So much for those two,' said Meredith as they left the Vicar's house. 'Now for Miss Boon. After that we can re-examine Pratt.'

As they were walking towards Number One, Long observed:

'There's one gentleman sitting pretty where Buller's death is concerned. If anybody's got a cast-iron alibi – he has.'

'Who?'

'Young Wade. We suspected 'im of the other job. We know 'e's got a darn good motive for this one. But he couldn't have done it, could 'e? Shanks fetched him over from Leckhampton Road and dumped 'im at the station somewhere round about eight-thirty. He's been there ever since. Waterproof, that is!'

They went up the steps of Number One, Long hanging back a little as if anticipating the wrath to come. Miss Boon and three dogs answered the door and it was difficult to distinguish her bark from the others. The gist of her remarks seemed to suggest that they were to come in quickly since they had to come in, shut the door after them and make the interview as brief as possible. Once seated in her untidy drawing-room, she ignored Long entirely and made it obvious that if she had to deal with officialdom then she preferred the Superintendent.

'The constable here has told you what the trouble is,' began Meredith. 'The question remains, Miss Boon, can you tell us anything that might put us on to a clue?'

'Nothing,' snapped Miss Boon. 'I told this boy here. He took down all I had to say. I've nothing to add.'

'I understand you were doing a crossword puzzle?'

'I was – this puzzle in the *Dog Lover's Weekly.*'

'May I see?' Meredith stretched out a hand and glanced at the paper. 'What time did you start this puzzle?'

'What an absurd question. I've really no concise idea!'

'About eight?'

'Before that.'

'And you've been working on the puzzle all the time?'

'Until your boy called – yes.'

Shanks winced and reddened a little behind the ears. Dash it! – this was a bit thick.

'I only ask,' went on Meredith quietly, 'because in the three-quarters of an hour at your disposal, you've only managed to fill in two words. I notice every clue is a breed of dog. If anybody could polish off a puzzle like this it should be you, Miss Boon. It seems funny you should have found it so difficult.'

'I ... I ... don't do these things often,' faltered Miss Boon, obviously put out by Meredith's perspicacity.

'For example,' continued Meredith in an even voice. '"Suggests an island off Canada." Surely that must have occurred to you at once. I don't consider myself very advanced in geography, Miss Boon, but that certainly seems obvious to me.'

'Really?'

'Yes – there *is* a dog called a Newfoundland, isn't there? And this, too "Suggests a large Scandinavian" – two words. I'm surprised you didn't get that, Miss Boon. Why, even the Inspector here–'

'Great Dane,' announced Long promptly. 'Simple! Any more?'

Miss Boon glared at him.

'But I don't see what–?'

'This,' rapped out Meredith, his voice suddenly hardening. 'From our investigations we find that the arrow which killed Buller was loosed from the direction of your house.'

'From here? Balderdash!'

'Furthermore you don't seem to be able to supply us with a very satisfactory alibi. Two words in three-quarters of an hour – with your intelligence? Do you expect us to believe that?'

'It's the truth,' barked Miss Boon furiously.

'Again,' went on the Superintendent, 'I happen to remember that when I called on you a short time back that you referred to Mr. Buller as "that inhuman monster." Why? What have you against Buller? Why don't you like him?'

'Is that anything to do with you?'

'It may be.'

'And if I refuse to answer?'

Meredith smiled. 'Well, in that case, we can only draw our own conclusions, can't we?'

'All right – if you must know. A year ago Buller deliberately killed a spaniel of mine. He swore it had snapped at him. It hadn't. Not unless he provoked it to attack him. He broke its back with a stick. I've never spoken to him or acknowledged him since.'

'I see. Can we have a look over the house? You realize, since Buller appears to have been shot from here, that the murderer might have crept in without your knowledge?'

'That is the only possible explanation, isn't it?' said Miss Boon icily. 'All right. Kindly wipe your boots before going into the bedrooms. I consider this all most unwarranted. Your insinuations have been little short of insulting.'

Methodically, beginning with the basement and working upward, they examined every room in the house. Again Meredith looked for a tell-tale wet patch on the floor. Again he drew a blank. No footprints on the carpets. Nothing suggestive. They climbed up to the attic and on the top landing, Meredith suddenly stopped dead. At his feet was a spreading pool of wet. He glanced up. Rain spattered on to his face.

'Good heavens!' he exclaimed, 'the skylight! It's open. Why?'

'You don't think Buller was shot from the roof? By Miss Boon?'

'Yes – or by anybody else. Here, give me a shove up. I'm going to investigate.'

Out on the rain-swept roof Meredith went over the ground with a pocket-torch. He worked along as far as the skylight of the Empty House and found it shut. Then on to a similar skylight in Matthews' house – again shut. Beyond was the peaked end of Fitzgerald's place and the little window from which he had kept watch on Cotton. A new idea flashed into his mind. The first murder. Suppose Miss Boon had had a hand in that? Wasn't it possible that she had got out on to the roof of her own house and entered West's place through the skylight? No key was necessary for that. She would have had no trouble in concealing her bow – a point which had considerably worried Meredith. She *said* she had been out with her dogs on the night of Cotton's murder. In proof of this statement she claimed to have seen Wade driving a car in Victoria Road. Was this really the truth? Or was Wade asleep, as he claimed, after that dose of morphia in April House? Those scratches on the roof of the shed, the footprints in the flower-border might have quite another significance. So far they had not had time to cross-question Wade on this matter. Suppose he offered a perfectly feasible explanation – wouldn't the case against Miss Boon be, *ipso facto,* strengthened? Of course she had not meant to kill Cotton that night. She thought it was Buller. They had already accepted the possibility of mistaken identity. But the motive for the murder – the malicious killing of that spaniel – did that sound likely? Perhaps in an eccentric woman with an overwhelming, single-minded passion for dogs, this incident might have provoked her to such a terrible expedient. But it was a big 'might.' There must be something more to it than that – some other, more convincing motive, which Miss Boon was concealing. And again – could she do it? She was reputed to be an indifferent shot. If she had done it then she must have practised in secret. But where? It needed a lot of space and, in her case, inviolable privacy.

Then: 'My God!' thought Meredith. 'The sheep!'

Had she been practising up on a lonely stretch of the wolds and hit that sheep by accident?

CHAPTER XIII

Probables and Possibles

Meredith realised, however, that he would gain nothing by cross-examining Miss Boon any further that night. She was already in a dangerous temper and by pushing things too far he might antagonize her to such a point that she would refuse to speak in the future. He did question her casually about the open skylight and received the answer which he had expected. It had been opened during the hot weather and Miss Boon had forgotten to close it when the rain began. Simple. Unassailable. Meredith had to take her evidence at its face value.

On their way over to Barnet's to take a final statement from Pratt, Meredith observed: 'Wade and West are our remaining concerns for to-night. I hope that chap you sent down to George Street has got West to come round quietly and sensibly to the station.'

Shanks then took down in the presence of his superiors the following statement from the doctor.

I was frequently asked to dine with Mr. Buller. On this occasion he had invited me because he was anxious to discuss his nephew's health. I arrived at the house at about seven and dinner was served at half-past. We remained at table for nearly an hour. I then saw Buller up to his study, having already apologized for having to desert him directly after the meal. I am working on a paper dealing with the Causes and Cures of Hay Fever. Up in the study Buller offered me a cigar and took one himself. I reminded him of his indigestion tablets and he pointed out that Mrs. Gannet had not provided him with his usual glass of water. He asked me to send her up with a glass on my way out. I stayed chatting for some few minutes and then took my leave. I was up in the study for about ten minutes. I sent Mrs. Gannet up with the water and returned to Number Nine. I left Buller seated in the armchair near the window, which, according to custom, was wide open. I had scarcely taken off my hat and overcoat when the Superintendent rang the bell and informed me that

Buller had been shot.

After they had had a drink, Meredith sent Shanks to collect Mrs. Gannet and take her round to Mont Road, whilst he and Long hopped into the police-car and headed for the station. On the steps under the crumbling portico a constable anxiously awaited them.

'Well?' asked Long. 'Did he come quietly?'

'Yes – he's inside, sir. Took it a bit flustered at first but as soon as I pointed out that it was only commonsense to clear himself if he wasn't implicated, he came willing enough. I think you'll find him ready to talk.'

'Anything else to report?'

'Yes, sir. Whilst I was hanging about outside his lodgings, a boy called at the place with a note. I naturally asked him who it was for. He said "Mr. West" and that a lady had given him a shilling to deliver the note. Seems that the lad met the woman just by Regency Square. Big, loud-voiced woman, he said.'

'With a dog at her heel, I'll bet,' put in Long with a wink at Meredith. 'Something up there, eh, sir? Fishy, to say the least of it. What time did the lad arrive?'

'Ten minutes to nine, sir.'

'And West turned up?'

'About five minutes later.'

'Right – that'll be all, Timms. If you've made out your official statement you can 'op it off home.' As they walked along the corridor to the Inspector's office, Long added: 'Think we ought to see young Wade first. After all we've kept him hanging about here since half-past eight.'

Meredith agreed that he should be shown in first and the sergeant-on-duty was sent to fetch Wade from the charge-room where he had been housed. He entered with his usual breezy unconcern.

'Well, well, well – I *am* having a night of it.' Then noticing Meredith: 'Oh, hello, old boy – so you've drifted along now, have you? It's a hell of a night, isn't it?'

'You can guess what we want to see you about, Mr. Wade?'

'Something pretty snappy, I should think, by the time you've kept me cooling my heels in that damned dungeon. Honest, old boy, I *feel* like a criminal if that's any consolation to you. Well, let's burrow down to the roots, shall we, and learn the worst? Shoot, sergeant!'

'It concerns the night of 13th June,' explained Meredith. 'The night that Dr. Pratt gave you an injection of morphia. We have reason to believe that you were seen later that same evening driving a car in the Victoria Road.'

'Gosh – that's a good one, I haven't heard it before. No, really old boy, it's marvellous the way you think of them. Have you ever seen a chap driving a car whilst under the influence of morphia? Worth seeing, eh? Matter of fact I can't drive a car when sober let alone when drugged up to the eyebrows with morphia. Somebody's seen my double or taken one on an empty stomach. Fact, old boy.'

'So you flatly deny that it was you?'

'Absolutely flatly, old boy.'

'I see. Ever had any reason to get on to the roof

of the shed under your bedroom window at April House?'

'On to the roof? Why, of course not. Bally waste of energy when you're old enough to have a key. The geezer may be mean in some directions, but she chucks in a latchkey *gratis* with the bed-sitter.'

'You're sure you've never been on that roof?'

'Sure, old boy? Why, of course I'm–' Wade paused and looked at Meredith with round-eyed astonishment and admiration. 'By Gad! – that's smart. Real ripe sleuthing. How the devil did you spot the criminal spoor? You're quite right though. I did go up on the roof one night. Left my key in another suit and rolled up so late I didn't dare disturb the old dragon.' Then confidentially, 'As a matter of fact, old boy, I was about three sheets in the wind. Met a lad I hadn't seen for years and went back to his hotel. Must have fetched up under Leckhampton about the middle of the death-watch. So I sneaked round the back, shinned up on to the shed and got in through the window. Real Raffles stuff. Smart, eh?'

'Except for one small point,' said Meredith with a faint smile. 'The footprints we found in the border beneath the shed had their toes pointed away from the wall. You don't mean to tell me that you shinned up the shed backwards?'

'A point, old boy. A *good* point. Any unpractised criminal would fall for that gag as meekly as a bally lamb. But we hardened toughs – well listen to this and match it up with the truth. You won't notice the difference. I *did* jump down off the roof. Why?

Because I couldn't get the window open without a knife. Had I a knife? No – I hadn't, but I knew the geezer kept one in the shed for scraping the leather off one's best boots. So what did I do? I nipped down and nabbed it. Fact, old boy.'

'I see,' said Meredith in a voice which gave no hint as to whether he believed his witness or not. 'And what did you do with the knife?'

'Shoved it in my pocket, old boy, and slipped it back in the shed next morning when the old geezer wasn't looking.'

Meredith nodded, then rising, said in a more serious voice.

'I'm afraid we've got some rather unpleasant news for you, Mr. Wade.'

'I know – you're going to arrest me for putting French pennies in a slot-machine. O.K. I'll plead guilty.'

'It concerns your uncle,' went on Meredith unruffled by the other's levity. 'It's the worst possible sort of news, I'm sorry to say. Mr. Buller was found shot this evening at about eight-thirty.'

For once Antony Wade discarded his mask of habitual light-heartedness.

'Uncle Teddy shot? But, good heavens, who would want to kill a harmless, decent old bird like him? You mean it was not accidental, don't you?' Meredith nodded. 'Murder, eh? Poor old Uncle Teddy ... murdered! It doesn't sound possible.' He added on a lighter note. 'Lucky for me that I was sitting in the police-station at the time. Otherwise I reckon you'd stick me down at the head of your suspect-list. I mean I come into the dibs and that's always supposed to be a cast-iron motive for murder, isn't it? Poor old boy. He had his faults but I've always liked the old chap. This has given me a bit of a jar. Rotten affair!'

'You've no idea, I suppose, if your uncle had any enemies among the inhabitants of the square?'

'That's a stock question, isn't it?' Wade gave a hollow grin. 'As a matter of fact he wasn't particularly popular with anybody in the square. He had the misfortune to win out in a tussle with one of Miss Boon's mongrels. Since then she's cut him dead. Matthews didn't like him because he didn't go to church and wouldn't subscribe to the funds. I don't know about that chap who's left – West, isn't it? I only know that whenever his name popped up my uncle used to change the conversation pretty quickly. Pratt seems to be the only one who was at all friendly with the old boy and I reckon half that was professional tact. But I don't see that his worst enemy in the square had good enough reasons to bump him off. Pretty rotten show, eh? No ideas, I suppose?'

'Not yet,' answered Meredith. 'We'll be keeping in touch with you, of course. You're the nearest relative?'

'Yes – that's the idea. I suppose I'd better get in touch with my uncle's solicitor johnnies and get things properly organized. If you don't want to put me through any more third-degree stuff, I think I'll ring through to-night before it's too late. They ought to know at once.'

'No – that's all, thank you, Mr. Wade. Sorry to have kept you hanging about here for so long. But now that you know the reason–'

'That's O.K. with me, old boy. Only sorry that I

should have wasted so much of your time through not being the criminal. More accommodating next time, perhaps. Cheero.'

The moment Wade had retired Long looked up from his desk where he had been taking notes, and scratching his many chins with his fountain-pen, observed solemnly: 'You know, the more I see o' that young blister the more muddled I get as to 'is innocence. 'E could talk the 'ind leg off a donkey and the donkey'd never realize it. Slippery-tongued – that's what he is, sir. Glib, as they say. I still think he got out o' that window on the night o' Cotton's murder.'

'So do I,' agreed Meredith quietly, 'but I can't for the life of me see why. Now what about having West in.' He turned to the constable who had just returned from seeing Wade off the premises and asked him to fetch the next witness.

West entered the room diffidently. He was neither nervous nor self-assured, just puzzled and a little bewildered. He was a different man from the one Long had interviewed the previous month. He had let himself go, with the result that his personal appearance no longer seemed to fit an erstwhile member of the Regency Square circle. It was obvious that West was passing through a pretty lean period.

Without preliminary Meredith explained what had transpired that night, tactfully pointing out that in the circumstances witness would be ready to appreciate the need for his immediate summons to the police-station.

'For instance, Mr. West – you realize that it is necessary for us to know where you happened to be at eight-thirty when the murder was committed.'

'Oh, naturally. Naturally,' replied West, his tone of voice belying his observation. 'At eight-thirty – now let me see – where was I exactly at eight-thirty? Somewhere in the High Street I think – looking around the shops.'

'You left George Street at what time?'

'Shortly after six o'clock. Mrs. Emmet, I feel sure, will be able to corroborate this fact.'

'Quite. And then where did you go?'

'For a walk. I went out of the town to just beyond Chariton Kings. I didn't hurry back but made a détour into the Old Bath Road and into the High Street again.'

'According to the constable you didn't turn up at George Street until just on nine. What were you doing between eight-thirty and nine?'

'Oh, just browsing around the shops. I went up Promenade and back into George Street via the Rotunda and Montpellier Terrace.'

'Did you meet anybody you knew?'

'No.'

Meredith altered his angle of approach, jumping his next question with disconcerting suddenness.

'That note – could you tell us who it was from, Mr. West?'

'Note – which note?' The ignorance, thought Meredith, was patently overdone.

'It would be better not to take that line, sir. Safer if you understand me. A boy delivered it five minutes before you returned.'

'Oh, that,' West laughed without much conviction. 'Yes, I was forgetting – there was a note

waiting for me when I got home, from Miss Boon.'
'Might I ask what it was about?'
'It was about a job she was trying to fix me into.'
'Really. Why not post the letter?'
'I suppose she thought the sooner I applied for the post the more chance I had of getting it.'
'What firm was it with?'
'What firm ... well, really ... I...' West began to stammer in the most pitiful manner. He stood there for a moment goggling at the Superintendent, obviously at an utter loss for an answer. 'You see,' he murmured weakly, 'there are certain confidences...'
'Look here, sir,' rapped out Meredith sharply, 'we're on a murder case investigation. You'd better realize that fact once and for all. We can't afford to respect any confidences when it comes to necessary explanations.' He thrust out his hand with an imperative gesture. 'Can I see that note?'
'I've ... I've destroyed it, I'm afraid,' blurted out the man with a desperate attempt to appear convincing. 'You see, I had no–'
'Now don't be absurd, Mr. West. You opened that note in the constable's presence and slipped it in your pocket. The constable accompanied you here and you've been in the sergeant's presence ever since you arrived – we *know* that note is in your pocket. Well?'
'I can't show it to you,' said West with sudden obstinacy.
'In other words Miss Boon was not writing you about a possible job but something – well, what shall we say – something a little more sensational perhaps?'

'What do you mean?'

'I mean that the substance of that note had a bearing on the murder. Miss Boon was sending you a warning. Why? Because you know something pretty vital about the crime, Mr. West! Come on – the truth is the only thing which will get you out of an awkward corner.'

'But what can I say? I know nothing about the murder. Nothing. Until you told me just now I didn't even know Buller was dead.'

'Then you're shielding Miss Boon.'

'I ... I...' West floundered miserably.

'So that's it,' cut in Meredith briskly. 'Well, you won't help her cause along by withholding evidence. If she did it and we can prove she did it, then you'll be arrested as an accessory after the fact. You know what that means? The game's not worth the candle, sir, believe me. Now what about that note?'

Suddenly West, with a sigh of defeat, capitulated and thrusting his hand into his pocket drew out the note.

'There it is – read it for yourself.'

Joined by the Inspector who looked over his shoulder, Meredith read the following brief message:

Say nothing to the police about your visit here. I have already put forward my story.

Kate Boon.

'So all your previous evidence is not worth a row of beans,' observed Meredith quietly when he had finished reading the note. 'Now, suppose, for a change, you tell us the truth, Mr. West.'

'Very well – I will. I suppose it's the only sensible thing to do. Actually when I left George Street at six this evening I went straight round to see Miss Boon. I hardly like to touch on the reason for this visit but I suppose I must. Briefly – I'm absolutely down to my last shilling. I've got no job. Nobody to turn to for help. I thought of Miss Boon who had always been very friendly with me in the past. I wondered if I had strength enough to sink my pride and ask her for the loan of some money. She was kind enough to help me – not only monetarily but with genuine sympathy for my present unbearable position. She did actually mention the possibility of getting me a job. I left her house shortly before eight-thirty, browsed round the shops as I have already said and reached George Street about half an hour later. You can imagine how surprised I was to find this note waiting for me. I couldn't see the reason why it had been sent. I can't now. I can't see any reason.'

'Unless...' prompted Meredith with a slight lift of his eyebrows.

'Exactly,' said West in a low voice. 'When I came in here and you told me about Buller, a horrible thought shot through my mind. A beastly, unworthy thought I grant you – but in the circumstances how could I think anything else. Can *you* tell me, Mr. Meredith, why she sent that note?'

'We're as much in the dark as you, sir – eh, Long?'

'Groping,' agreed Long with a doleful grimace. 'But women do do funny things and she'd probably do funnier things than most.'

'And you'd be ready to swear that you returned direct from the square to George Street?' asked Meredith.

'Yes – except that I made that détour via the Rotunda.'

'Thank you, Mr. West. I'm glad you saw fit to tell us the truth about that note. I can quite appreciate your sentiments. As it is I've an idea your candour will help to clear the fog a little. Nothing further, eh, Inspector? No? Right, Mr. West. Good night.'

'Which leaves us, as I said before,' muttered Long as soon as they were alone, 'groping. It strikes me that we might as well put a list of names in the hat and draw for it! If I've got any fancy that I feel inclined to back – well, between you and me, it's the ole grey mare. Mind you, I start off with a natural prejoodice where she's concerned. I don't like 'er and she don't like me. No doubt that she sent that note, eh?'

'Oh, she sent it all right, but she's probably got a very simple explanation,' answered Meredith. 'But I'm damned if I'm going to ask for that explanation to-night. We've done all we can for the moment, Long. Suppose you come round and meet me at Number Eight about nine o'clock to-morrow morning?'

But despite the lateness of the hour Meredith did not go to bed the moment he got back. He sat for a long time in his room puzzling and pondering over every aspect of the two murders. As far as he could see there was no lack of suspects. The trouble, so far, had been that there were too many suspects. There was plenty of evidence, a number of useful clues, a lot of strange discrepancies in various people's statements – yet when this collection of data was viewed and examined as a whole there seemed to be no relation between any one fact and another. As usual, to clarify his thoughts, Meredith jotted down the outstanding points which had come to light during the investigation. As a basis on which to work he wrote down a list of the suspects and entered up against their names the details which he had gathered about their movements and so on. His completed notes ran thus:

THE COTTON MURDER

Probables

(1) WEST. *He had motive. Alienation of his wife's affections. He had key to Empty House from which arrow was fired. He was unable to supply a water-tight alibi. He was a good, often brilliant shot.*
(2) FITZGERALD. *He had motive. Cotton was blackmailing him because Mrs. F. imagined that she had married Cotton. He had no water-tight alibi. He had access to roof through small landing window of Number Four and might have got into Empty House through skylight.*

Possibles

(1) MISS BOON. *No known motive but could have got into Empty House through her skylight and West's. Although stated she was walking her dogs no*

corroborative evidence. Said she saw Wade in car. Wade denies having left April House that night.
(2) PRATT. *No known motive. Was a good shot. Unless working with Wade had a sound alibi. Did he really inject Wade with that morphia?*
(3) WADE. *No known motive. Was not known to have been an archer. But evidence points to fact that he may have left April House on night of murder. (Miss Boon's statement and footprints below shed.) If in criminal collaboration with Pratt may not have had that morphia injection.*

Impossibles

(1) MATTHEWS. *Unshakeable alibi.*

THE BULLER MURDER

Probables

(1) WEST. *No known motive. But might have re-entered Miss Boon's after his visit via the Empty House and skylight of Number One. Could not put up a water-tight alibi. Detour via Rotunda to George Street possibly false evidence,*
(2) MISS BOON. *Had a motive of sorts (The dog). The arrow appeared to have come from her window. The note to West was suspicious. Was in the house alone (apparently) when the murder was committed.*

Possibles

(1) MATTHEWS. *No known motive. But was in*

the square near No. 1 just after the murder. Had been in Public Library (Newspaper Room) but could not claim to have been recognized by anybody. Could have got into Miss Boon's via his own skylight and that of No. 1.
(2) FITZGERALD. *No known motive. Could have got into No. 1 by same route as suggested in Cotton murder. No water-tight alibi.*

Impossibles

(1) PRATT. *Because he had only just left Buller's house. Could not have taken up position to have loosed arrow in the time. No motive anyway.*
(2) WADE. *Strongest of motives. But soundest of alibis. Was in the police-station when murder was committed.*

Other Possibility

That Cotton and Buller were murdered by somebody not in the square circle.

'Possibles and Probables,' thought Meredith as he glanced down the list. 'Umph – sounds rather like a Rugger trial. But what's to be gained by it? Confound it! If anybody has a good motive for the murder they've got a cast-iron alibi. If their alibi's rocky then they've got no motive for committing the crime! Strikes me that every single fact cancels out every other fact. Curse!'

Wasn't there, he wondered, at least one illuminating point to be gleaned from a perusal of his list? He examined it again more closely. And suddenly a thought struck him. West was the common denominator of the Probables! He alone figured in that section in *both* murders. And wasn't it fairly safe to assume that whoever killed Cotton, killed Buller? After all the method of murder was unusual – it was not one that might have been repeated in so short a lapse of time. Granted that murderers were reputed to emulate each other – that one trunk-crime might be followed by a veritable spate of trunk crimes. But, in this case, the murder-method was specialized. It called, not merely for an archer, but for an expert archer – a really brilliant shot. This West was reputed to be. Again, the type of arrow favoured in each case was identical save for the dabs of luminous paint – the same erasure of the maker's imprint, the same home-made barb. On the other hand, what reason had West for murdering Buller? If Buller had been murdered first then the possibility of mistaken identity might enter in. Would it be too much to hope that a motive might come to light during the next few days' investigations? And if so would they be justified in arresting West on suspicion? Turning the facts, once more, over and over in his mind, Meredith persuaded himself that if this second motive could be found then the outlook from West's point of view would be decidedly grave.

CHAPTER XIV

A Flutter at Number Seven

Shortly after nine o'clock the following morning Long and Meredith found themselves facing once more a very irate and unhelpful Miss Boon. To the Superintendent's practised eye she appeared to be abnormally keyed-up and suffering from the aftermath of a sleepless night. Hoping to startle her into telling the truth, Meredith sprang his first question at her, the moment they were seated in the drawing-room.

'That note – why did you send it? That's what we're after. That's the reason we're here again.'

'Note?'

'To West.'

'Did I send him a note?'

'Yes,' snapped Meredith, pulling it quickly out of his pocket. 'This one.'

She looked at it, nodded and made as if to tear the note in pieces. With a swift gesture Meredith took it from her and apologized with a smile.

'Sorry – but we can't have evidence destroyed, you know. Well, Miss Boon – we're waiting.'

Miss Boon stared at him balefully.

'I should have thought you'd have hit on the explanation at once. Very simple. Perhaps I overrate your intelligence.'

'Easily done,' agreed Meredith genially.

'I sent the note because of Arthur.'

'Arthur?'

'Yes – West. You know where he was last night, I imagine?'

'Here,' answered Meredith promptly.

'Quite. Confidential visit, understand? Well, Arthur left here just before eight-thirty. About nine o'clock your boy came in and said Buller had been shot. I knew, of course, that you already suspected West over the Cotton affair. Perfectly unjustified, let me say at once. I knew you'd be after him again. It struck me that if he walked back to his lodgings and was not recognized by anybody, he'd be in a nasty fix. I felt and still feel very sorry for Arthur. That man's been through purgatory these last months. I wanted to spare him more trouble. So, in an unthinking moment, I sent him that note. My idea was that if we concealed his visit he could say he had not left his rooms. Foolish of me, I admit. But that, at the time, didn't occur to me. The moment your boy had left I scribbled that note, slipped out into the square, found a lad and tipped him to take it to George Street. That's all.'

'You realize that you might easily have prejudiced the police in their attitude towards Mr. West?'

'Quite. But how did I know that the note would be discovered. I suppose you intercepted it?'

'Not exactly. Mr. West read the note all right. It was not until after we had questioned him that the real truth came out. Your attempts to help him only put him into a very awkward situation. You realize that?'

'I've already told you that I now consider my action foolish,' barked Miss Boon. 'Isn't that enough?'

'But why should you think that West would *want* to murder Buller?' cut in Meredith, neatly switching the conversation.

'Good heavens,' cried Miss Boon, 'it's common property that–' she stopped dead, suddenly realizing her mistake, hesitated and ended tamely. 'When have I suggested that he wanted to? As far as I know he–'

Meredith suddenly got up and crossed over to the hearth. He was no longer genial. All his powers were concentrated on the vital need to extract from Miss Boon the information which she was so patently concealing. Once grant that West *had* a good motive for the murder then the case against him would be a strong one. The Common Denominator of the Probables! She must be made to talk.

'Look here, Miss Boon, I'm going to speak frankly. I warn you that it is a criminal offence to withhold evidence from the police. You *know* that West had a motive for the crime. You've as good as told us that already. You say it's common property – well, it isn't to us. So you'd better prime us now, eh? If you don't tell us, somebody else will.'

'But it's only hearsay,' protested Miss Boon, subdued by her stupid error. 'You know how people chatter.'

'There's often the germ of truth in gossip,' pointed out the Superintendent.

'Very well. But remember I don't *know*. I've only *heard*. You knew, of course, that Arthur lost his money in a bad deal on the Stock Exchange? You didn't? Well he did. Some months back I heard – never mind who from – that Buller had been responsible for his crash.'

'You mean that West's losses were Buller's gains – is that it?'

'Yes. I don't understand how the trick was done. I've only heard that it was. I don't even know how my informant found out. At any rate, West knows about this. He told me so yesterday. Perhaps now you can understand my foolishness better – in sending that note?'

Meredith nodded.

'How long has West known about this?'

'Some weeks, at least – possibly longer.'

'And you refuse to tell us who told you this?'

'Absolutely.'

'Very well, Miss Boon. We can't make you.'

The interview terminated at this and the two men crossed over to discuss matters in Aldous Barnet's study. The crime-writer had gone out directly after breakfast to have a round of golf on Cleeve Hill.

'You know,' began Long, dropping with a grunt into a deep armchair, 'I can't 'elp feeling that that woman's up to some sort o' hanky-panky. I mean, all these notes an' things and desire to be 'elpful. Seems fishy to me. Looking at it square, it strikes me she really *wanted* to get the fellow in an awkward corner. She sent that note so as we'd be suspicious of 'is doings – see? An' that slip of 'er tongue was deliberate to my mind. She *wanted* us to know that 'e had a motive for the murder.'

'In other words, Long – you think she did it?'

'I do,' said Long with profound emphasis.

'After all, how could West have done it? There was his bow for one thing. How did he get it through the streets? How did 'e get back into Miss Boon's after he'd left at 8.30? Why didn't he shoot from the Empty House? 'E had the key. See how I mean? Nothing really seems to fit in against him.'

'On the other hand Miss Boon took the trouble to conceal the fact of his visit. That seems genuine enough.'

'Artistic ornament,' explained Long with a slow wink. 'Dressing up her lie pretty so as we'd swallow it more ready.'

'For all that,' contested Meredith, 'I can put up just as many objections to Miss Boon being the murderer. First and foremost, she had no real motive. Personally the death of that dog strikes me as being insufficient. Cotton was shot at from the Empty House. Why the devil did Miss Boon take the trouble to break into West's place when she could have done the job from one of her own windows?'

'That's easy,' said Long. 'She did it, as I said before, to put the suspicion on West. Shouldn't be at all surprised to hear that she's got something red-hot against that poor devil.'

'Then why the deuce didn't she shoot from the Empty House this time?'

'I've an idea about that too, sir. We reckon that if she did loose the arrow in the first murder she must have got into the Empty House through the skylight. Well, last night it was raining. She couldn't very well go up on the roof without getting her feet wet and leaving footprints all over the Empty House.'

'Might have worn over-shoes,' argued Meredith. 'And taken them off before getting through the skylight. No, frankly, Long, I think there is less reason for us to suspect Miss Boon than West. And in either case we're up against one very strange and inexplicable fact which you appear to have overlooked.'

'What, me!' exclaimed Long on a note of incredulity.

'Even you,' smiled Meredith. 'What about the wet patch left by the open window when the arrow was loosed?'

'There wasn't any wet patch. We looked for it.'

'Exactly. Why not?'

'Why not? Why because ... because...' Long broke off, stared at Meredith, scratched his head and wheezed. 'Crikey! That's funny. Slipped my mind. *Do* you know why there wasn't a wet patch, sir?'

'I don't, Long. There can be only one feasible explanation.'

'And that?'

'That the arrow was not fired from Miss Boon's *or* the Empty House. In other words, due to some movement of the body, our calculations are wrong. This leaves us with one other possibility – and as far as I can see *only* one – that the arrow was shot from one of Matthews' windows.'

'Or from the square itself,' corrected Long.

Meredith shook his head.

'Impossible. No movement of the body could counteract the obvious upward angle of an arrow shot from the ground-level. For another thing, Buller's head would have barely been visible at all above the back of the chair.'

'But good Lord, old Matthews couldn't 'ave done it. A bloomin' parson! Besides, 'e's got nothing against Buller, has 'e?'

'Nothing as far as we know. But neither Miss Boon nor West appear to have motive either, so that's no basis for argument. Wish we could find out a bit more about West's slip-up on the Stock Exchange.'

''Ere,' suggested Long suddenly blessed with inspiration, 'what about those old biddies next door? They look the tittly-tattly sort – you know, seed-cake and scandal. What about dropping in and putting them through a spot of questioning? Cause a flutter in the 'en-roost, I dare say, but we're more likely to get the truth out o' them than anybody else.'

'O.K. Inspector. Get your hat and we'll drop in now.'

The sight of the two men coming up the front-path roused in the maidenly breasts of the Misses Watt something more than a flutter and only just less than sheer panic. For days they had anticipated this visit. They had visualized it over and over again. The unexpected arrival of the police, the dramatic confrontation, their own inadequate replies to cunning questions and the final, awful moment when they would be arrested on suspicion. They were innocent, of course. But could they make the police realize that in time? How dreadful if they were seen by the square, handcuffed, being escorted to the police-station.

And then – oh, terrifying thought – a night in the cells before the dreadful error was rectified. There might be mice, even rats in the cell, and the shame of it afterwards! They would never be able to live down such a slight on their previous iron-sided respectability.

'You're sure it's the police, Nance,' fluttered Miss Emmeline, peering over her sister's shoulder from the upper window. 'You're quite sure?'

'Certain,' answered Miss Nancy, releasing the curtain from her trembling fingers. 'The tall one is the Superintendent from next door and the little, fat one is the Inspector.'

Miss Emmeline cast a furtive eye round the room, even in the midst of her alarm anxious that everything should be in its accustomed place.

'Now listen,' she went on hastily. 'We must be quite calm and unhurried. And we mustn't say too much. I read somewhere that the police always suspect a witness who talks too much. So remember, Nance.'

'Do we sit?'

'Of course we sit.'

'Do you think we ought to offer them some coffee and a slice of cake? It's nearly half-past ten.'

'Most decidedly not!' snapped Miss Emmeline. 'They might consider that bribery, Nance.' Adding as a portentous afterthought, 'or even corruption. Now go down at once and let them in. We mustn't keep them waiting too long. Show them up here and ask them to wipe their feet, won't you?'

With a few deft twitches Miss Emmeline rearranged one or two flowers in a vase, took a dent out of a cushion and straightened a lace antimacassar. When she looked up from these little duties her sister was back in the room with the two men standing hatless, respectfully behind her. To her distorted vision the room seemed full of men.

Meredith stepped forward and looked from one to the other of the prim, rather defiant figures confronting him.

'May I introduce myself? Superintendent Meredith. I think we've seen each other in the square. Miss Watt, isn't it?'

'I'm Miss Emmeline Watt – this is my sister Nancy.'

'And this is Inspector Long of the Borough Police.'

Long bowed like a stage duke, whilst the Misses Watt seated themselves side by side on the sofa.

'We want to ask you a few questions,' went on Meredith as Long drew out his note-book with a flourish.

The sisters glanced quickly at each other, registered this statement with an infinitesimal nod and stiffened as if in anticipation of some long-awaited ordeal.

'It concerns the death, indirectly, of Mr. Buller.'

Almost imperceptibly, they shuddered.

'But we know absolutely nothing about that,' affirmed Miss Emmeline in a dignified voice. 'I fear we shall only be wasting your time.'

'No time is wasted in a murder investigation when we want information,' Meredith assured her with a smile.

Was that smile a little malicious? A little sinister? wondered Miss Nancy. He looks kindly enough and he has had the good manners to remove his hat. But we mustn't be led astray by that. The little fat man seems to be looking at us queerly.

Oh, golly – what a couple of old 'ens, Long was thinking. Like those old aunts o' mine on my mother's side. Fossilized – that's the word! Poor old dears look as if they're sitting on eggs. Couldn't look more guilty if they'd done Buller in themselves.

His hand went up to conceal an ill-mannered grin which had been born of the thought. He could just see them up in a window drawing a bow on old Buller! Crikey!

'Now you've lived in the square for a good many years,' Meredith was saying, 'and I expect you know a good deal about your neighbours. Mr. West for instance. Have you any idea if he was on good terms with Mr. Buller?'

Miss Emmeline looked puzzled. She felt sure this was some very subtle trick. After all there was no other reason for dragging in poor Mr. West. She must be careful – on guard.

'I really can't say. I'm afraid Mr. Buller was not understood by most of the people in the square.'

'And Mr. West among them?'

'Mr. West again! Possibly,' said Miss Emmeline.

'You've never heard, for example, that Mr. Buller was responsible for Mr. West losing all his money?'

Miss Emmeline started. How had the police managed to learn this piece of news? Surely dear Mr. Matthews?... She recalled with startling clearness the night of Mr. Buller's delirium and another night, not so long ago, when she and Nance had unwillingly overheard another conversation.

Should she speak of these things? After all they could not possibly have any bearing on the dreadful crime which had been committed. That unfortunate Mr. West, whose wife had run away from him, could not possibly have been the murderer. Not possibly. Then, as she heard Meredith's insistent voice repeating the question, she suddenly saw like a revelation that Mr. West had a good reason, a very good reason for doing such a terrible thing. And if a man had a *very* good reason for murder wouldn't the police, perhaps, decide to let him off. Now what was the phrase they used in the newspapers? Justifiable something – ah yes, justifiable homicide. Perhaps if she told this man, who really seemed very quiet and polite, all that she knew about poor Mr. Buller and poor Mr. West, he might not do anything more about the matter. She felt certain, now, that the police did not suspect that she or Nance had anything to do with the crime.

'I have heard something about that – yes,' she acknowledged. 'I feel sure that Mr. West had a very good reason for not liking Mr. Buller.'

Long and Meredith pricked up their ears and exchanged a quick glance of triumph. Nancy peered sideways at her sister, obviously puzzled. Surely Emmeline was falling into some verbal trap by talking too much? She nudged her sister, who nudged her back violently and shook her head.

'In fact,' went on Miss Emmeline in slighter louder tones, as if to show her sister that she knew very well what she was up to, 'in fact, I was the first person in the square to learn of Mr.

Buller's deception.'

'Could you explain?' asked Meredith politely.

'Oh, but you couldn't do that!' exclaimed Miss Nancy quickly. 'It would be a breach of confidence.'

'Nonsense,' snapped Miss Emmeline. 'And kindly allow me to conduct my affairs as I wish. One naturally doesn't want to speak ill of the dead but I'm sure it's my duty to speak up and save poor Mr. West from any wrongful persecution. It all happened some months back when Mr. Buller had an attack of influenza. You remember there was quite an epidemic shortly after Christmas? Dr. Pratt, who attended Mr. Buller, asked me to sit with the patient one evening as he was finding it impossible to obtain a professional nurse. Of course, I was only too pleased to help, particularly as Mr. Buller appeared to be very feverish. Later that evening he grew delirious. I didn't understand. I think at first he thought he was being chased by bulls. He kept on talking about bulls. Then it was bears. Bears and bulls. It was really quite frightening to sit in that darkened room listening to him. Then suddenly I heard him mention Mr. West's name. Then he began to laugh. Really it was not a nice laugh. He seemed to be sneering at poor Mr. West in a most unchristian manner. He said something about "an easy pigeon to pluck" and mentioned some cement shares. Gradually I began to see what he was talking about – that by some sort of trick he had managed to swindle Mr. West of a great deal of money. I remember some other phrases he used because they were so unusual – unusual to me that is. He talked of "forcing the shares down" – then something about "make him unload at a rock-bottom price and wait for the rise." He seemed to know for certain that the price of the shares would go up. He kept on saying "they'll treble their value in a few weeks." Naturally I was very worried over this matter and, not knowing what I ought to do, I went to Mr. Matthews for advice. He seemed to know exactly what Mr. Buller had done on the Stock Exchange and felt sure that Mr. West had been very seriously swindled. It appeared that Mr. Buller had also advised Mr. West to invest the money he got from selling the cement shares in something that proved quite worthless. Mr. Matthews said something about "a bucket-shop" but I really didn't understand what he meant.'

'And what did he advise you to do about it?' asked Meredith, profoundly impressed by Miss Emmeline's evidence.

'Oh, not to say a word to anybody. From that day to this neither my sister nor I have breathed a word to a soul. We have been puzzled, very puzzled indeed as to how Mr. West got to hear about the matter.'

'How did you find out that he knew? Did he tell you?'

Miss Emmeline seemed flustered by the question. She realized, but too late, that she was now faced with another explanation. Her sister looked at her with a glance of withering pity. Emmeline was making a nice fool of herself!

'No – he didn't actually tell me. I ... I heard indirectly.'

'How?'

Miss Emmeline coloured a little.

'It was something we overheard, wasn't it, Nance?'

'Was it?' asked Miss Nancy, flatly unhelpful.

'Really, I don't know what you must think of me,' went on Miss Emmeline. 'I don't make a practice of eavesdropping. It's all most unfortunate. But it happened a few days before Mr. Buller's untimely end. Let me see now – it was Thursday of last week – a very sunny day if you remember. My sister and I were sitting out on the balcony – yes, that's right, the one you see through that window. I was doing a little sewing for the Church bazaar and Nancy was reading. As you realize Mr. Buller's house adjoins ours and, as he always sits in his study – or I should say as he always *sat* in his study with the window wide open, we really couldn't help hearing something of what was being said in the room. That evening, Mr. West called at Number Six shortly after tea. We saw him come across the square and, much to our astonishment, enter Mr. Buller's gate. Later we heard voices coming from Mr. Buller's study, just ordinary polite voices at first, then presently, much to our alarm, we heard the sound of a violent quarrel. We tried not to listen but the voices were so overbearing that we couldn't help hearing something of the conversation – could we, Nance?'

'As I was reading I only heard a very little,' said Miss Nancy, thus insinuating that her sister had heard a great deal.

Miss Emmeline went on: 'I heard Mr. West say in a very angry voice: "I've heard all about that trick of yours – never mind from whom – the point is what are you going to do about it?" Mr. Buller laughed – it was the same sort of laugh I had heard when he was delirious. A very unpleasant laugh indeed. "Nothing," he said. "I'm going to do exactly nothing about it and I'll leave it to you to make out a case against me." He said this in the coarsest voice – rather crowing we thought, as if he were actually *gloating* over poor Mr. West's predicament. "I warn you," shouted Mr. West – yes, I mean shouted – "I warn you, Buller, that you've not heard the last of this. You've ruined me completely!" After that, Mr. Buller – whom I had always considered a gentleman – used the most improper language, I couldn't possibly repeat the words he used. They were so unsettling that I sent Nancy indoors to find my spectacles. Then after a few more high words, which I was unable to catch even from the far end of the balcony – not that I wanted to overhear, of course – I heard the slam of the door and presently Mr. West appeared down below and walked off quickly across the square. And that,' concluded Miss Emmeline, with a sigh of exhaustion, 'is all.'

'And very kind of you too,' commented Meredith with a pleasant smile. 'How do you think Mr. West got to hear of the swindle?'

'Incredible as it must sound, I think Mr. Matthews must have told him. Very tactless for a man in holy orders. I feel he should have respected my confidence. However...'

'Well, I must compliment you, Miss Watt, on the clarity of your evidence. You certainly have a very remarkable memory.' Meredith laughed. 'Luckily for us!'

'Shall I tell you the secret?' asked Miss Emmeline, as the Inspector rose and made toward the door. 'Pelmanism. A really wonderful system. I think I can claim, without boasting, that I know the whole of the Prayer Book by heart.'

'Remarkable!' exclaimed Meredith politely as he edged towards the door. 'Thank you so much for your information. Good morning.'

'Good morning,' echoed the sisters in unison.

As they walked briskly toward the station the two men fell into a prolonged discussion. More and more Meredith felt inclined to the theory that West was the wanted man. He pointed out the known facts, once more, to Long. West had a motive now for both murders – in each case a powerful motive. Cotton – because of his wife's affair. Buller – because of the swindle. He could not put up a successful alibi for either of the murders. In the first he swore he had not left his rooms in George Street after returning there at tea-time. His landlady, Mrs. Emmet, had last seen him on the night of Cotton's murder at 8.45 when she cleared away his supper things. The murder was committed round about 9.30. This would allow West plenty of time to slip away from George Street to Regency Square, enter the Empty House and commit the murder. In the second case he had left Miss Boon's shortly before 8.30 and reached George Street (on the constable's evidence) at 8.55. Meredith reckoned, and Long agreed, that if West had gone direct from the square to George Street he should have taken some fifteen minutes, perhaps less. Instead he had taken at least twenty-five. West accounted for this by explaining that he had made a détour via Promenade, the Rotunda and Montpellier Gardens. He had not hurried but browsed in the shop-windows on his way. Unfortunately he had not stopped to speak to anybody or been recognized *en route*. To say the least of it – both his alibis seemed weak. On top of this he was a good and often brilliant shot with a bow and arrow. The two outstanding points which remained unaccounted for were *(a)* How had he managed to smuggle his bow through the streets in the first murder? *(b)* Why hadn't the rain driven in through the open window when the Buller crime had been committed. Both Number One and Number Two had been searched and in each case the expected clue was missing. On the other hand it *was* possible that the arrow had been loosed from the roof. In which case, after leaving Miss Boon's, West must have sneaked into the Empty House, got out on to the roof via the skylight and shot Buller from there. Granted there had been no sign of wet footprints in the house, but as Meredith calculated, West could have worked the business in this manner: On entering the front door he could have discarded his boots and walked up to the top landing in his stockinged feet. Before climbing out through the skylight on to the wet roof he could have taken off his socks. On returning through the skylight he could have put on his socks, walked dry-shod down the stairs and put on his boots again before going out into the square. He would have to chance being seen when he entered the Empty House, because it was still light, but as the rain was keeping most people indoors this would be fairly safe. He might even have approached the house from the back lane and left the same way. He couldn't, however, have entered by the back door because that was bolted on the inside. Matthews had come into the square almost directly after Buller had been shot, but as he hadn't encountered West it seemed pretty certain that he must have left via the lane at the back. So far so good, argued Meredith, but in his opinion, endorsed by the Inspector, they were still not justified in making an arrest. For example, the truth of West's second alibi ought to be meticulously tested. It was a bad business if the police made a blunder and arrested the wrong man when there were loose ends lying around which ought to have been followed up.

'Let's see,' pondered Meredith as the pair swung into the High Street. 'West would have reached Promenade, if his story were true, about 8.40, wouldn't he, Long?' Long agreed. 'Right. Have you got that photo on you – that snap which Stinns managed to get of West? You have? Good. Now I want you to comb down both sides of Promenade and find out if anybody saw West round about 8.40 on the night of Buller's death. Most of the shops would have been closed, of course, but not all of 'em. Besides a lot of people live over the premises. It's a long shot but it may come off, Inspector.'

'O.K., sir – and what about you?'

'I'm off to see that expert of yours – let's see, Bryant, isn't it? I've got an idea about the concealment of that bow.'

As luck would have it Bryant had just returned

for lunch when Meredith arrived at his house. As at his previous interview Bryant led him out to the summer-house where there was no chance of them being overheard.

'Well, Superintendent, still at it? What's the trouble this time? Don't say there's been a third murder!'

Meredith shook his head.

'No – I want confirmation of an idea. Tell me, Mr. Bryant, would it be possible to shoot with a hinged bow?'

'A hinged bow! Good Lord! I've never heard of such an atrocity. Whatever put that idea into your head?'

Meredith explained how puzzled he was by the way in which the murderer had smuggled his bow through the streets.

'After all, a six-foot bow would be sure to arouse *some* comment. It isn't often you see a man carrying a bow through the street anyway. We inserted a paragraph in the local papers asking anybody to come forward who had seen a man with a bow on the night of 13th June. We haven't had a single reply. It made me wonder if a bow could be folded up in any way – say in two. It wouldn't be at all conspicuous like that wrapped in paper, would it?'

'But a hinge!' exclaimed Bryant with a dubious shake of his head. 'That would weaken the very section of the bow which takes all the strain. But wait a minute, Mr. Meredith – now you come to talk of it, there's an American patent on the market now. A beastly affair in my opinion. It's made of steel and the two halves are joined by a socket. Perhaps your man fancied something of that sort.'

'Perhaps!' exclaimed Meredith delightedly. 'There's no perhaps about it. I reckon you've hit on it. A steel bow fitted with a socket. Can they be bought in England?'

'Oh, yes – at any of the recognized sports people in town. Ayres, Gamages, Harrods. But I don't think there are many in use in this country. We're pretty conservative as a whole.'

'Then I might be able to trace the sale?'

'You might – unless it was a cash transaction. Then you'll have to rely on the salesman's memory for faces, eh?'

'And believe me,' said Meredith, rising and holding out his hand, 'people remember faces far more clearly than one might imagine. You may have put us on to a red-hot clue – thanks.'

Directly after Meredith had lunched with Barnet at Number Eight, he put through a call to Long at headquarters.

'Well – what luck?'

Long's excited wheeze drifted over the wire.

'The most unbelievable bloomin' slice o' fortune you ever come across! Thank God you had the common sense to follow up that alibi before you made an arrest. We're ditched, sir. Ditched proper – at least, where that chap West is concerned. *'E didn't do it!* Don't see 'ow he could 'ave – not after what I've found out. What's that? Did anybody see 'im? No, sir – nobody *saw* 'im exactly. But 'e's got his alibi fixed up as snug as a bug in a rug now. And 'oo do you think fixed it for him? I did. Quite by chance, o' course, but that makes no difference to 'im, does it? If you can come round straightaway I'll show you something – then you can draw your own conclusions.'

Puzzled and intrigued by the Inspector's cryptic insinuations, Meredith strode off down the Winchcombe Road utterly flattened out by this latest setback. If Long were right in his supposition and West wasn't the murderer, then they were right back at the beginning again. Flummoxed! Confound these dead-end investigations – these inviting by-ways along which one unsuspectingly wandered to fall into a deep pit. Confound the whole case! He was sick of it!

He found Long seated at his desk, grinning from ear to ear, triumph written all over his big, round face.

'Damn you!' snapped Meredith. 'You've properly put the kibosh on our investigations this time. Why the devil did you have to be so conscientious?'

Long winked. 'We couldn't have 'ung the wrong man, could we, sir?'

'He wouldn't have been hung anyway,' answered Meredith with polite sarcasm. 'He would have been *hanged.* Well, what's it all about?'

'This,' answered Long, taking up a large photograph from his desk and handing it over. 'Nice, artistic bit o' work, eh?'

'Where did you get this from?'

'Borrowed it this morning from the *Courier* offices. Saw it in their windows and took a sudden fancy to it. Recognize the subject? The Neptune fountain by night. One of their photographers was out with one o' those new-fangled cameras which take photos in the dark. Doing a series for the paper called *Cheltenham After Dark.* And since they've flood-lit the fountain 'e reckoned it would make a first-class subject. 'E's right there – it has!'

'But what the devil has this got to do with West?' demanded Meredith angrily.

'If you look closer you'll see.'

For a moment Meredith stared at the photo, then: 'Good heavens,' he cried. 'West! That's him right enough. Over here in the right-hand corner.'

Long nodded.

'That's just what I thought when I saw the photo in the window. And when I saw the title and the date typewritten underneath I didn't stand upon the order of my going. I nipped in quick, saw the manager and in two shakes I was putting the photographer chap through a spot of third-degree. Not that 'e wasn't ready to talk. Vulnerable wasn't the word...'

'I'm sure it wasn't,' said Meredith with a twinkle. 'Well – go on.'

'That photograph was taken last Monday night *at exactly eight-forty.* Chap was certain about the time because 'e had to look at his watch to time the photograph, see? Always sets it, moreover, by the Post Office. So our friend West was standing by the Neptune fountain in the Promenade at eight-forty on the night Buller was murdered. And if 'e was standing by the fountain at that particular time 'e couldn't possibly have been in Regency Square drawing a bead on ole Buller. And if 'e didn't do the second murder, then I reckon 'e didn't do the first. And if 'e didn't do either of the murders, then we've been barking up the wrong tree. And if we've been barking up the wrong tree we're now properly in the soup and I shouldn't be at all surprised if the Old Man doesn't 'av something pretty snappy to say to us. And that, sir, is about all there is to be said.'

CHAPTER XV

The Raid at Charlton Kings

Long's pessimistic prophecy was fulfilled early the next morning. Meredith had scarcely finished his breakfast when a call came through from borough headquarters asking him to go round at once. He and Long found the Chief Constable waiting for them in the latter's rather dark, old-fashioned office. His first words showed well enough which way the wind was blowing.

'Stayed up late last night to read through your latest report on the Cotton and Buller investigations, Long. And quite frankly I didn't find it very pretty reading. I suppose you realize that over a month has gone by since Cotton was killed? Mind you – I'm not exactly blaming you. I realize well enough that the case has been overloaded with all manner of tricky complications. The theft, for instance, of that three thousand and the blackmailing of Fitzgerald. But the point is this. We can't afford to enter up two unsolved murders on our books. Already a certain amount of pressure has been exerted on me from higher up to hand over the whole thing to the Yard. It's only your reputation, Meredith, which has enabled me to have my own way. This morning, moreover, I had a letter from Major Forrest, hinting very broadly that he'd like you back at Lewes as soon as possible. You realize, of course, that your ticket-of-leave can't be extended indefinitely?'

'Quite, sir.'

'Now I'm going to put you both a straight question – what hope is there of either of the two cases being cleared up in the near future?'

Both the men hesitated a moment before speaking and looked at each other as if trying to ascertain what line they ought to take. Finally Meredith announced with a slight lift of his shoulders:

'Candidly, sir, very little hope at all as things stand at present. We're at a deadlock. Agreed, Long?'

The Inspector nodded dolefully.

'It 'urts but I've got to agree. Now that the West supposition has fizzled out we're really in the soup, sir. Look at the list o' suspects, possible suspects that is, and see for yourself. West, Fitzgerald, Miss Boon, Pratt, young Wade, that parson chap and the couple of old dears at Number Seven. We've checked up and it looks as if none of 'em could have done the job. Mind you, we 'aven't exactly had time to readjust ourselves to the noo situation brought about by the clearing o' West. Out o' fairness, sir, I reckon the Superintendent and me ought to be given another twenty-four hours to lay our heads together. We may hit on a flaw in our line o' argument, see?'

'You take the same attitude, Meredith?'

'Yes, sir.'

'All right. We'll call it a deal. If, at this time to-morrow morning, you've nothing further to report then you'll have to resign yourselves to working with the Yard. At least in your case, Long. Where you're concerned, Meredith, I'm afraid Major Forrest has got the prior claim. So unless anything new *does* turn up you'd better be prepared to leave for Lewes to-morrow. Sorry and all that – but there it is. It's results that count!'

'O' course,' said Long, back in his own office after the interview, 'the Old Man's very fair. 'E's given us a decent run for our money and it's our own bloomin' fault that we 'aven't pulled any plums out o' the fire. Now, sir, if you've got an idea for 'eavens sake let's have it. For my own part I'm flummoxed. Properly flummoxed!'

But Meredith, despite the need for urgency, was as barren of ideas as the Inspector. Try as he would he could not see where they had tripped up. Some tiny, vital clue was missing – a minute pointer which would show them the exact direction to take in their investigations. But what had they overlooked? For two hours without a break they pored over statements and reports, argued over possible new theories, tested and retested alibis, entertained the most unlikely suppositions in the hope of hitting on some illuminating point. But of no avail. At eleven o'clock they left Clarence Street to attend the inquest on Buller. The proceedings had already opened when they arrived, but, much as they had anticipated, the affair was brief and in no way controversial. Cotton's death and the findings at his inquest acted as a perfect pointer to the present verdict. Buller had been murdered by person or persons unknown.

The Coroner added no further comment. It was all very cut-and-dried.

When Meredith left for lunch at one o'clock the situation remained unaltered. Their afternoon session produced no further result and at six o'clock they agreed that any further discussion of the two cases was a sheer waste of time. They would have to acknowledge that they were beaten and let in the Yard!

But with a curious waywardness for which Fate is notorious, certain events took place that evening which not only proved stimulating to their jaded brains but sent them racing off on an entirely fresh line of inquiry. The *deus ex machina* of this dramatic, last-minute twist was Constable Shanks.

Shanks had been keyed-up since waking that morning. He had been detailed by Inspector Swallow to form one of a party who were to carry out a raid that evening. Now a police raid in a respectable, well-behaved spa like Cheltenham was an unexpected and unanticipated treat for a young constable. Moreover this was Shanks's first raid. He felt ready to distinguish himself.

The house which had come under police notice stood just off the London Road in a quiet part of Charlton Kings. It was not a large house but it stood isolated and almost concealed in its own well-wooded garden. It belonged to a retired London lawyer whose arrival in the Cheltenham district had been discreet and unostentatious.

But it was not many months before the long arm of the Metropolitan Police reached out and pointed an accusing finger at Harold Kenton, Esq. Not directly, of course – that was not the way of the police. A dossier of considerable thickness found its way into the pigeon-holes of the borough police office. The dossier contained two photos of Mr. Harold Kenton, alias Jervis Rake – one full-face, one profile. It also contained a set of his finger-prints – eighteen prints in all (for the police are very thorough) – five individual prints of the left hand, five of the right and two sets of the fingers of the right and left hand taken simultaneously. It also contained a very, very detailed description of Mr. Jervis Rake, not only of his appearance but of his past activities and last, but by no means least, his convictions. He was referred to more than once in this dossier as 'The Rake' or 'Jervis the Rake.' His particular line was the running of good-class gambling houses. He had a *penchant* for roulette.

The little group, all in plain clothes, huddled in the shadows of some overhanging laburnum trees.

'Now you lads know exactly where you've got to go,' Inspector Swallow was saying in a low voice. 'One to each window on the ground floor, not bothering about the small windows at the back. Fletcher at one door, Green round the back, Hartley, Goddard, Hammond with me. And for God's sake don't make a noise. This has got to be done quickly and slickly. Get that? Right – let's go.'

Nearing the house the little group seemed to melt away magically in the dark. The house in

Shanks's opinion seemed deserted, for no light showed in any of the windows. He had an idea that he was going to be diddled of the fun after all. For all that he crept silently up to the house in the best Boy-Scout-cum-Red-Indian fashion and took up his arranged position before one of the french windows which gave out on to the shrubbery. On nearing the window he realized with a thrill why there were no lights to be seen – the windows were blanked out on the insides with stout wooden shutters. Flattening himself against the wall of the house he waited there keyed up with suspense, listening.

For five minutes nothing at all happened. He thought he could detect the faint murmur of voices behind the shutters, a confused buzz as if many people were all talking at once. Then suddenly, drawing his muscles up taut, he heard this buzz swell into an uproar, an uproar punctuated with individual cries and shouts and the strident shrilling of police-whistles. So old Swallow was in! Good for the old boy! Sound chap, Swallow. Pity he hadn't been picked as one of the Inspector's bodyguard. Those lucky devils inside would naturally have all the fun. Might tumble into a decent scrap if there was any proper resistance. Out here there was nothing to do but–

Shanks held his breath. Somebody was rattling the shutters. He held himself ready to spring.

The shutters swung open and for a brief instant the constable saw the outlines of a man silhouetted against the blaze of electrics hanging from the ceiling of the room. Good heavens – the chap was trying to make a getaway! In another minute he'd have those windows open and then it would be up to him to leap forward in a sensational tackle and snap the bracelets over the chap's wrists. Ye gods! this was something like.

Then with disconcerting rapidity a series of unexpected events upset all Shanks's careful calculations. To begin with, the man didn't open the window. He simply lifted a foot and with a couple of violent kicks shattered the glass of one of the lower panes. Some of the splinters whizzed outward and the constable was suddenly aware of an acute pain in his right wrist. Then, inside the room, the lights went out and plunged the whole scene in darkness. But before this happened Shanks received another shock. As the man crouched to crawl through the hole made by his boot in the large pane of glass, the constable recognized him. His identity was impressed on his eye in a flash but he was certain that he had made no mistake. Lunging forward he grappled with the unseen figure as it swiftly straightened up. For a moment they swayed in a violent struggle, then, without warning, the man jerked up his knee and caught the constable a thudding blow in the diaphragm. He doubled up gasping for breath, staggering with the pain. His hand groped for his torch which had been struck out of his grasp but before he could direct its rays among the ink-black shadows under the shrubbery the man was gone. With a badly lacerated wrist, still gasping for breath, Shanks crawled through the broken window and, with murder in his heart, went to seek out his superior and put in his unheroic report. In more than one sense he felt deflated!

'Let him go!' exclaimed Swallow when one of the constables had located the switches and turned up the lights. 'But heavens alive, you knew he was coming!'

Shanks explained what had happened and, as if in alleviation of his failure, added: 'But I recognized the chap. I'm prepared to swear to his identity in court.'

'You recognized him? Who was it?'

'Dr. Pratt.'

'Pratt? Good Lord, that's the chap that lives in Regency Square. Buller's doctor, wasn't he? Respectable sort of chap I should have thought. Fat lot of good you putting forward evidence of identity unless we can *prove* he was out here. Your word against his if he denies it. We must get corroborative evidence and there's no chance of his pals out here squealing. They'll hang together right enough.'

'I've an idea, sir,' said Shanks hastily. 'Why not put a call through to Superintendent Meredith. He may be in and he's staying next door to the doctor in the square. He'll let us know at any rate, sir, what time Pratt gets back.'

Swallow considered the idea for a moment, then nodded.

'Righto, Shanks. Find out if there's a phone here and get through. Explain what has happened and ask the Sooper if he'd be good enough to find out what he can. I've got too much to occupy me here.' And he nodded towards the sheepish group huddled in one corner of the room. 'Otherwise I'd speak to him myself.'

In five minutes Shanks was through to Meredith

and the latter had been primed with the details of the raid. He promised to do what he could.

Meredith did not have to wait long in the doorway of Number Eight. A car swished into the square and drew up before the doctor's gate. Meredith sauntered down the path, smoking a cigarette and hailed Pratt as he stepped out.

'Evening, doctor. Just the man I want to see. Can you spare me a minute?'

'What is it?' asked Pratt shortly. 'Important? I've a lot of writing to do.'

'It is rather.'

'All right. I'll give you ten minutes.'

As soon as the door of the doctor's study was closed Meredith dropped his casual air and said officially:

'See here, Dr. Pratt, I've just had a phone message. Do you deny that you have been out to Charlton Kings this evening?'

'Charlton Kings! What the devil are you talking about?'

'I'm talking about a house known as–' Meredith consulted his note-book '–as "The Lilacs," London Road. Owned by a retired solicitor, Harold Kenton, alias Jervis Rake. You visited him this evening, I understand.'

'Kenton? Never heard of him. Haven't the faintest idea what you're getting at.'

'Very well,' said Meredith quietly. 'Let me put my question in a different form. You haven't been out to "The Lilacs" – in that case where have you been?'

'Running around in the car.'

'Any special reason?'

'I really don't see–' began Pratt in an angry voice, dropping into a chair.
'It's essential I should have an answer, sir.'
Pratt hesitated and then said curtly: 'I've had trouble with my car so I was taking it for a test run.'
'And you went–?'
'Confound it! This is preposterous! What the devil are you after? Am I supposed to have done something criminal? If so, let me know what, so that I can at least have the satisfaction of clearing myself.'
'I merely want to know what route you took in the car,' went on Meredith, unperturbed by the other's outburst. 'That shouldn't cause you any worry, sir, if you're telling me the truth.'
'The truth! Of course I'm telling the truth. I took a run out to Bishop's Cleeve and back along the main road. Does that satisfy you?'
'So that the man who tried to escape from Rake's house tonight when it was raided was *not* you?'
Pratt laughed sarcastically.
'You must be crazy, Mr. Meredith. I've already told you–'
'And it couldn't have been you who broke a pane of glass in one of the french windows and had a tussle with one of the constables?'
'That's obvious, isn't it? I couldn't have been at Charlton Kings when I was at Bishop's Cleeve, could I?'
Meredith crossed over slowly to where the doctor was seated by the hearth.
'On the surface of things I'm inclined to agree

there, Dr. Pratt. On the other hand,' added Meredith suddenly pointing down at one of the doctor's ankles, 'how do you account for that?'

The doctor started slightly and looked down at his feet.

'Account for what?' he stammered, obviously puzzled by the Superintendent's action.

'This,' said Meredith quietly as he stooped down and slipped something from the turn-up of the doctor's right trouser-leg. He held it up to the light and slowly twisted it, watching the doctor's face closely.

'Glass!' exclaimed Pratt.

'Exactly. A long splinter of glass from the window which you smashed out at "The Lilacs" this evening. Come along, sir – it's no use trying to fob me off with that story about a run to Bishop's Cleeve. I may as well point out that you were recognized by the constable who tried to stop you. His evidence, combined with this.' And Meredith again held up the long, triangular piece of glass, 'is all that's needed for us to get a conviction. Lucky piece of observation on my part, I admit, but it's told me all I want to know. Care to make a statement now, sir? I must warn you, of course, that anything you may say will be taken down in writing and may be used as evidence. Well, Dr. Pratt?'

There was a long silence. With shaking fingers the doctor drew out his cigarette-case and lit a cigarette. With a neat gesture he flicked the match into the fireplace. With a faint smile on his face he got to his feet and faced the Superintendent.

'All right. You win, Meredith. I suppose the game really *is* up. You realize that if this business comes into the courts it will mean the ruin of my practice? You *would* choose to raid the place the one night I was there. Still, if you've got your notebook handy I may as well make a statement. I suppose it will be better for me in the long run if I do. Ready?'

In a flat, precise voice the doctor gave out the bald facts of his visit to Jervis Rake's establishment, the details of his attempted escape and his struggle with the constable. Meredith then read through the deposition and the doctor signed it with a flourish. Now that he knew what he was up against, he seemed quite resigned. After refusing a drink, Meredith returned well satisfied to Number Eight.

He found Shanks waiting for him. Inspector Swallow had sent him round to learn the result of Meredith's cross-examination.

'It's O.K., Shanks. We've got him by the short hairs.'

'Thank heavens for that, sir. Things would have looked bad if he'd got clean away. Lucky I spotted him.'

'Had a lively time, eh?'

'Yes, while it lasted. By the way, the Inspector nabbed another one of your friends, sir.'

'Oh?'

'Wade, sir.'

'Wade!' Meredith stared fixedly at the constable. 'Good Lord! Are you certain about this?'

'Dead sure, sir.'

'All right, Shanks. Here's Pratt's signed statement. I'll be along at the station first thing tomorrow morning if the Inspector wants to see me.'

Wade! So Wade was mixed up with this gambling establishment was he? Wade and Pratt – both of 'em. But hadn't Pratt denied that he knew Wade socially and hadn't Wade sworn that he only knew Pratt professionally. So they had both lied. They must have done. Rake's gambling *coterie* would be too exclusive for two members to attend the tables without getting to know each other. (And there was no reason to suppose that this was the doctor's only visit.) And they had lied for a reason. What reason? Was it illogical to suppose that the two men were in some way connected, after all, with the murders of Cotton and Buller? If they were in conspiracy then it was pretty certain that Pratt had not given Wade that morphia injection and that Miss Boon's evidence was true. Wade *had* been driving a car in Victoria Road round about the time Cotton had been murdered on 13th June. But whose car and why had he been there? Pratt could not possibly have reached the square in time to commit the murder. This had already been proved by their test runs to and from April House. He had stayed to chat with Mrs. Black. Did it mean that Wade had murdered Cotton?

Meredith reviewed the facts. Whilst Pratt was engaging the landlady in conversation downstairs Wade could have slipped out of the house via his bedroom window. Hence those footprints in the flower-border. Somewhere, somehow he had a car waiting. He jumps in and drives all out to Regency Square, parks his car round the corner, enters the Empty House by means of – Meredith's thoughts stopped dead. Snag Number One. How had Wade managed to enter the Empty House? Well, that could be tackled later. His thought-stream went on. Wade then shoots Cotton, gets back into his car and drives off and is seen by Miss Boon in Victoria Road. Possibly Wade had chosen this route to avoid driving directly through the town where he might be recognized. Then: 'Snag Number Two,' thought Meredith. Was Wade an archer? So far this fact had not been elicited. Assuming that he wasn't – what about the sheep which had been killed out at Winchcombe? Wasn't it possible that Wade had been responsible for this when having a private practice with his bow and arrow? Had he meant to kill Cotton? No – that was a case of mistaken identity. He thought the man, with the bald patch, sitting in his uncle's favourite chair *was* his uncle. A very natural mistake. And why had he wanted to do away with his uncle? Here Meredith smiled. He'd got a red-hot motive now right enough. Thank the Lord! that Jervis Rake's activities had been unearthed by the police! Wade was probably in debt to Rake. He knew his uncle's peculiar and inflexible views about money and dared not ask him for a loan. Moreover he realized that if Rake went to Buller with the tale of his gambling, his uncle would almost certainly cut him out of his will. Rake himself was playing a dangerous game but he knew well enough that none of his clients would dare face a scandal if his activities were given away. Even Buller would not give evidence to the police if it meant his nephew's appearance in a local court.

Meredith sighed. But, in heaven's name, how could Wade have committed the second murder? His alibi was absolutely unassailable. He was sitting in the police-station at the exact time Buller had been shot. Did it mean then that Pratt had been responsible? But Pratt couldn't have done it either because he couldn't have taken up his position on the other side of the square in time to loose the arrow! Then, who, who, who?

Meredith listened. Across the hall he heard the phone-bell ringing. Barnet was out dining with friends. Should he answer it himself and save the maid the trouble? He crossed the hall into the study and picked up the receiver. To his astonishment it was Long on the other end of the wire.

'Hullo – what the devil's the matter with you?'

'Have you ever felt like throwing yourself into a river with your feet in a weighted sack and your hands in a pair o' bracelets? You haven't? Well I have! Of all the thundering, bloomin', one-eyed bits o' loonacy.'

'Meaning you?'

'Meaning me,' agreed Long with disarming cheerfulness. 'In a minute you can call me what you like and I'll take it sitting, sir. I've never slipped up like this afore and I 'ope, for the sake o' my future in the force, that I'll never do so again. Of all the thundering, bloomin', one-eyed–'

'Could you possibly come to the point, Long? I can't hang on all night.'

'Sorry, sir. I will. Now listen to this. Remember the arrow what was sticking into Buller's head? 'Course you do. I tested it for finger-prints, didn't I? 'Course I did. And did I find any prints on it? No – I didn't. All well an' good. But that arrow, sir, *held the most important clue in the murder.* And we missed it!'

'Missed it – what the deuce are you driving at?'

'Listen again,' went on Long, growing more and more excited and triumphant. 'Do you 'appen to remember what sort o' weather we were having on the night Buller copped it? Remember, sir?'

'Yes, of course I do,' snapped Meredith, impatiently. 'It was raining cats and dogs.'

'You've said it, sir! It *was*. It was fair pelting. And that arrow was shot from the far side of the square through the rain. Then, why the 'ell, *wasn't the shaft speckled with raindrops when I made that fingerprint test?* It wasn't. I remember now. And there wouldn't 'av been time for the water to evaporate. It was dry as a bone. I'll swear to that! Well, sir, why wasn't it wet? Why, eh? Any ideas? I'm flummoxed. Properly flummoxed!'

CHAPTER XVI

Pure Deduction

'And now,' said Meredith to himself as he settled into an armchair with his pipe, 'let's see if we can find out exactly what this means. One thing's certain – the Chief will have to postpone his call to the Yard. This clue alters the whole aspect of our investigation. We're in a position to start moving again.'

He settled deeper into his chair and began to theorize. So the arrow had apparently not come from across the square? His suspicions of West and Miss Boon were, therefore, unfounded. The skylight in the roof of Number One was open for the reason put forward by Miss Boon – it had been open in the warm weather and she had forgotten to shut it. The note had been sent to West because Miss Boon had an idea that West might be suspected of the crime. West had lied about the note for exactly the same reason – he wanted to shield Miss Boon. So much for that line of inquiry. It had petered out into thin air.

And if the arrow had not been loosed from the other side of the square where, precisely, *had* it come from? One of the balconies on either side of Buller's place? Impossible surely? For one thing the angle would be too acute, the shot too chancey. For another, neither of the balconies was hooded, and the arrow would in consequence have been wet. Only one possibility remained – the arrow had been loosed in Buller's study. But how? By whom? And when?

Buller was not dead when Pratt left him just after eight-thirty and yet when Mrs. Gannet entered the room a few minutes later with the glass of water the arrow had been discharged. So whoever had loosed the arrow must have seized the very limited opportunity between the doctor's departure and the housekeeper's entry in the study. A matter, Meredith reckoned, of not more than two minutes. This pointed to two further facts – either the murderer was hidden in an adjacent room where he could keep secret watch on the study door or else he was concealed in the room itself. The next point which arose was – how had the murderer made his getaway? Certainly not down the stairs because then he would have met Mrs. Gannet coming up with the water. There was another risk – the doctor might have stayed half a minute or more in the hall putting on his coat and collecting his outdoor things. No, that way, argued Meredith, would have been far too dangerous from the murderer's point of view. There were two other explanations as far as Meredith could see – the murderer had escaped via the balcony or he had slipped into one of the upper rooms and hidden himself until he judged the coast was clear for his escape. He tackled the possibilities in order.

The balcony? Again the risks seemed to overweigh the chances. Some fifty windows or more looked out on to the square – Buller's balcony was visible from the majority of these. There would be traffic and pedestrians passing along the main road which ran across the open end of the square. Moreover Pratt had only just left, a fact which the murderer must have realized, and the chances were he might glance back before he entered his own house and spot the man on the balcony. No – that way of escape seemed out of the question.

The upper rooms then? Well, if that had been the murderer's move it was certain he wouldn't have attempted his getaway whilst the police were still buzzing about the place. The last people to leave Number Six on the night of the murder were Mrs. Gannet and Shanks. Shanks had been told to escort the old lady home. He recalled the constable's report on the following morning.

'I will say that the old thing's got a highly developed sense of duty, sir. She wouldn't leave without making a tour of every room to see that the windows were shut. I went round and helped her lock up because it was pretty obvious that she was just about all in. Wonderful old dame though – plenty of pluck.'

Shanks had not noticed anybody. How did this fit in with his theory? Well, the murderer might have hidden in a cupboard, behind a piece of furniture, a curtain, anything. Wouldn't it be a sensible plan to slip along to Number Six and take a look round for himself? One of the keys had been in his possession since the inquest and, loath to waste a minute of his time, Meredith scrambled into his coat and went out into the square. A few minutes later, with all the blinds drawn, he was making a thorough investigation of the house. He tried the attic rooms first and to his astonishment found that only Mrs. Gannet's room was furnished. It was, on second thoughts, quite understandable – Buller wouldn't use all the rooms in so large a house. He lived by himself and seldom entertained. Moreover the housekeeper's room was the only one on the top floor boasting a built-in cupboard and Mrs. Gannet must have gone to this cupboard when packing her clothes. The unfurnished rooms were as bare as a bone, offering not the slightest cover for a hiding man. It was obvious that the murderer had not concealed himself in the attic.

On the floor below there were four rooms – Buller's study and bedroom, a guest-room and bathroom. The first two could be ruled out. The body had been laid on the bed in Buller's own room and the door locked on the outside by the

Inspector. There was a sheer drop of twenty feet beyond the two windows which looked over the back garden. The bathroom offered no cover at all. This left the remaining bedroom. Here the layout of the room was more satisfactory from the murderer's point of view. Several hiding-places suggested themselves at once – the vast mahogany wardrobe, the long, thick window curtains, a screen and the bed itself. If the murderer had, therefore, lain low until the coast was clear this was the one room in which he could have done it.

So far so good. Assuming that Mrs. Gannet and Shanks have left – what then? The murderer creeps down the stairs and gets out either through the back door or a ground-floor window. Shanks, in his report, had assured Meredith that the front door had been securely locked. But – confound it! thought Meredith, if the murderer had escaped in this manner then either the back door was unbolted or one of the window catches unfastened. Wasting no time, he made a brisk tour of the basement and ground-floor windows. No result. Every window was still fastened on the inside and the back door bolted. Then how–?

In a puzzled frame of mind Meredith went upstairs to the actual scene of the crime. He tried to reconstruct the events which must have taken place in that room on the fateful night. Buller seated in the armchair – there. The murderer concealed – where? Behind that curtain perhaps or the big armchair set back in a far corner of the room. Very well – Pratt leaves. Buller takes a cigar ready to light it. Stealthily the murderer creeps out from his hiding-place, his arrow already set to the string and, taking up his position directly behind his victim, shoots. But could he have done this without Buller realizing? Taking into consideration the position of Buller's chair, the angle at which the arrow had entered and the proximity of the wall, Meredith was uneasy about this point. He knew from one of his talks with Bryant that an arrow to be effective and 'truly-flighted' must be drawn back to the full extent of the bow. Taking up his stance directly behind the dead man's chair, arming himself with an imaginary bow and arrow, Meredith aimed and drew. He found, to his surprise, that the tip of the arrow must have been within a few inches of Buller's head if the murderer were to avoid jamming his elbow into the wall directly behind him. But surely Buller would have had time to notice him before he could have got so close? One senses the close proximity of a presence by a kind of instinct. It was inconceivable that Buller could have sat there, unaware, without glancing back over his shoulder. And if he had had time to do that the arrow would have not entered the back of his head. The only other explanation was obvious. Buller's head had not been square with the back of his chair but turned slightly to face the far corner of the room – the corner beyond the window in which stood the other large armchair. All the murderer had to do then was to bob up, take aim, loose his arrow and arrange the position of the body in such a way as to suggest that the arrow had come through the open window. The more Meredith thought about it the more certain he was that, however the crime had been committed, the murderer had intended to suggest that the arrow had been discharged *outside* the room. That could be the only reason why he had chosen such a cumbersome weapon as a six foot bow. An automatic fitted with a silencer would have been a more natural choice. The fact that Buller always sat by the open window may have put the idea into his head. Yes – and the fact that Cotton had been killed in just this peculiar manner. Did it mean that, after all, this was a crime of emulation? That the two murders were not the work of the same man? This theory certainly had a feasible ring about it.

And had the first murder been committed by Wade? The raid that evening had established one fact beyond doubt – Wade and Pratt knew each other socially. On that new piece of evidence he had already reconstructed the first murder with Wade in the role of the murderer. But since Wade was in the police station when the second crime was committed, somebody else *must* have been the murderer. Who? Once again Meredith looked through his list of possibles and probables, but this time viewing the crime from an entirely different angle.

His Probables in the Buller murder were West and Miss Boon. They had been marked down as Probables because at the time the police suspected that the arrow had been shot from either Number One or Number Two. How did their alibis stand up to the recently discovered facts? Take West. He left Miss Boon's house at 8.30 or thereabouts according to his own statement and Miss Boon's evidence. He was by the Neptune fountain in Promenade at 8.40 – that was undeniable. And as Buller must have been shot at about that time, West could be ruled out. Miss Boon too, since she would have had no opportunity to conceal herself in Buller's study on account of West's visit. So much for the old Probables.

His Possibles were Matthews and Fitzgerald. But now, as Meredith saw it, they could no longer be suspected. He had seen them both about five minutes after Buller had been killed and set them to watching the exits of the Empty House. And he had already satisfied himself that the murderer could not have made his getaway from Number Six directly after the crime.

His Impossibles included Wade and Pratt. Wade's alibi for this murder still held good. This left Pratt.

Was Pratt the murderer? Dropping into one of the study armchairs, Meredith refilled his pipe and ceremoniously lit it. A faint glimmer of light was glowing in the far recesses of his mind. Pratt. Why not Pratt? Pratt *could* have done it – there was no doubt about that. And if Pratt had done it then Buller was dead before he left the house. He was dead when Pratt called down to Mrs. Gannet for that glass of water. And wasn't it possible that Pratt had used one of those steel bows which Bryant had mentioned – the American patent which folded in two. He could have slipped it inside his overcoat on leaving and easily smuggled it unnoticed back to his own house. But how then had he smuggled the bow into Buller's? That would be far more tricky. He would be expected to remove his overcoat in the hall when he arrived.

Had he planted it previously in the stockbroker's study? He often visited Buller professionally. He might have managed it. Mrs. Gannet would know, of course, if he had visited Number Six just before the night of the murder. But good heavens! how had he actually committed the crime? Buller, as his host, would have been on the alert, probably insisted on him having a drink or taking an arm-chair. Surely Pratt would have had no opportunity to take the socketed bow from its hiding-place, fit it together, set the arrow to the string, aim and fire without Buller's knowledge. The supposition was fantastic! And yet Pratt, of all the possible suspects, had a reasonable chance of killing Buller.

'Damn it!' thought Meredith, 'if it isn't one snag, it's another. If I hit on a theory to explain away how the murder was done, I find I can't get my murderer out of the house. If I find an easy way for him to walk out then I can't fathom how he engineered the crime.'

Pratt, Pratt? Pratt! Surely he was thinking on the right lines at last? All right – accept Pratt as the murderer. What motive? None. Suddenly Meredith sat upright and whistled softly to himself. Half a minute – that was not quite true. Pratt might have had a very good motive if he were working hand in glove with Buller's young nephew, Wade. Wade knew he was going to inherit and he had probably let Pratt know this, unless the doctor knew it already. Well and good – they were both gamblers. Suppose Wade *and* Pratt were both in debt, heavily in debt to Jervis the Rake? That was more than possible and, in any case, these facts could be wheedled out of Rake himself in the near future. They needed money. Only Buller stood between Wade and a very tidy fortune. Had they talked matters over and decided to do away with the stockbroker? Cold-bloodedly planned to murder him?

If this were the case then Cotton's murder had been accidental. Long's theory of 'mistaken identity' was right. Either Wade or Pratt had been misled by that bald patch and scored a – now what was the technical term? – a 'gold' on the wrong target. This, as Meredith was quick to realize, fitted the known facts better than any other theory. Wade and Pratt in collaboration. Wade's inheritance as the prize-money. Pratt's interest in the crime ensured by Wade's promise to clear up his debts when Buller was dead. That morphia injection had not been given. Wade had probably done the first job, and when he discovered that he had made the terrible mistake of killing the wrong man, had got cold feet and jibbed at doing the second. Besides it was unfair that he should take all the risks. Pratt, realizing that Wade had got cold feet, must have taken on the entire job by himself. This, at any rate, would account for the two arrows being identical. If the murders had been committed by two entirely different people, not even in collaboration, then it was absurd to suppose that the arrows would have borne such a family likeness.

But what about that sheep? How did that incident fit into this new theory? Was Pratt up on the wolds for practice? Why not? That new steel bow – surely he would have to accustom himself to its peculiarities since he normally used a 6 ft wooden bow when target-shooting? Wade might have used it in the first murder, after extensive practice, and handed it on to Pratt when he refused the second job.

On the other hand, thought Meredith, it seemed a trifle unnecessary to practise when the victim was to be shot from such close quarters. Did it mean that Pratt had changed his plans, perhaps thinking his second scheme of shooting Buller in the room itself far less risky? Had his original intention been to discharge the arrow, as in the Cotton murder, from the Empty House?

Meredith's mind jerked back once more to the facts of the first crime. He was beginning to feel now that the Empty House had been chosen, not simply because it was empty, but because the house belonged to West. Pratt and Wade must have heard something about the low-down trick which the stockbroker had played on West. They realized that here was a good motive for West wanting to murder Buller. The fact that Cotton had been killed by mistake, luckily for them, by no means upset their scheme to foist suspicion on the owner of the Empty House. If anything West had a stronger reason for wanting to kill Cotton. Of course they could not be sure their plan would work out in detail, because it was on the stocks that West would be able to serve up a perfectly good alibi. And that elm tree which had been cut down – had Pratt cunningly egged on West to go to the authorities about it? The fact that West had been the prime mover in having it felled had certainly earned him another black mark. West ought to be questioned about this.

But how the devil had Wade (assuming the fellow had killed Cotton) managed to get into the Empty House that night? A skeleton key was one possibility, but a risky one since it would mean engaging an expert to make it. Besides how had the impression been taken and when? Only two keys existed, one in possession of the house agents, the other with West himself. But if Wade hadn't entered through the front door then how on earth *had* he got in? The skylight? But to do that he would have to get up on to the roof. How? He couldn't have scaled any of the buildings to the left of the square – too difficult, too dangerous. On the other hand there was an easier method of attaining the roof. What about the skylights of Number One and Number Three or the landing window of Fitzgerald's house? Could Wade have entered any of these three houses, sneaked up the stairs and scrambled out through one of the skylights or that window? The Matthews' *ménage* was at home, so were the Fitzgeralds – but what about Miss Boon? Meredith snapped his fingers. Good Lord – yes! Miss Boon's house had been deserted for a whole hour – from approximately nine till ten on the night of the murder. Hadn't she been taking her dogs for a walk and, later, noticed Wade driving down Victoria Road? It was a warm evening. She might have left a window open. Miss Boon would have to be questioned about this.

Another point occurred to him – if Wade had worked with a car, which now seemed certain, he must have parked it somewhere whilst he was entering the Empty House and committing the murder. Somewhere close and handy since speed was essential if he were to get away from the scene of the crime without being noticed. Somewhere in the main road, perhaps, or just round the corner in Willingdon Square, which abutted Regency Square. To-morrow he would put a couple of men on to cross-questioning all the people overlooking the roads in the near vicinity. There was just the chance that somebody would have remembered seeing a parked car or a man (carrying a bow, thought Meredith) answering to Wade's description.

With a sigh of satisfaction he rose, went down the stairs, switching out the lights on his way, and let himself out into the square. It was a perfect starlit night, cool and fresh, after the stuffy atmosphere of the sealed house. Meredith filled his lungs with the clean air, knocked out his pipe on a lamp-post and, stuffing it into his pocket, returned in an optimistic frame of mind to Number Eight. The case, like the sky, he thought, had cleared considerably during these last hours. A lot of the murk had been blown away and small points of illumination were beginning to twinkle from the darkness of unsolved problems. The Chief ought to be pretty pleased with Long. After all he had been responsible for this sudden clearing away of the clouds. He'd boost him for all he was worth in the right quarters. A sound and amusing chap!

CHAPTER XVII

Jervis The Rake

Meredith had not been over optimistic in supposing the Chief ready to shelve his idea of calling in the Yard. As soon as he had learnt the new facts from Long and the Superintendent, he got through to Major Forrest at Lewes and obtained his consent to Meredith prolonging his stay in Cheltenham. As he put it to Forrest: 'It's hardly fair to expect Meredith back, now that the train is just steaming into the station after a beastly uncomfortable journey. If there are going to be any plums let him stay here for the share-out.'

Long was delighted with the result of that nine o'clock interview. He had not looked forward to working with entire strangers from the Yard now that he had got to know Meredith and his methods so well. He kept on thanking his lucky stars that he had hit on such a vital and, in his later opinion, obvious clue. As soon as they had left the Chief's office Meredith put forward the full details of his overnight theories. Long was impressed. He himself had suspected that Pratt and Wade might be mixed up in the crimes, but he had by no means formed such a plausible theory as his superior.

'And what now?' he asked when Meredith had finished speaking. 'Find out about the parked car if possible, I suppose? Shanks and Fletcher can tackle that job for us without tying 'emselves in knots. Take 'em a good time, I reckon, but if they bring 'ome the goods time's of no account, eh? What about me? Shall I tackle West and leave you to deal with the 'arpy? Be most sensible like that, wouldn't it?'

Meredith laughed. 'You seem to have an immortal terror of that woman, Long. Why?'

'She's got just the same glint in 'er eye as my ole woman,' said Long with a wink. 'And if ever I 'ave a nightmare I dream I've got the pleasant little job o' putting Mrs. Long through the third-degree 'oop. I wake up in a fair sweat.'

'All right – you tackle West and find out if he knows anything about Pratt or Wade. See that those fellows get off at once on the parked car investigation. I'll deal with your ogre.'

Long sighed with relief and went in search of Shanks and Fletcher. As soon as they had been dispatched Long walked round to George Street to find West. This time he was recognized by Mrs. Emmet, who announced without waste of time: 'Yes, he's in. First door on the left. You know your way.'

West looked up startled from the book he was reading over a late breakfast, when the Inspector entered in response to his: 'Come in.'

'Well – what's the trouble, Inspector? Serious?'

Long grinned amiably.

'Not for you, sir, if that's what you mean, I'm 'ere for a little private confab – that's all. D'you mind if I park myself in this chair and put a few questions while you finish your 'addick, sir? No objection? Good. Well, sir, to come to the point without any shilly-shallying – you know Dr. Pratt, that used to be a near neighbour of yours? What sort o' fellow is 'e? Reserved and efficient – so that's your opinion? Ever seen 'im and young Wade together? Never. Well that doesn't surprise me, o' course. 'Ow was he off for money, d'you think? Not so well off as he seemed. What makes you think that?' Long whistled. 'I see. You 'appen to know that he still owes Marks and Redwood a couple o' hundred or so for 'is new car. Surprised they let 'im have it. Yes, o' course, it's all credit, credit, credit these days. Really, sir. Rumour going round that 'e was in debt to a number o' local people. Mind you, I partly blame the tradespeople for being such mugs, but there it is – they don't dare offend for fear o' losing custom. Oh no, quite – confidential, o' course. Very kind of you, sir, to have given me the time. No – don't you trouble to get up. I can see myself out – at this hour o' the day at any rate.'

And with a broad wink Long retired to the door and went out. He felt quite pleased with himself. The Superintendent ought to give him a pat on the back for gleaning this new evidence. So Pratt was in debt all round in the locality? This fact fitted neatly into Meredith's latest theory.

An hour later Meredith walked into the police station. His step was springy, and it was all he could do to conceal his pleasure and excitement. Long handed over his information and the Superintendent's grin broadened.

'Our lucky day, Long!' was his triumphant observation as he lifted a cigarette from the Inspector's box. 'Your bit of news fits in perfectly. But listen to this. I've just got another statement from Miss Boon, and if her new evidence isn't of vital importance I'll eat my hat. I tackled her first about seeing Wade in that car on the night of 13th June. I wanted to get more details out of her. I was particularly interested over the time factor. You see, in her previous mention of this encounter she put the time at just after 9.30. Cotton, as we know from Buller's evidence, was murdered at exactly half past nine. I'd never really suspected Wade of the murder until last night. We had a fleeting thought that he might be the murderer, remember – but we never took that theory very seriously. Well, this time, I got Miss Boon to define a bit more clearly what she meant by "just after 9.30." It might have meant five or ten minutes after. The point is, Long, it didn't. When she said "just after" she meant that the St. Peter's clock–'

'That's the church at the corner of Victoria Road and Park Street, isn't it, sir?' put in Long, anxious to miss no point in Meredith's story.

Meredith nodded. 'And this clock had only just struck the half-hour. You see the significance of that, Long?'

'Well, I can see this,' began Long laboriously. 'If young Wade was driving along Victoria Road at 9.30 then 'e couldn't have been up in a window of the Empty House taking a pot-shot at his uncle.'

'Exactly.'

'But, good 'eavens, sir, that blows a darn big 'ole in your theory, doesn't it?'

'Yes – but it may bring us nearer to the truth. I've always been puzzled about the fact that Wade was not known to be an archer. It was a very tricky shot at the best of times and when one considers the strain and excitement – well it was brilliant shooting to say the least of it.'

'I still don't quite see what you're driving at?'

'Pratt. That Pratt loosed both arrows – that Wade was merely a confederate in the background.'

'Pratt was at April House,' objected Long stolidly.

'Yes – we've held to that opinion all along, I agree. But are we right about that? If we could only prove that Pratt left April House ten minutes earlier than he did – well–'

'But Mrs. Black seemed certain he didn't leave until 9.15. She even compared the hall clock with the one in the kitchen when Pratt asked her if it was the right time.'

'I know,' mused Meredith, staring at the smoke of his cigarette, 'but doesn't that fact strike you as a little odd, Long? Why should Pratt ask? He had his own watch – a pocket-watch – I noticed it when I saw him last night. He's also got a radio and I've a strong feeling that he's the sort of man to set that watch regularly. Doctors have to keep appointments and so on. Then why should he ask Mrs. Black if the hall clock were right?'

'Funny, I admit.'

'I was only wondering, Long, if he asked the time simply to draw Mrs. Black's attention to the clock. He was relying on her to provide him with his alibi.'

'Yes – but, look 'ere, sir, you made a couple o'

test runs from the Leckhampton Road and *proved* 'e couldn't have been in Regency Square in time to commit the murder. 'Ow can you get over that?'

'There's just one explanation,' said Meredith slowly, as if anxious to give weight to his theory. 'Mrs. Black's clocks were fast. Both of 'em. And they were fast because young Wade had arranged the matter before Pratt's visit. He had a perfect opportunity to do this when Mrs. Black was out of the house phoning for Pratt. Say he put them on ten minutes. The fact that he had put them *both* on would allay any suspicion where Mrs. Black was concerned, but that extra ten minutes would have enabled Pratt to reach the square in time to commit the murder.'

Long rubbed his chin thoughtfully.

'Umph – it all sounds nice and comfortable to me, but I still don't see why Wade was in Victoria Road at 9.30.'

'No – that's still puzzling me. I can't see his reason for leaving April House at all.'

'Yes and, in any case,' went on Long with an air of malicious triumph, 'how the deuce did our friend Pratt get into the Empty House when 'e did arrive there? There's still that little snag to be cleared up.'

'It is,' said Meredith with a grin.

'Eh?'

'Thanks to Miss Boon.'

'How does she come into it?'

'She doesn't,' answered Meredith neatly, 'she walks out and leaves the door ajar – that's all. The door of Number One.'

'But good Lord, 'ow was Pratt to know that?'

'Because our Miss Boon is a woman of routine like hundreds of women who live alone. Remember how she told us about her nightly promenade with her damned dogs? Always left the house at nine o'clock and returned at ten. Always took the same route. And always left her front door ajar so that she wouldn't have to find the key-hole in the dark. She confessed to-day that she's a bit short-sighted. Too proud to wear glasses of course–'

'And spoil her manly beauty,' put in Long with a disparaging grunt. 'The vanity of some women passes all understanding. You'd think they was all Helens of Troy or Greta Garbos by the trouble they take over making-up their faces. Past 'ope, most of 'em.'

'May I go on?' asked Meredith politely.

'Sorry, sir – carried away. You're suggesting that Pratt 'ad noticed this fact about the door?'

'Of course he had. He also knew that Miss Boon was always out of the place between nine and ten. So all he had to do was to enter Number One, climb out through the skylight on to the roof, and drop through the skylight of the Empty House. The moment the crime was committed he gets out the same way. Plausible, isn't it?'

'It's certainly plausible,' admitted Long, 'but it's a pity we can't lay our 'ands on a bit more proof.'

'I think we can over this particular point,' went on Meredith with justifiable smugness. 'Pratt – always assuming, of course, that we're on the right track – Pratt overlooked one thing when he thought of utilizing Miss Boon's house. *He forgot that dogs have noses.* It was strange that Miss Boon should have noticed the peculiar behaviour of her dogs when she returned from her stroll that night. "Uneasy" was the way she put it – sniffing round the house and eventually congregating on the top landing under the skylight.'

'Well of all the–' began Long, grinning from ear to ear. 'Strikes me if I stays 'ere long enough listening to your words o' wisdom, you'll end by drawing a warrant for arrest out of your pocket with the blanks filled in. Beats me, sir – 'ow you do it! It does straight.'

'Luck,' said Meredith. 'Luck combined with your observation, Long. And, perhaps, a little reasoning thrown in to make weight.'

'And now what are we going to do?'

'We're going to slip along to the cells and have a word with Jervis the Rake. I hear he asked for bail when he was charged.' Meredith chuckled. 'The cheek of these old lags needs a lot of beating. If he's dropped on this time it'll be his fifth conviction.'

Proceeding along a corridor, they turned left, went down a few stone steps and eventually arrived at the detention cells. A constable came forward with a bunch of keys and opened up to them. Rake was seated on a chair in the far corner of the cell, reading a book. He was lounging back as far as the chair allowed, with his legs crossed, and a silk handkerchief sticking up perkily from the breastpocket of his well-cut suit. Rake had always been very much the dandy and he saw no reason, whatever the circumstances, to abandon this pose. As the officials entered he rose elegantly, placed the book, face down, on the chair to mark the place, and fixed a welcoming smile on his pseudo-handsome face.

'Anything I can do for you?'

'I'm Meredith – this is Inspector Long. We want to have a little informal chat with you, Rake.'

'I'm always ready to oblige. I can't ask you gentlemen to sit down because there isn't enough seating accommodation to go round – so if you don't mind standing–?'

'We're used to it,' said Meredith with a faint smile. 'I wouldn't like to say how many hours, all-told, I've stood in the witness-box. A tiring job, Rake.'

'That's not a very politic remark,' answered Rake. 'Witness-boxes are a sore point with me just now, Mr. Meredith. I suppose you don't know yet who'll be hearing my case?' (Meredith shook his head.) 'No – I thought not. It makes such a difference … to one's near future, I mean. Well, what exactly can I do for you?'

'Be frank, Rake – that's the most important thing. I'm not going to make you any rash promises about any possible information you may give us helping along your case. You know as well as I do that we can't bring any influence to bear on the court decision – but you may have some information which we can do with, Rake, and I'll tell you straight that these inquiries are connected with a major case.'

'A major case, eh?' Rake's dark brows went up in a note of interrogation. 'Not murder by any remote chance?'

'Possibly,' said Meredith. 'Possibly not. Now first of all what do you know of a young fellow called Antony Wade?'

'Never heard of him.'

'That's more than probable. You've never heard of him under that name. Perhaps you recognize this?' And Meredith pushed an enlargement of one of Stinn's excellent snapshots under Rake's nose.

'Wilfred Black! Gracious! I know *him* well enough.' Adding slyly: 'And you do, too, don't you? I had an idea that he was among those present the other evening when … when...'

'Quite right he was. So he was calling himself Black was he? After his landlady no doubt. That shows a lack of invention, eh, Long?'

'Bloomin' cheek if you ask me, but just about what I'd expect from 'is nibs. Lively lad, Wade!'

'Been one of your clients long, Rake?'

'About three or four months.'

'A *lucky* client would you say?'

Rake beamed: 'Do you mean from my point of view? If so, the answer's in the affirmative. A godsend, Mr. Meredith.'

'Does he owe you anything?'

Rake coughed and replied in a deprecatory voice: 'Come. Come, Mr. Meredith. That's a little too confidential.'

'Not a bit of it,' said Meredith breezily. 'It's bound to come out in court. You know how the most confidential matters do under cross-examination. The point is I can't wait until quarter-sessions – well, Rake, going to be nice to us?'

'Oh, very well. Very unprofessional, of course, but since you insist. Yes – he owed me quite a tidy sum.'

'Meaning?'

'About a couple of thousand. Foolish of me, perhaps, to have allowed him to run up a debt of this magnitude, Mr. Meredith, but in my particular line one can't afford to refuse credit. The financial side of my ... er ... type of establishment is naturally a very...' His fingers twiddled in the air '–a very *delicate* matter. To offend a good client is usually very unprofitable in the long run, I assure you.'

'Quite. And you naturally expected to see your money, if not at once, in the near future?'

'Oh, naturally, naturally. *All* my clients are invariably on the verge of inheriting or pulling off a good deal on the exchange. It's a recognized thing.' Rake smiled wryly and fastidiously detached a piece of fluff from his lapel. 'This young gentleman, for instance, assured me that it was only a matter of days before he would be able to make good his losses. He was a trifle upset when I suggested that I should go to a certain relation of his, whose opinion he seemed to covet rather highly. One hears things of course, and I happened to know that this uncle of his was a very wealthy man. I felt sure, though Mr. Black didn't endorse my opinion, that his uncle would be only too ready to settle his debts for him out of hand. I mean, if, by any remote chance, things got into the paper, it would have been extremely unpleasant for such a respectable old gentleman. I mean, *his* nephew. People will talk so.'

'But you didn't take the risk?' asked Meredith.

'The risk? Oh, I see what you mean. Of course, it *was* possible that the old gentleman might look upon me as the greater criminal. A hateful word, but I can't think of another. But you see, Mr. Meredith, in my line one has to take risks ... of a kind. But a knowledge of psychology does help considerably to minimize these risks. I'd gleaned quite a lot of information about this old gentleman. I think I should have been safe in going to him.'

'And you didn't?'

'It was hardly necessary, was it, when I learnt that he had been murdered? I knew then that Mr. Black would have no difficulty in settling his debt with me. You follow my line of argument?'

'Only too well,' grinned Meredith. 'It's flawless. What about Pratt? Oh all right – you've never heard of him.' Meredith produced a second enlargement and showed it to the imperturbable Rake. 'I'm interested to know what this gentleman called himself. Smith, Jones or what?'

'Watt,' said Rake promptly.

'Watt!' Long chuckled. 'Brother of the dear old biddies at Number Seven, I'll bet. That's ripe.'

'Look here, Rake,' said Meredith brusquely. 'You're wasting our time with all these subtleties. You knew Black was Wade, otherwise you wouldn't have known Buller was the lad's uncle. You know quite well that Pratt happens to be a doctor and you know where he lives. Now then, I want straight answers to three questions. How long had Pratt been coming out to your place? Was he friendly with Wade? Was he, like Wade, in debt to you?'

'He came out for the first time with Wade three months ago or a little over. That answers two of your questions. And he owed me about five hundred pounds. Does that satisfy you, Mr. Meredith?'

'You'd be prepared to swear in a court of law that Wade and Pratt were intimate friends?'

'Since Wade introduced him to my establishment – yes.'

'Right – that's all I want to know. The Inspector here has made notes of our conversation. You probably noticed that?'

'I did. That's why I was so particular about the wording of my sentences. I detest a badly constructed statement, don't you? Shall I read through now and sign?'

'If you will,' said Meredith politely. 'Fountain-pen?'

CHAPTER XVIII

Startling Climax

Meredith was worried. Three days had gone by, and progress in the case was at a standstill. He had been out to April House, without Wade's knowledge, and re-examined Mrs. Black about the night of 13th June. But she had told him nothing new. She still stuck to her previous statement that Pratt had left at 9.15 according to both the hall and kitchen clocks. As far as she remembered it had not struck her the following day that the clocks were wrong; in fact, since she always set them by radio, she felt fairly certain that she would have noticed a fifteen-minute discrepancy. But, as Meredith saw at once, there was nothing to prevent Wade, on his return to the house that night, from altering the clocks back again. If he had advanced them to give Pratt his alibi, then it was pretty well certain that he would have been fly enough to cover up the fact. No – April House had nothing to surrender in the way of an unsuspected clue. The sole information gained from Mrs. Black was of a negative nature – Wade, so far as she knew, had never possessed a car, and she hadn't noticed a car standing in the lane behind the house on the night of the murder. There may have been, but if so she hadn't noticed it.

Shanks and Fletcher after two days' intensive cross-examination had also come back empty-handed. Nobody within the vicinity of Regency Square had noticed a parked car round about the time of the murder. Or, if they had, they had forgotten it. It was not easy to recall events which had taken place at least seven weeks before, and, in any case, there was nothing at all remarkable in a parked car. Most of the people round about had cars, their friends had cars, cars were always being parked in those broad, residential roads. The description of Pratt's car, hawked round by the constables, was the description, they declared, of half the cars in the neighbourhood. It was a popular make.

'So much for those lines of inquiry,' thought Meredith. 'What now?'

He considered the points which still puzzled him. (1) The sheep incident. (2) The manner in which Pratt had managed to shoot Buller, without the latter being aware of his intentions. (3) The reason for Wade's escape from April House? Again and again he hammered away at these points – points which, if elucidated, would further incriminate Pratt – perhaps definitely. If he could only prove that it was Pratt who had shot that sheep – surely then he would be justified in asking for a warrant of arrest?

But could Pratt have driven up to Cleeve Hill, obviously more than once, without arousing interest? He was well-known in the locality, a member of the golf club, whose premises he would be bound to pass. Surely he would have been recognized by an acquaintance? If the subject had cropped up in conversation, of course, Pratt would have hidden the real reason for his journeys out to Cleeve Hill under the pretext of visiting a patient. Would it be worth a visit to the golf club on the offchance of picking on somebody who recalled seeing Pratt in that direction round about the time when Farmer Bates had lost his ewe? Umph – a long shot and nothing really proved if he did obtain the evidence he was after.

Over lunch that day, however, he casually asked Barnet: 'I suppose you've never seen Pratt driving in the Winchcombe direction when you've been up at the club? Particularly during these last few weeks?'

'I'm afraid I haven't,' said Barnet. 'But, of course, the clubhouse stands back from the road – so my evidence means next to nothing. I've seen him at the club naturally, and once or twice I've played against him in foursomes. He gets out pretty frequently for a man with an extensive practice. He's as keen on golf now as he is on archery.'

Suddenly Meredith sat upright and set down the glass from which he was just about to drink. The germ of an idea had settled in his mind. An idea which seemed to grow and grow the more he considered it. Golf. A keen golfer. The golf club – was that Pratt's alibi? Had he been able to slip away unnoticed from the golf-course to practise with his barbed arrows? Meredith wished he knew more of the lie of the land.

He asked Barnet: 'Suppose, by any chance, a man wanted to reach Bates' farm from the course, could he do it without being noticed?'

Barnet's eyebrows went up quizzically. He whistled softly. 'So that's how the wind's blowing, is it? Pratt! Good heavens, Meredith, you don't seriously think it's the doctor?'

'Perhaps. I may feel even more certain about it when you've answered my question, Mr. Barnet.'

'Well – yes – I'm inclined to think it would be possible. At the twelfth, for example – there's a sudden dip on the left of the fairway. The slope at this point is pretty thickly dotted with gorse bushes and once a man was down in the hollow he could walk for a mile without being spotted from the course itself.' Then 'good heavens,' exclaimed Barnet, 'Pratt, of all people, could have managed it without the fact being noticed! We've been pulling his leg about going out of bounds on the twelfth. You see, you've only got to hook slightly to drop your ball bang in the middle of those gorse bushes. When Pratt had a limited time, say between two appointments, he used to go out on his own. He never engaged a caddy except when playing an opponent. And now I come to think of it – more than once people have exchanged a few withering remarks with him when he was in the gorse bushes looking for his ball. Quite a clubhouse joke – Pratt and the twelfth.'

'And your idea is that he could have slipped away, once the coast was clear, under pretence of looking for his ball?'

'Easily. Nobody would have noticed how long he was absent. They might think, if they thought at all, that he'd packed up in disgust and gone home without even coming in for the nineteenth. He often went direct to his car. I've seen him myself.'

'And this has been happening recently?'

'Well, the joke's been going round the club for the last month.'

'Any idea when Pratt first joined?'

'Yes – about the middle of May. So he's a comparative newcomer out there. Apparently he had never played golf before then – rather despised the game so I understand. He's always been so enthusiastic about archery that his appearance out at Cleeve Hill rather surprised the people that knew him.'

'Umph,' mused Meredith. 'I wonder if anybody has ever actually seen him sneaking off from the course. It might be worth an inquiry.'

'It might,' agreed Barnet, 'but most of us are so keen on keeping our eye on the ball that we're liable to miss anything extraneous to the game. I think you're more likely to strike lucky with the caddies than the members. At any rate they always seem to be looking in the wrong direction when you get a snorter up the fairway. Their principle seems to be to keep their eye on anything *except* the ball! And damned annoying too.'

Struck by the common sense of Barnet's suggestion, Meredith, finding that his host was at a loose end after lunch, got him to drive out to the clubhouse. Barnet, who naturally knew his way about, piloted Meredith round the back of the main building, to the professional's shed. Outside the adjacent cleaning-room, a number of nondescript individuals in flannel trousers and moth-eaten pullovers were hanging about in a desultory fashion, smoking and talking. It was barely two o'clock and the afternoon rush had not yet begun, so, as the professional explained, Meredith would have at least half an hour in which to make his inquiries.

'What's more,' he added. 'You've got pretty well the whole bunch collected on the spot. There may be one or two still out but not more.'

In the circumstances Meredith decided to hold a sort of mass cross-examination and, at the professional's bidding, the seedy, rag-and-bobtail group of idlers clustered round, their faces reflecting both their interest and curiosity. Meredith stepped up on to a providential beer-crate and began to address his little meeting.

'Now then, lads, I want you to think carefully. Don't answer unless you're quite sure of your facts. I don't want any second-hand rumours, see? The point is this – the police have an idea that a member of the club may have slipped off the course during a round of golf and used that as his alibi. Know what an alibi is, eh?'

'O' course,' said a lean, hatchet-faced man. 'It's when a bloke swears 'e's in a place when 'e isn't.'

Meredith grinned.

'Yes, that's about right. In this case we have an idea that the gentleman in question may have gone out of bounds on the twelfth.'

A general laugh greeted this statement. The twelfth seemed to be quite as much a joke with the caddies as the members.

''Ooked his drive maybe.'

'Yus – into them ruddy gorse-bushes.'

'Ah, you've said it – we're always getting 'ang-ups on the twelfth.'

'You seem to know the spot all right,' commented Meredith. 'Lot of gorse-bushes there, eh? Chap could easily lose his ball there and spend a lot of time looking for it.'

'*And* never finding it,' said a voice.

'Exactly – but what I want to know is this – have any of you lads seen any member of the club cutting off back over the wolds from that particular spot? Think it out. I won't hurry you. And remember I want first-hand information.'

A silence settled over the group. Meredith anxiously waited. Was he going to pull another blank out of the hat? A long shot, of course, but he had known similar cases when– He looked up suddenly. There was a slight commotion in the crowd as a tall, shambling figure in a patched fairisle and a pair of old army breeches pushed his way importantly to the fore.

'Well – have you got something to say?'

'Aye.'

'All right. Let's go inside and have a talk there.'

'Well?' said Meredith, once they were behind the closed door of the professional's shop.

'I 'aave seen summerbody cuttin' off like you say. Sometimes t'waard the end o' June t'would be, if my reck-nings 'bout right. I waas in them prickly gaarse pokin' around for lost balls an' I seed summerbody lower down the slope a-doing of the same thing. 'Aad his bag with him so I knew aas 'ee was a member.'

'I see. Yes?'

'Well, after sumtimes this summerbody – I'm not takin' no liberty to mention names – this summer-body takes a look round, like a startled hare might do, and not thinkin' to be noticed makes off at a raare pace a-down the paath that leads to Bates – Farmer Bates that is in case you're not famillyer with these paarts.'

'Still carrying his bag?'

'Oh, aye – 'ee haad his sticks with him right enough. T'was that aas struck me as quare.'

'Did you see him return?'

'No. Though t'was half-hour or more afore I come back to the sheds I never seed the gentleman again.'

'But you recognized him?'

'I'm not saying it wasn't summerbody I thought aas I knew and I'm not saying aas it waas.'

Meredith went on reassuringly.

'There's no need for you to worry your head over that point, Mr.–?'

'Aadams. Nick Aadams.'

'Naturally, Mr. Adams, you don't think it's quite your place to give us information about a club-member. Dr. Pratt has probably tipped you handsomely when you've caddied for him. You feel it wouldn't be playing the game to give him away. That's about it, eh?'

'Aye, thaat's just how I looks aat it. More'n once I've carried for the doctor and 'ee's always been free with his tips. I'm not saying 'e 'aasn't. So it's natural like for me to play fair by him, isn't it?'

'Well, you have,' remarked Meredith, struggling to keep a straight face. 'I think you can congratulate yourself on your loyalty, Mr. Adams.'

'Why, I don't know about thaat, but my motter 'aas always been "Do 'aas you would be done by." I seed *summerbody* – thaat's as much as I know. You'll just 'aav'e to content yourself with the fac' thaat I seed summerbody an' not go pressin' me for any names.'

Hastily thanking Nick Adams, Meredith made for the spot where Barnet was waiting with the car. As he dropped down beside the driving-seat he began to roar with laughter. Barnet looked at him bewildered,

'What's the joke, Meredith? Did you have any luck?'

'Luck,' exclaimed Meredith through his laughter. 'I should say! *And* a model witness. If this doesn't mark the beginning of the end then I'm a bigger fool than I thought I was!'

As Meredith turned over the new evidence in his mind he realized more and more clearly how significant it was. Later, of course, he'd get a signed statement from Nick Adams but he didn't want, at the moment, to frighten his witness into stubbornness. Those simple sort of fellows could be amazingly stubborn if one tried to force their hands. That it was Pratt he had seen, Meredith did not doubt. The manner in which he had obtained that part of his evidence made it pretty well certain. Moreover, his question about the golf-bag had not been asked without a definite reason. Pratt had walked off with his bag still slung over his shoulder. Why? Because he wanted to practise his shots in private, away from the withering observations of his fellow members? Well, that might be the doctor's line of defence over this point. But the prosecution had a good point to make there – a sound, incriminating point. A steel-socketed bow, when in two parts, would fit neatly and unobtrusively into a golf-bag. There was no doubt that Pratt had been devilish clever in providing himself with an alibi which in itself was watertight. If only he hadn't slipped up in other directions – been recognized during that raid on Rake's establishment, for instance – the police would have had no reason to connect the mysterious shooting of Farmer Bates's ewe with Dr. Pratt.

Back once more at Number Eight, in the privacy of his own room, Meredith reconsidered the points which still baffled him. There had been three – three major points. Now there were only two. Why had Wade left April House on the night of Cotton's murder, to be seen at nine-thirty by Miss Boon driving that car down Victoria Road? How had Pratt managed to shoot Buller at such absurdly close range without the latter realizing his murderous intentions? He'd take the Wade problem first.

Wade's reason for sneaking out of April House

must have been connected in some way with the murder. In some way he was essential to Pratt's scheme. It was more than likely that he had tampered with the clocks. So far so good – but why this elaborate hoax to get him out of the house without Mrs. Black realizing? His faked illness, the pretended morphia injection, Pratt's strict injunctions that he was not to be disturbed. And the car? Why the car? Whose car? Stolen? The police had not been informed. Borrowed? From whom? Whom, among Wade's circle of friends possessed a car? Somebody he had met, perhaps, out at 'The Lilacs.' Or Pratt perhaps? No – Pratt needed his own car to hustle him full speed from Leckhampton Road to Regency Square. Funny that nobody had noticed *his* car parked that evening. Surely somebody from some window or other would have seen–

Meredith sat up with a jerk! Pratt's car! Was that the explanation? Good Lord – yes! Why the devil hadn't it occurred to him before? He had already learnt something of the doctor's amazing thoroughness, his brilliant eye for detail in the planning of his cold-blooded plot to do away with Buller. The fact that his car might have been recognized in the vicinity of the square must have occurred to him. So what then did he do? Avoided the parking of his car by keeping it on the run whilst he was entering the Empty House via Miss Boon's front door and skylight. *Wade had chauffeured him!* That must be the explanation. Yes, whilst the doctor was engaging Mrs. Black in conversation in the hall, Wade slips out of his bedroom window, cuts out through the garden gate behind the house and thus round into Leckhampton Road. There he nips into the doctor's waiting saloon, probably hiding himself under a rug on the floor of the rear seat. Pratt comes out. Mrs. Black sees his empty car waiting. Pratt drives off. Clear of April House they change over and Wade takes the wheel, Pratt sitting beside him, his socketed bow and the barbed arrow carefully arranged inside a raincoat, perhaps, ready to spring out and slip in through Miss Boon's open door. Arriving at the corner of the square Wade slows up. Pratt takes a quick look round to see if the coast is clear and covers the few yards which will take him up the steps of Number One. Wade drives off and keeps on driving until the prearranged time shall have elapsed. Then he drives back to the square, Pratt watching for his return from the safety of Miss Boon's house. Pratt slips out, takes the wheel and leaves Wade to return either by bus or on foot to April House. Where was the flaw in that? Surely this theory held water?

'At any rate,' thought Meredith elated, 'it gives me something further to work on. It's not a question of a parked car now. We've got to find out if anybody saw a car slow up and a passenger alight, very possibly with a coat over his arm.'

There and then he decided to take a look round in the vicinity of Number One. At once a significant fact emerged. Almost directly opposite Miss Boon's a narrow road entered the main road, which crossed the end of the square. This road entered at right-angles and was bordered on each side by the high, brick walls of the gardens of the two corner houses which faced on to the main road. Brick walls! No windows from which to be overlooked. Surely this was the point from which Pratt had left the car? But had anybody in the near neighbourhood noticed the fact? Well, that was a job for Shanks and Fletcher – another house-to-house investigation, examining witnesses on the new point which had arisen.

He walked round to Clarence Street and found Long in a bad temper writing up a report on a petty larceny case.

'And bloomin' waste o' the golden hours which ought to be devoted to the major case. No forrader, eh, sir?'

Meredith explained what he had been up to in the interim. Long was obligingly impressed. There and then he sent for Shanks and Fletcher, who were luckily in the building, and sent them off on their chase for corroborative evidence. He turned to Meredith.

'What about a warrant of arrest? Think we've got enough to go on? What about sounding the Old Man?'

They went along to the Chief's office, where Meredith brought him up-to-date with the progress of the case. He, too, was impressed, but, conscious of his responsibility, proved cautious.

'I'm not saying the application wouldn't be granted. The case against Pratt is, in my opinion, conclusive, but let's make dead certain, Meredith. You'll gain nothing by being too hasty. You'd better detail a couple of men to keep a watch on Pratt in case he gets wind of our suspicion. One mobile unit, say, to keep on the track of his car.

Another posted at your friend's place, if he's no objection. In the meantime Shanks may bring back something definite. If so let me know at once and I think we'll take a risk and have that warrant drawn up.'

'Right, sir. Thanks.'

But Shanks and Fletcher after two days' exhaustive cross-questioning again turned up empty-handed. Three, four days went by – no development. Pratt seemed to be going about his customary routine, worried no doubt by the impending trial in connection with the activities of Jervis the Rake, but otherwise carrying on with his usual efficiency.

Then, with startling unexpectedness, came the climax. The Chief's foresight in providing that 'mobile unit' proved to be the doctor's undoing. How was he to suspect, as he set out in his car late on Saturday night, that he was being deliberately followed by the helmeted and goggled young man on his powerful motorbike? He drove out through the town, over the railway, along the main road in the direction of Stroud. Behind him, at some distance, purred the innocent-looking young man in goggles. Through Shurdington, past the A.A. box at the cross-roads, leaving Brockworth on the right, up the winding, beech-covered hill to where the sign-post pointed to Cranham. Here Pratt turned and swung down the tree-arched lane between the celebrated woods. At a deserted spot, about a mile from the little village, he drew up, running his car off the road under the trees. There he switched off his lights and waited. A motorcycle droned by, its headlight sliding over the car.

Pratt shrank back and listened to the sound of the engine receding. Then hastily he took a spade from the back seat and a small brown-paper parcel. He moved as quietly as possible deeper into the wood and, in a little clearing, began to dig a hole. He threw up the loose soil and piled it at the side of the hole, then placing the parcel in the hole he began to replace the earth, stamping it down firmly with his feet.

'Well. Well. What's all this?'

The blaze of a pocket-torch struck directly into the doctor's eyes, blinding him. With a sudden cry of alarm he dropped the spade and stood there, for a moment, as if paralysed. He seemed to crumple up queerly inside his clothes. Then with an oath he sprang aside and began to run through the wood. A low-lying cluster of brambles tripped him and brought him crashing to the ground with the young man in the leather helmet on top of him.

'It's no cop. Better keep quiet.'

'Who the devil–?'

'Police – get that?' The constable was twisting the doctor's arm with one hand, groping in his pocket with the other. He drew out a pair of handcuffs which glistened in the rays of the torch which shone up from the ground where it had dropped.

'By God – you don't,' cried Pratt, with a superhuman effort, breaking free and struggling to his feet. His fingers were fumbling in his waistcoat pocket, but the constable was too quick for him. The handcuffs snapped over one wrist, then, after further resistance, over the other. A small white object slipped from the doctor's nerveless fingers and fell directly in front of the pocket-torch. The constable snatched it up and with a muttered, 'So that's your little game is it?' pushed it carefully into his breast-pocket.

Twenty minutes later Colonel Ridgeway was talking to the sergeant-on-duty at Clarence Street.

'Yes – about two or three hundred yards from the main Stroud Road. The Cranham turning. He flagged me as I went by. Wants some of your fellows out there as soon as possible. He's got him all snug and tidy in the car, but wants help in getting him back. Wilson he said. Get that? Said you'd know all about it. Suggested you got in touch with – here wait a minute – took it down. Yes – Long and Meredith. Right. Got that? I'll nip back and keep him company until you turn up.'

CHAPTER XIX

Post Mortem

'Well,' beamed Long as the police-car hummed merrily along the Stroud road, 'this looks like the end, eh? A red-handed catch! Providence serves something up on a plate! Though the devil only knows what kind o' monkey-tricks 'is nibs was up to in Cranham Woods. Well, we'll know that soon enough, I suppose.'

Presently the car slewed into the verge and drew up with a screech. Meredith sprang out and walked over to the stationary saloon.

'Well, Wilson?'

Tersely the constable made his report, lowering his voice so that Pratt should not hear. Meredith came to a rapid decision and drew out the warrant, which had been hastily drawn up before leaving Clarence Street.

'Well, Pratt – anything to say? Usual caution, you know. Anything you say will be taken down in writing and may be used in evidence.'

'Nothing,' said Pratt in a husky voice.

'O.K.,' said Meredith briskly as Long joined him. 'Get him over to the other car. He's to be detained of course. Understand that Pratt? You'll be charged tomorrow with the murder of Captain Cotton and Edward Buller. Still nothing to say?'

Pratt dumbly shook his head.

Then, 'I reserve the right–' he began.

'Of course,' broke in Meredith. 'You'll be at liberty to arrange your own defence, but we can't discuss that now.' He turned to Wilson. 'Now then, constable, let's see about it.'

The two men made off into the wood until they came to the little clearing where the spade was lying. In silence Meredith picked up the spade and began, with extreme caution, to dig. In a few minutes he reached down and drew the paper parcel out of the hole. With even greater caution he unwrapped it and examined its contents in the light of the constable's torch.

Then, 'Good heavens!' he exclaimed. 'What the devil's this? Here, Long! Long! Take a look here.'

The Inspector loomed up out of the darkness,

tripping and swearing as he blundered through the undergrowth.

'Hullo. Hullo. What's the trouble now?'

Meredith extended his hands and held the open parcel in the rays of light.

'What d'you make of this packet, eh, Long?'

'A pistol, isn't it? Sort of old-fashioned blunderbuss. You're not trying to kid me that anybody was looney enough to *fire* that thing? I wouldn't fire it electrically from half a mile off in a concrete dug-out – not if I was paid to, I bloomin' well wouldn't.' He looked closer, a puzzled frown on his usually cheerful countenance. 'Glass too – bits o' broken glass. Wot's it all mean, eh, sir?'

'I've got a vague idea, Long, but I don't want to start airing my opinions until I've had time to examine this little lot properly. One thing I feel sure about – there's enough evidence wrapped up in this bit of brown paper to hang our friend Pratt twice over. Anything else, Wilson?'

'Yes, sir – this,' said Wilson, fiddling in his breast-pocket and fishing out the little white object which had dropped from the hand of the arrested man. Meredith took it on his open palm.

'Umph – sort o' tablet,' observed Long. 'Like an aspirin.'

'Not a sort of tablet,' corrected Meredith with a grin. 'It *is* a tablet. Though I reckon it's not an aspirin. How d'you get hold of this, Wilson?' Wilson explained. Meredith let out a low whistle. 'Suicide, eh? Poor devil must have realized his number was up when you walked in on his digging party. Wonder what poison he fancied? We'll have to have this analysed at once, Long. Let's have a scrap of that brown paper.'

Back in Clarence Street, despite the lateness of the hour, things began to move. The police surgeon hustled over to make an immediate analysis, not only of the little white tablet but of the minute white specks still clinging to the broken scraps of glass. The Chief Constable was already waiting for the return of Long and Meredith. They stood in conference round the former's desk on which reposed the curious looking pistol.

'There's no doubt that this is what he used in the second murder,' Meredith was saying. 'The idea couldn't have occurred to him at once because we know that after the Cotton murder he practised with his steel bow up on the wolds. You can see for yourself, sir. There's a powerful spring inside the barrel and a catch just in front of the trigger to hold it in place before the release. All he had to do was to fix the spring, ram the arrow down the barrel and pull the trigger. Simple, eh?'

The Chief agreed.

'Simple to hide, too,' was his comment. 'It could easily be concealed in the lining of his coat.' He smiled sardonically. 'Our friend wasn't going to make any mistake the second time. One case of mistaken identity was enough for his nerves, I imagine. A sitting-shot, too! Couldn't have missed!'

'On the other hand,' said Meredith quietly, 'I don't think he killed Buller with this contraption.'

'What!' exclaimed Long and the Chief in unison.

'As soon as Dr. Newark has made his analysis I shall know for certain, sir – until then it must still be pure guess work.'

'And your theory?' asked the Chief.

'Buller was poisoned,' said Meredith bluntly. 'He was dead before the arrow entered his head. As you said just now Pratt didn't want to take any chances the second time. I reckon the Cotton slip-up must have scared him stiff. Remember that the first person he saw after taking that shot from the Empty House was the very man he thought he had killed – Buller! Chap must have had an iron nerve. The point was that if he relied solely on this spring-gun affair he could never be certain that he'd have the opportunity to use it. Buller might have waved him into a chair, being his host, and sat facing him all the time. Awkward, eh, sir? You couldn't have pulled a damn big thing like that out of your pocket, levelled it and fired without attracting notice.'

'True enough,' murmured Long. 'About as 'andy as a 'owitzer when you come to think of it.'

'But there was one way,' went on Meredith, 'in which Pratt, without arousing the slightest suspicion, *could* have murdered Buller. Buller suffered from dyspepsia. Pratt had prescribed anti-acid tablets to be taken directly after meals. Mrs. Gannet always left a tumbler of water ready in the study on Buller's smoking-table, together with the box of tablets. According to the evidence on the night of Buller's murder this tumbler was *not* placed ready. Mrs. Gannet thought it was – but, apparently, she was wrong. I say, *apparently*, sir, because I'm very much inclined to think that the housekeeper was right. The tumbler of water was there on the table when Pratt and Buller entered the study after dinner. What more natural for Pratt to–'

'Hand poor old Buller 'is number nine or whatever it was,' cried Long, suddenly realizing the trend of his superior's argument. 'Only instead o' one of them indigestion pills 'e slips 'im a dose of rat poison and stands back to watch the results.'

'More or less,' grinned Meredith. 'Though I'm inclined to think the poison – whatever it was – was slipped into the glass of water first and that Pratt did actually hand Buller one of his usual tablets.'

'The point being, Meredith?'

'This, sir. Pratt wanted an instantaneous result – a compressed tablet wouldn't work quickly enough, but a shot of this stuff dropped, even dissolved in the water, would send the old chap out in a flash. He might even have had a liquid phial of the stuff already made up. Buller tosses the stuff down and Pratt, who seems to have been a canny sort of bird over the details, shoves the used tumbler into his pocket. He waits for the poison to work, then fires the arrow into the dead man's head.'

'To confuse the issue,' put in the Chief with an understanding nod. 'To suggest that Buller had been shot from across the square as Cotton had been shot.'

'Precisely, sir. He even tried to suggest by the angle of the shaft that the arrow had been loosed from the Empty House. And there,' concluded Meredith, 'was his alibi. He was in the house – ergo – he couldn't have been anywhere in the square.'

'Ergo,' said Long. ''E bloomin' well wasn't the

murderer.' Then in a tone of infinite disbelief, coupled with an enormous and knowing wink: 'Sez you!'

There was a rap on the door. Dr. Newark entered. The three heads swung round questioningly toward him.

'Well?' said the Chief.

'Veronal,' replied Newark shortly. 'About twenty grains in the tablet. Deposit on the broken glass the same. Impossible, of course, to say how many grains had been added to the fluid.'

'Not a convulsive or a corrosive is it?' asked Meredith anxiously.

Newark shook his head.

'Produces very little external effect, if that's what you're after.'

'I am,' smiled Meredith. He turned to the Chief. 'Do you think my theory holds water now, sir?'

The Chief nodded slowly.

'Everything seems to point to it, Meredith. I can apply for an exhumation order if you can bring forward enough corroborative evidence. Then the mystery will be cleared up once for all. Pratt hasn't got an earthly anyway – as I see it.'

Three further pieces of evidence were diligently collected by Meredith and Long before the necessary permit was obtained. The broken pieces of tumbler corresponded in thickness, size and shape with those in use at Number Six. Mrs. Gannet declared that since the set was new, there should have been a full dozen glasses. There were only eleven. Finally, in the left-hand pocket lining of Pratt's dinner-jacket there were found undeniable traces of veronal.

The body was exhumed. An autopsy was performed. Veronal was discovered.

'Which only goes to show,' said Long in his slow, lugubrious voice, 'that things more often than not are not what they appear to be, and what they appear to be, more often than not, they're not!'

Meredith felt inclined to agree.